The Senator
The Lonely Heroes Series Spinoff
Sam E. Kraemer

Copyright

This book is an original work of fiction. Names, characters, places, incidents, and events are the product of the author's imagination and are used fictitiously. Any resemblance to actual persons, living or dead, business establishments, events, or locales is entirely coincidental.

Copyright ©2024 by Sam E. Kraemer

Cover Designer and Formatter: KSL Designs

Editor: Sam J. Keir, Keir Editing & Writing Services

Formatting: TL Travis

Proofreaders: Mildred Jordan, I Love Books Proofreading

Published by Kaye Klub Publishing

These characters are the author's original creations, and the events herein are the author's sole intellectual property. The novel has been edited and recovered for this rerelease. No rights to the content of this story are forfeited due to the previous versions of the manuscript.

All products/brand names mentioned in this work of fiction are registered trademarks owned by their respective holders/corporations/owners. No trademark infringement intended.

No part of this book may be reproduced, scanned, or distributed in any form, printed or electronic, without the express permission of the author. Please do not participate in or encourage piracy of copyrighted materials in violation of the author's rights. Purchase only authorized editions.

Note: NO AI/NO BOT. The author does not consent to any Artificial Intelligence (AI), generative AI, large language model, machine learning, chatbot, or other automated analysis, generative process, or replication program to reproduce, mimic, remix, summarize, or otherwise replicate any part of this creative work, via any means: print, graphic, sculpture, multimedia, audio, or other medium without express permission from the author. I support the right of humans to control their artistic works.

Blurb

Their story --
What happens when a sitting United States Senator gets caught with his pants down—literally? The U.S. Senator from Virginia is about to find out! Welcome to Washington, DC, where the Power Players are more intriguing than anything happening under the Capitol Dome.

A romantic getaway to an exotic island with forty-five-year-old Spencer Brady's lover leads to being outed to the entire world. The blowback costs Spencer more than he bargained for, but the impact on his family is more agonizing than he ever imagined.

Twenty-seven-year-old Nashville Lincoln is working two jobs to survive in Washington, DC—one as a bartender for a catering company that services parties for the Washington elite. The other job involves servicing many of those same heavy hitters in a more intimate way.

In the nation's capital, if someone isn't scratching your back, they're stabbing it. Can Spencer recover from a devastating professional loss? What does the future hold for his marriage, and will he ever learn the identity of the person responsible for outing him?

How does Nash Lincoln play into Spencer's future? Is he more hinderance than help? Is Spencer's wife, Vanessa, pushing them together? Can Nash help save The Senator?

A Note to Readers

Surprise! I've hinted about this book for a while now. It sat dormant for a couple of years because I got busy doing other things, but when I was checking my WIP list, I went back to it. I posted it on Patreon, and they gave me some great feedback, so I'm giving it to you!

You may also notice some familiar characters mentioned in this story—Raleigh Wallace and Congressman Benjamin Hoffman. When I was writing "Positive Raleigh," this story popped into my head, so there's the "Heroes" tie!

At first blush, some might want to label "The Senator" as a story of infidelity, and I know a lot of readers aren't attracted to that sort of thing. I hope you'll give it a chance. I love the characters, and I think you will too!

Thanks for all your support,
Sam

Contents

1. Chapter One — 1
2. Chapter Two — 18
3. Chapter Three — 26
4. Chapter Four — 40
5. Chapter Five — 58
6. Chapter Six — 73
7. Chapter Seven — 86
8. Chapter Eight — 102
9. Chapter Nine — 112
10. Chapter Ten — 125
11. Chapter Eleven — 138
12. Chapter Twelve — 150
13. Chapter Thirteen — 165
14. Chapter Fourteen — 181
15. Chapter Fifteen — 193
16. Chapter Sixteen — 213

17.	Chapter Seventeen	223
18.	Chapter Eighteen	236
19.	Chapter Nineteen	250
20.	Chapter Twenty	261
21.	Chapter Twenty One	278
22.	Chapter Twenty Two	293
23.	Chapter Twenty Three	310
24.	Chapter Twenty Four	320
25.	Chapter Twenty Five	329
26.	Chapter Twenty Six	340
27.	Chapter Twenty Seven	350
28.	Chapter Twenty Eight	360
29.	Epilogue	372
30.	♥♥♥	387
About Sam E. Kraemer		388
Other Books by Sam E. Kraemer/L.A. Kaye		389

Chapter One
Spencer Brady

"Is this correct? This can't be accurate. Ladies and gentlemen, bear with me while I verify breaking information." The news anchor's mumbling was picked up by the microphone in his hand as he conferred with the production assistant handing him a tablet. Finally, he glanced at the camera, seeming to have gathered himself—or remembering he was broadcasting live—and cleared his throat.

"Ladies and gentlemen, I've been informed that NBS is projecting the winner of the Senate election in Virginia to be..." Blaire Conner hesitated, as if he was afraid to say the results out loud.

The room went quiet as everyone waited on tenterhooks for the next words out of the reporter's mouth—words I dreaded to hear as much as he likely didn't want to say them.

I was seated in the formal living room in one of the navy wingback chairs, it's mate now empty after my wife left the room. I, too, was anxious to learn what the Fates had in store for us; however, I wasn't exactly thrilled the news would be delivered to the world at large at the same time I was learning it.

Our home in Great Falls, Virginia, was filled with my campaign staff, office staff, friends, supporters, and lastly, my small family, though my son had refused to come downstairs to listen to the returns. To say it had been a bad year for me was a vast understatement.

It was never a good sign when the incumbent became immersed in scandal so close to an election. In my case, I was *literally* caught with my pants down three months earlier. My weak defense was that I still couldn't figure out how it happened.

I felt a gentle hand on my shoulder, fingers quivering as much as my own. I glanced up to see my long-suffering wife with a pained look on her weary face. Standing, I led her back to the kitchen where she'd originally gone to make coffee and probably gather herself, while the world as we knew it tilted on its axis.

We'd learn the election results from the sounds emanating from the living room anyway, so there was no need to risk someone in my circle of acquaintances taking pictures of us at a vulnerable moment and releasing them to the media. We'd been in the spotlight more than anyone needed to be. I was done with it.

"Vani, love, did you call Bertram as I suggested? I won't fight you for anything. Take what you want. I can be out of the house by tomorrow if that's what you need." She didn't deserve being dragged through my mud, and the sooner I was out of her life, the better it would be for her.

All our friends had taken sides during the three months between the revelation of my affair and election day. I didn't mind that everyone was sympathetic to Vani. The nasty things they said about me, I could handle, but my loyal companion of twenty years would not fare the same.

"Spencer, I refuse to allow you to go through this alone. What we do, or don't do, in our bedroom is our business. Outing you as they did is unconscionable. Whoever did that to you deserves to be horsewhipped. Thankfully, Blaire wasn't caught up in it, too, but I refuse to allow you to suffer the judgment of a bunch of hypocrites! We had an arrangement, and it was—and still is—nobody's business." Vanessa's conviction in her statement was admirable.

A collective groan sounded from the living room, and I knew it was over. I looked into Vanessa's eyes and saw the sadness, but all I felt was relief. "Come here." I opened my arms for her, and she stepped forward, clutching the kerchief in her hand while crying softly against my chest.

In my heart, I knew she was relieved, but the fact my reputation was effectively in the shitter was sort of tragic, which was likely why she was upset.

I didn't want her to be tainted by my mistakes, so I made up my mind to stay out of the spotlight as much as possible. It would give Vani a chance to seriously consider what I'd tried to get her to understand—I was damaged goods, and being supportive of me would only bring her down as well. Our time in the sun had ended in a shitstorm.

I found a baseball cap in my closet and grabbed my glasses from the nightstand, having popped out my contacts after everyone had finally left—some a lot more intoxicated than was necessary under the circumstances.

Getting elected with a scandal over my head was a no-win proposition, but I appreciated that my Senate and campaign staff had remained optimistic—the ones who hadn't deserted the sinking ship in August.

I was confident that all the folks who'd staffed my Senate offices in the Capitol would find employment easily, and the paid campaign staff would be snatched up quickly because in every campaign, there was a winner and a loser. Besides, once a government wonk, always a government wonk.

Those who walked out the day the scandal hit the papers hadn't fared so well, most of whom were still trying to find jobs, if what the rumor mill was ginning out had any basis in truth. Sadly, in a town like Washington, DC, loyalty—under any circumstances—weighed more heavily in one's favor than fleeing the scene before being touched by the stench of disgrace.

"You sure this is a good idea, Spence?" my Senate chief of staff, Mario Fernandez asked, glancing in the rearview to change lanes. That poor bastard had been through hell and back with me, starting when we both graduated from UVA and then staying on for law school together. He knew me as well as

Vanessa, but I supposed that's why he still hung around.

It was like I had two spouses—two spouses and no sex to speak of, especially after the scandal overtook the headlines. What a load of horseshit it all turned out to be.

"I gotta go talk to him. Clearly, everyone believes I'm a dirty son of a bitch, so I expect Attorney General Milson will begin an investigation any day now. You'll all be under the microscope with me, but I still want to ensure Blaire stays out of the fray. He just got promoted to a network job. I won't be *his* downfall, too.

"I'm considering taking some time away at the end of the year, but I'll stay in touch so you can find me if I need to come back to testify before the Ethics Committee or something. Just drop me at the corner up here." I pointed to the end of the upcoming block.

Mario shook his head in disagreement, but I was doing what was best for everyone. Since the scandal broke, my parents had cut off all communication with my family, and our adopted son, Jay, was having a hell of a time keeping a low profile at college. He'd come home for election night, but I was certain he was leaving in the morning as soon as he could pack his Escape and get on the road. It was mind blowing how quickly everything went to hell.

Three Months Earlier

"Come on, Spence, we can't take a vacation together. What will Vanessa say if she finds out?" Blaire hissing into the phone made me chuckle. I was outside the Senate chamber, having cast my vote for the last bill on the agenda before the August recess.

"Vani and Jay are going to Portsmouth to see her folks before Jay starts school at Tech this fall, and I want to go away for a week before I start campaigning around the Commonwealth. Vani's going on the campaign trail with me, but it was her idea that I take a week to myself. I'll take care of everything, sweetheart. Please come with me?" Begging wasn't my usual MO.

Blaire Conner, a local network newscaster, and I had met at a fundraising dinner in January hosted by prominent lobbyist, Sean Fitzpatrick of The Fitzpatrick Group, and we hit it off extremely well. It was an unwritten rule in DC circles that media members who were invited to such events didn't share information they learned through casual conversations, or they weren't invited again. The town worked in mysterious ways, but most people followed the same code of conduct, or they quickly found themselves on the outside looking in.

"Are you sure this is safe? I mean—"

I cut Blaire off. "I'm not telling anyone, are you? Look, we won't travel together. I'll fly out on Saturday, and you can join me on Sunday. I'll text all the details from my personal phone and make sure there's a car to pick you up at the airport. I'm looking forward to this, Blaire, so please, make it work on your end. I've missed the fuck out of you." It was my last-ditch effort to talk him into the trip.

I hoped to hell I was being convincing because I really wanted to see him. I wasn't in love with Blaire Conner, but I was sure I could find myself there eventually if we continued to see each other as we had been.

"Okay, fine. I'll do my best. Call me tomorrow. Be safe. Bye." Blaire ended the call. Mario was standing to the side, holding off a few senators who wanted a piece of my ass for voting for/against their spending bill—which hadn't gone according to their plan. *Fool me once—fuck you.*

I'd agreed to vote in favor of a joint resolution some members of the Senate had introduced regarding funding for an infrastructure project along the district boundaries on both the Virginia and Maryland sides. It would have improved the commute for many of my constituents who worked in the downtown area, and the Memorial, Key, Fourteenth Street, Purple Heart, and Wilson Bridges were all long overdue for an overhaul, which would have been included under the spending bill.

I was on board with it, even though it included a lot of pork—namely, an assload of money for a highway improvements project through the state capital of Georgia. I was backing it, even though I wasn't keen after Senator Turner put his label on it, but there was still a lot of the bill worth passing, and I'd been rallying my fellow senators on the blue side of the aisle to support it as well.

All was going well until I saw a news clip where the senator from Georgia made some nasty comments about one of the *out* members of the House, calling him a "limp-wristed fruit fly" because the younger man had contributed to a competing bill in the House that would also include laptops and hot spot devices for children in the low-income parts of DC.

The House bill was a solid piece of legislation, and it would do a lot for education in and around the district while only siphoning off a small percentage of the infrastructure funds to underwrite it—namely, some of the money that would go to Georgia for its bloated highway spending project. All things considered, I had no problem supporting the House bill when it came over to the Senate, and I'd pulled my support from the Senate bill, much to the *disappointment* of a few Senators—and that was putting it mildly.

Once I slid my phone into my pocket, it was game on. Senator Frank Turner, Republican from Georgia, raced over, his face as red as his tie. We'd worked across the aisle on a few pieces of legislation dealing with the federal tax rates on capital gains and income equality. For being a staunch conservative, the man had a few liberal tendencies I could respect, and I found myself liking him most days. That particular day was not to be one of them.

"Senator Brady, I thought you and I had struck a deal on that bill. I've always known you to be a man of your word," Turner snapped, his anger on full display.

The corridor outside the chamber was suddenly quiet, and I imagined every Gossipy Gertie taking careful notes about the interaction. I glanced to my right to see Mario with his usual worried expression, so for his sake alone, I vowed to keep my temper in check.

I was running for re-election, so I'd been on my best behavior and minded my manners, but when I'd seen the sound bite of Turner and his comment about the new junior representative from North Carolina, Benjamin Hoffman, I lost my shit.

Maybe it was because I was so deep in the closet that I couldn't find my way out with Alexa *and* Siri's help, but the young guy was recently elected because the senior congressman had left under somewhat dubious circumstances. Congressman Benjamin Hoffman handily beat his opponent in a special election, and he was a fellow Democrat, who had an impressive record in a mostly conservative North Carolina.

Congressman Hoffman had spearheaded a pushback of North Carolina's infamous "Bathroom Bill," which banned trans persons from using the restroom of their current gender, forcing them to use the restroom assigned at birth. I might have been lying about who I really was, but I was still supportive of my fellow members of the LGBTQ+ community.

Ben's ability to effectively serve North Carolina in the U.S. House of Representatives had nothing to do with being married to a man. From everything I'd heard, Raleigh Wallace worked in DC for a New York security company, Golden Elite Associates, and the man was effective at his job. Turner would be smart to steer clear of Mr. Wallace. I'd seen the man at a Fourth of July function once, and he was the size of a brick shithouse.

"Yes, Senator Turner, we had a deal. That was, until I saw you on television, bad-mouthing one of the junior congressmen for supporting competing legislation instead of pushing your bill in the House. Derisive language against anyone is reprehensible, but against a fellow member of Congress, who is still learning the ropes and looking out for the underprivileged, is bullying at its worst.

"If he'd have backed your bill, you'd be telling everyone what a breath of fresh air Congressman Hoffman is in the House, and how much you look forward to watching his career grow. Instead, you're putting another nail in the wall between our parties."

The more I spoke, the redder his face turned. I hoped to hell the old blowhard didn't have a stroke right there. That wouldn't be a good look for me any way you framed it.

I wasn't done talking, though. "And to think, I believed you to be one of the standouts who supported bipartisanship when it came to legislation benefitting the citizens of our great nation. Now, I stand corrected." It felt good to get it off my chest.

Turner was the epitome of a pompous southern politician, what with his potbelly that hung over his belt and a cigar in the pocket of his shirt. The way he rode roughshod over his staff was legendary in the Russell Office Building. I'd heard the stories myself for the two terms I'd been in office. Thankfully, my staff seemed to like me and worked hard to promote our agenda, not just use me to pad their resumes.

"That snot-nosed little bastard has no business in Congress. I'd have blackballed him if he was a member of my party. No faggot should ever..." Turner trailed off as I turned and walked away.

I wasn't about to listen to his bullshit. I had a vacation to plan with a guy I enjoyed spending time with, and no bigoted asshole was going to spout venom to taint it.

"Come on, Spence. The beach is private. Nobody will see us." Blaire demanded as we made our way outside the villa I'd rented and onto the private beach. Blaire wanted to fuck outside, and I was so dick whipped by him, I complied without a second thought.

We were at Jumby Bay Island, a beautiful private resort community in Antigua, and our accommodations happened to have a hammock strung between two curved palms near the shoreline. Blaire said he wanted to ride me in the hammock, and while I was worried about the laws of gravity, seeing the beautiful look of pleasure on his face made the decision for me— as perilous as it might be.

I pulled my shorts down enough to release my hard prick, but the way the hammock was strung between the trees, there was no way one of us wasn't going to fall off and break his neck, or something more important.

When Blaire started to climb on, I stopped him. "Babe, we're about one swing away from an ambulance ride. How about you lie crossways, sex swing style, with that gorgeous asshole in the air, and I'll keep my feet on the ground." He stepped back so I could haul myself out of the swinging death trap.

Once I was up, I helped him on, and I knelt, burying my face in his delectable ass. He'd arrived midafternoon, but he had a few reports to file before he was officially off the clock, so I worked in the study to give him space and privacy. It wouldn't do for anyone to recognize me lurking in the background while he had Zoom meetings with his colleagues back in DC.

As I spread his cheeks, I spit in his crack, and that pink star lured me in. Without hesitation, I swirled my tongue around his hole, enjoying the sounds he made as they echoed off the water.

I reached into the pocket of my shorts for the lube and condom I'd grabbed on the way outside, and in my haste to bury myself in his ass, my swim shorts fell around my ankles. Thankfully, it was a private beach, so nobody would see my forty-five-year-old white ass. The sun burned overhead, but I was looking forward to a weeklong fuck-a-thon, and I couldn't wait to get started.

Blaire had been away on assignment, reporting on recovery efforts from a category-two hurricane, Stanislav, which had made landfall in Newport News, Virginia, in mid-July. We'd seen each other there briefly when I'd toured the damage with the Governor and my fellow senator from Virginia, John Buford, another card-carrying bigoted southerner. Due to the fact it was a day trip, I didn't even get to speak to Blaire, so I was eager to reconnect.

"I'm ready." Blaire's breathy voice was my signal to pounce. I slid the condom down my cock and slicked his hole and then myself. I pulled his hips forward so his legs were hanging off the hammock, and I pushed my way inside until I was fully seated, both of us gasping at the feeling of being together again. I slowly slid out halfway and pushed back in, beginning a steady pace in pursuit of bliss for both of us.

"Yeah, baby, make it sting." Blaire's moan was hot. He liked a little slap and tickle while he was getting fucked, and I was only too happy to give it to him. One swift blow turning his right cheek bright pink revved my motor, so I did the same to the left.

I changed the angle to hit his prostate, dragging the head of my rod against it such that Blaire yelled, "I'm about to come! Do it again!" *Gladly.*

Blaire's hard cock had worked its way through the ropes of the hammock, so I tightened the netting like a cock ring to restrict him from blowing. "Not yet, baby. I'm not there yet." I was mesmerized by the visual of my dick sawing in and out of his velvet vice.

"Come on, Spencer, let me come," Blaire whined as my balls drew up, signaling I was there with him. I released the netting and jacked his cock twice, getting a tantalizing visual of him shooting his load onto the sand. I pounded into him a few more times before blowing my load in the condom buried deep inside Blaire's heavenly ass.

After catching my breath, somehow managing not to collapse, I grabbed onto the rubber and pulled out, holding it on my dick with one hand while helping Blaire up with the other. He turned to me and kissed me passionately, the action causing me to let go of the condom to pull him into my arms. The damn thing slid off my dick and splatted onto our feet, causing both of us to jump. "Gross!" Blaire yelled before we both laughed.

We pulled up our swim shorts and went into the ocean to rinse off before we ventured back to the hammock, collecting the used condom and walking arm in arm into the villa to start our five days in paradise—or so I thought.

It all came to a crashing halt two days later when Vani forwarded to me the link to an article on a gossip website showing my old white ass—blurred for the kiddies—and enough of a view of Blaire's right flank to give away the fact the recipient of my dicking wasn't Vanessa.

Chapter Two
Spencer

Present Day

"Send me a text if Andy Bennett calls, will you? I'd like to explain myself to him since he supported me early in the campaign season by attending a few events. I'm sure he's pissed at me, but he's a good friend, and I owe him the truth," I requested as Mario turned down Edgewood Terrace. Thankfully, the traffic was light so we wouldn't be spotted.

"Have you talked to Andy since the pictures hit the papers?"

Sadly, no. I hadn't spoken to Andy since the scandal broke. He'd clerked for my father and had acted as a mentor to me when I was beginning my legal career. I could only imagine what he must have thought of my complete career implosion.

I needed to try to explain the situation to Andy without tromping on Vanessa's privacy. It was a fucking no-win proposition, really.

Mario stopped at the corner of the Edgewood Terrace and Woodmont Road in Alexandria to let me out near Blaire's townhouse. It was midnight, but I doubted the man was asleep because the hood of his car, which was parked on the street in front of his home, was warm. The house was dark, which wasn't a good sign that I'd be welcomed inside.

The sliding door in the kitchen was unlocked, so I quietly stepped inside and closed it, locking it behind me. "In the living room." His voice was quiet.

I walked into Blaire's living room, squinting in the darkness to find him. The floor lamp suddenly illuminated in the corner of the room, but the bulb only offered a dim glow, so I couldn't make out Blaire's expression.

The nerves coursing through my body had to be palpable in the room. "Are you okay?"

Two beats of silence before he spoke. "No, as a matter of fact, I don't think I am. Imagine this—I got fired today, which wasn't expected. I was identified in a photo of the two of us in the infinity pool in Jumby Bay. Someone had a telephoto lens and took pictures of us all week.

"They were sent to my boss during last night's broadcast, and when you lost the election, it didn't go unnoticed I'd fumbled the announcement. I got called into his office first thing this morning."

"I'm sor—" Oh, he wasn't done.

"*You've compromised your objectivity as a journalist, and when the country finds out you've been fucking a well-respected,* married, *Senator, you'll lose all credibility with the public. NBS has no desire to allow you to ride out the storm at a desk and then attempt to salvage your career when the country has moved on to the next scandal.*"

I tried again. "Look, Blaire, I'm real—"

"My epitaph will read, 'Here lies a man with many possibilities but one weakness—a big dick.' I assume Vanessa has filed for divorce since she saw the story and sent the link to you?"

I'd never explained to Blaire the intricacies of my marriage because I couldn't fully trust him with the details. He was a journalist, ruled by his ambition, so while I was pretty certain he wouldn't out himself and me in the process, I didn't want Vanessa compromised in any way.

"Uh, not yet, but I told her that she should, and I'd give her everything. She's really a wonderful woman, and she's loyal to a fault, which is more than I can say for ninety-nine percent of the people in the DC area." I put my hands on my hips, waiting for the other shoe to drop.

Blaire drained the crystal glass in his hand before walking back to the kitchen. The lights over the kitchen peninsula were flipped on, and the tinkling of ice into glasses echoed through the room. I followed him. I could damn well use a drink if he was pouring.

I took off my baseball cap and tossed it on the floor next to a stool where I plopped my ass. Seeing Blaire in the harsh light of the kitchen showed how much the whole mess was affecting him—his hair, which was usually smoothed neatly, was standing on end, and the worry lines around his eyes made him look considerably older than his thirty-five years. It was yet another smack in the face to remind me regarding how my poor decisions had damaged others in my orbit.

I hadn't seen Blaire, except on the news, since the scandal broke, not for my lack of trying. He'd refused to take my calls, even though I used a burner cell to contact him, not willing to tie us together by using my official cell. I knew the speculation around town regarding the identity of my sex partner had been bandied about in living rooms, bars, and offices all over the city, which brought another question.

"Why now? Why was your identity *just now* disclosed and only to your boss? This happened back in August, so if someone knew it was you, why did they wait to tell anyone?" I was thinking out loud, which was a bad habit I'd developed back in law school.

Blaire reached into the cabinet and pulled out a bottle of Glenlivet, my drink of choice, pouring it over a large ball of ice, just as I preferred. I'd bought him the mold to make the larger cubes when we started spending more time together, and he'd become accustomed to using them as well. It was the same mold we had at the house in Great Falls.

"Oh, I don't know? Maybe someone thought it would be funny to prolong the agony of discovery. I've been waiting for this exact moment for months. I think I have the start of a goddamn ulcer." Blaire took a seat next to me at the counter.

I tentatively reached out a hand, placing it in the middle of his back as I kissed his temple. "I'm so sorry about this, Blaire. I never intended for you to get hurt."

Blaire chuckled ironically. "I was starting to fall in love with you, you know. I knew you were married, which broke my rule of never fucking a straight guy, but I don't think you're exactly straight, are you?"

It was a crossroads: Accept and finally embrace who I was or pull the closet door tightly and nail that fucker shut from the inside. I glanced at my companion and saw the pain of his current predicament—one I'd put him in—and I couldn't help but give him some truth. "No, I'm not straight."

"Bisexual, maybe? That makes the most sense to me. Your wife is a stunning woman, and the two of you have been married for years, so there must be chemistry between you, but everyone gets bored. I guess I'm just a new plaything, which, at my age, isn't a boost to my confidence as it might have been when I was younger."

I sighed heavily. "Not Bi. I'm gay. I've been gay my whole life, and Vani knows. She's known since we met in high school," I admitted.

Vanessa Hawkins Brady was a small-town girl at heart. We'd been best friends since her family had moved down the road from us in Portsmouth. By her family, I meant her mother, Velma, grandfather, Roy, and grandmother, Patsy. Her father was never in the picture, and to add insult to injury, Vani was raped by one of her mother's boyfriend's when she was seventeen. Her mother, that harping shrew, didn't believe her and blamed Vani that the guy took off on her.

At the time, I was in my first year of college at UVA, and when Vani found out she was pregnant by the man, she called me, her best friend. She didn't know what to do, especially with her mother's guilt trip being heaped on her every day. I, being a bumbling idiot with my head up my ass, decided I knew how to fix it.

I went back to Portsmouth, taking her away from that awful mess, and we got married, planning to tell everyone the baby was mine and we'd been undercover lovers since she was sixteen. Sadly, she lost the baby a week after the wedding, and with it, any ability to have children in the future. She'd had her sights set on being a mother, so we adopted Jay years later.

Vani and I never consummated our marriage, though that shouldn't surprise anyone, really. She had PTSD from the violent rape she'd endured, and hell, I was gay. We loved each other more like siblings than anything else, and we made a life together. She looked the other way when I found a lover. There was one rule: not in our home. In turn, Vani worked hard to make herself into someone other than the sweet, shy girl I knew from Portsmouth.

She took night classes to get a liberal arts degree in design, followed by classes to become a Realtor in Virginia, DC, and Maryland. I was proud of her and encouraged her every step of the way. She was an unbelievable woman who had me in awe.

Blaire touched my arm, bringing me back to the shitstorm at hand. "Who do you suspect followed you to Antigua, Spencer? This isn't just happenstance."

I was caught off guard for a moment by his comment, but he was right. It wasn't dumb luck that someone stumbled upon us at such an out-of-the-way, gated resort on a small, private island. For the first time since my blurry ass appeared on the front page of every paper across the country, I realized it was a targeted attack on *me*.

"You think someone followed me intentionally?" Blaire nodded, and I felt the rug being pulled out from under me.

Chapter Three
Spencer

I took an Uber home after saying goodbye to Blaire, letting myself into my home in Great Falls at four o'clock in the morning. I could smell coffee, so I walked into the kitchen to see Vanessa at the table with her tablet. "Morning, Vani. Why are you up so early?"

I walked to the pot and poured myself a cup, taking a seat across from her to try and determine her mood, which seemed cold as ice. "I spoke with Jay. He's upstairs in his room, but he's leaving in a few hours. You need to sit him down and talk to him, Spencer. I won't betray your secrets, but he needs to know I'm not the aggrieved wife taken by surprise because of her husband's infidelity." The snap in her voice told me she was pissed off.

"Tell me what's wrong?" Out of everyone involved, Vanessa and Jay deserved to be hurt the least. We adopted Jay after he came to live with us as a foster child when he was seven.

Jay was in a group home around the block from a house in Springfield that Vani was trying to sell. On the day of the open house, a beautiful little boy strolled nonchalantly in through the front door.

Vani talked to him for a few minutes and decided he was curious, so she showed him around. She figured it was good practice since it was her first solo open house, and at the end of it, the little boy said, "I'm gonna have a house like this one day so I can have a family."

When Vani found out where Jay lived, she insisted on walking him home. What she saw at the group home upset her, and the next week, we petitioned to be his foster parents.

A year later, we adopted him, and we became the family we never thought we'd be. Knowing my son was upset with me broke my heart. He was never meant to be touched by anything I did. Yet another thing I didn't contemplate when I took off for a wild vacation in Antigua with a fuck buddy.

"I'll talk to him when he wakes up. How are you doing?" I was worried about her.

"Mother called. She's asked that you not come for Thanksgiving because she doesn't want her church group to turn their back on her for welcoming the queer into her home. Her words, not mine. I told her to go fuck herself, and that I wouldn't be there either." Clearly, Vani's anger wasn't directed at me, which was a relief. Her mother was truly a piece of work.

I chuckled quietly because Vani sounded like the girl I knew back in Portsmouth. "I'm sorry, but Velma has always hated me. She's always looked for a reason to remind you how much better you could have done."

Vanessa's grandparents had died several years ago, never knowing what had happened to their granddaughter when she was a beautiful young woman full of light. They never knew that Velma was indirectly responsible for that beautiful light being extinguished in Vani's eyes.

I wanted to tell them what happened to their only granddaughter, but Vani begged me not to, so I kept my mouth shut with them. I did, however, remind Velma at every chance I got that it was her fault for leaving the man alone in the house with her precious daughter.

It galled me that she chose to pretend it never happened. That was my biggest beef with the woman. The years of therapy Vani endured at the hands of Velma's inability to judge a person's character never failed to anger me.

"I'm sorry, Vani. I didn't mean to come between you and your mother. I swear, I won't go anywhere near her, but you and Jay should go. He'll be going back to Tech after the holiday anyway, and he and Velma always got along. I'll be fine.

"I'm going to catch some sleep. I need to go into the office later. I'm sure the troops are nervous. Why don't you go back to bed, too?" I knew she had a showing at eight, but she could sleep for a couple more hours. Hell, even if she didn't, she'd still look fresh as a daisy when she went to meet her clients.

"How was Blaire?" Vanessa didn't look up.

I sighed. I didn't want to discuss it, but she deserved answers. "NBS fired him. Somehow, his boss got pictures of the two of us in Antigua and held onto them until last night. Blaire didn't really give a reason why, but he asked something interesting. '*Who followed you to Antigua?*' And it made me wonder if I really *was* followed.

"I only told my travel plans to you, Mario, and Blaire. You didn't mention to anyone that I was going on vacation, did you?"

The look in Vanessa's eyes was one of pure venom, and I'd never seen it before in all the years we'd been married. "Are you asking me if I had you followed, Spencer? After everything we've been through, do you think I'm behind the complete chaotic disaster our lives have become? My client canceled the showing this morning and pulled the listing from me. My boss called to tell me he was sorry you lost and suggested I take some time off to get my private life in order. He offered me the name of a good divorce lawyer and told me to call him after the first of the year." Clearly, that was why she was up—she hadn't been to bed.

Guilt swamped me again. What a shitstorm! I rose from my chair and walked around the table, lowering myself to my knees before taking her hands in mine. "I cannot tell you how sorry I am this whole thing happened, dear one. I never meant to hurt you, and I'm not accusing you of anything." I kissed her palms and rested my head against them.

I was so fucking tired of it. Going to work since the scandal came out had been a goddamn trip to hell for me. The whispers. The nasty looks like I was shit on the bottom of their shoes. I endured it with a smile and limited my interactions with others, not yet ready to crawl into a hole and die.

Oh, it was fucking tempting to disappear, but I was made of stronger stuff than that, or so I believed until that moment as I sobbed into Vanessa's hands.

"Oh, Spence, I'm sorry this happened. We've had a life we both loved, you living your way, and me living mine, both of us supporting Jay in everything he did. We didn't hurt anyone. We love each other, and for someone to try to tear you down, it hurts me as well." She bent over and kissed the back of my head, crying along with me.

I'd been holding it inside since the news broke about the events in Antigua, but I wondered how long Vanessa had been hiding her feelings on the matter. We cried for a long time, mourning the happy life we'd lost that seemed to be free-falling and sucking us down. Sadly, I didn't know how to stop it.

★★★ ★★★

The term lame duck was apt for the way I was treated on the Hill after my loss. I still owed my constituents the work they'd hired me to do when they voted me into office, and I was going to give them all the bang for the buck I could muster.

Vanessa and I had been in a holding pattern regarding the future since we'd lost the election, but we had been combing through the house to discard things we'd held onto for too long as we prepared the house to sell. I'd finally convinced her to *consider* filing for divorce, but she refused to kick me out, for which I was secretly grateful. Regardless of the outcome, we agreed we didn't need the two-story house in Great Falls.

Jay had left the day after the election to go back to school, skillfully avoiding any conversations with me. I was relieved to have dodged his questions for a little longer, but thankfully, he had started calling Vani to talk to her.

Mario was running the Senate office, notifying me when it was time for a vote in the chamber. One good thing about the clusterfuck was that I could finally vote my conscience instead of what my party expected of me. There was no one trying to make a deal with me to support their piece of legislation in exchange for supporting something I was trying to do. I was political poison—not surprisingly.

Everything I'd recently submitted to the Speaker's Office for consideration had miraculously disappeared, and that was that. I was the lamest duck on the pond.

It was the week before we adjourned for the holidays—my last week as one of the senators from Virginia, and I was busy cleaning out my office, sending records to the archives and shredding anything personal I found, which wasn't much.

I had ordered boxes to pack my things so I could send them to the house, which I was expecting at any moment, so when there was a knock on the door after regular office hours, I called out, "It's open."

I glanced up to see one of my former college interns standing in the doorway, and I was shocked. Clearly, she didn't know not to be seen talking to me. It would be a detriment to any career aspirations she might have.

"Miss Renfro, what can I do for you?" The young woman's familiar smile was a comfort in the strangest way.

Ava Renfro was a beautiful young woman. She'd interned for me a few years earlier, and she was now working for the Congressional Liaison's Office of the Library of Congress, or so I thought. I'd given her a glowing recommendation when I was contacted by one of the recruiters, and I had heard through the grapevine she was highly valued in her job.

"Senator Brady, sir, I wanted to pass along how sorry I was that you lost the election. I voted for you, as did my folks." It was kind of her to say.

Ava lived in Arlington and had graduated near the top of her class at George Washington University. I'd met her folks once when Vani and I went to dinner at a Thai place in Arlington Forest, and the Renfros were waiting for a table. They seemed like nice WASPs, so it was surprising they voted for the newly outed gay senator from Virginia.

"I appreciate it, and I'm sorry I let all of you down. Please, take a seat and tell me how you're doing." I rose from my seat and walked around the desk, moving the guest chair so I could face her.

Ava sat, a nervous smile on her face. "I'm doing well, sir. I'm leaving the Library of Congress at the end of the year to work for Fitzpatrick and Associates." I nodded, not surprised by the news at all.

Sean Fitzpatrick was a self-made success story in the tech world before selling his dating app—*Love Under the Rainbow*—to one of the big social media conglomerates. He became an advocate and lobbyist on behalf of the LGBTQ+ community to push for equal rights and protections afforded to every American except for those under the rainbow.

Sean had taken DC by storm, and he was well liked by folks on both sides of the aisle. I'd met with him many times over my years in the Senate, and he'd been a staunch supporter of my campaigns—even the one I'd recently lost.

I was concerned by Ava's visit, remembering Sean hadn't reached out to me since the election. Since I'd been caught having a gay tryst with a reporter—a reporter I'd met at a party he'd hosted—the guy was probably cutting his ties with me because of the scandal, as he should to maintain his credibility. God knew, I'd lost all of mine.

"Oh, that's great. Sean's a really nice guy and whip smart. I'm sure you'll learn a lot from him and be happy there."

"Sean asked me to drop by to give you this." She offered an envelope with *Senator and Mrs. Brady* scrawled across the front in fancy calligraphy. Before I could open it, she spoke again. "He asks that you and your wife come to his birthday party next Monday night. He wants to speak with you in person." My interest was piqued.

"Do you know why?" The nerves in my gut balled into a knot as I tossed the envelope on my desk.

Ava's face flushed. "He told me to say it had something to do with Antigua."

I exhaled, trying to reason out why Sean Fitzpatrick would want to talk to me about the most embarrassing thing that ever happened to me. If he wanted to further exploit my fucking humiliation, his goal was obvious.

"Uh, yeah. So, tell Mr. Fitzpatrick that I'll take a pass, but I wish him…" I instantly had a speech prepared in my brain before she pulled out her cell phone and handed it to me. I didn't see her touch the damn thing at all.

"Hell—hello?"

"Senator Brady? It's Sean Fitzpatrick. I have information you need to hear, so don't give young Ava a problem, and tell her you agree to come to my party. Her employment depends on your attendance." Was he threatening me with the girl's job? I was fucking stunned.

"How so? Not going to hire Ava if I don't show at your damn birthday party? That's a bit childish, isn't it? Oh, and that breaks about six of the workplace harassment and discrimination laws."

"Ava, pull up the guest list for Senator Brady, will you?"

Ava took the phone and pressed the screen a few times, turning it back to me. I glanced down the list of names, recognizing most of them, but one stood out. "Seriously? When did you become acquainted with him?" Fitzpatrick knew exactly who I was referring to.

"Cock of the Walk on I Street. He was cruising, I swear on my homophobic brother's grave. We talked for a few minutes, and we've had lunch a few times. He told me you were going to Antigua with your latest fuck buddy. Wonder who else he told?" Fitzpatrick teased, catching me by surprise.

I took a deep breath and made a decision. "I'll be there."

Who knew I was so eager to go to a fortieth birthday party? Not this fucking idiot, but I was going. I had plenty of questions to ask.

★★★ ★★★

"Who has a damn birthday party on a Monday night?" Vani climbed into the sedan I'd secured for our impromptu appearance out on the town.

I wasn't going without her. I had no idea what Fitzpatrick's game might be, but I was taking my best weapon in case it was all a ruse to demean me again. Yes, my ego was beaten to hell, but the chance to find out why a man I'd believed was straight for years was cruising a well-known gay bar was too tempting to pass up.

"If that's a riddle, I give up. The real answer is a narcissistic lobbyist who can demand people be wherever he wants them to be on any night of his choosing. You look fabulous, by the way! Remember, all the men here are gay, so don't get your heart broken." It was better to joke about it than continue to seethe.

Vani laughed. "You as well, darling." We stepped out of the car in front of the Four Seasons Hotel in Georgetown, which was the venue of the soiree.

"Don't forget, I'm unaffected by handsome men or beautiful women. I'm asexual, remember?" That was something she'd learned about herself during her therapy.

I could heartily agree that accepting one's true self was liberating, and Vani was certainly coming into her own. I was so proud of her that I was busting buttons.

I wrapped my arm around her shoulders and kissed her temple. "You're the best, Vani."

We followed the fancy sign in the lobby up the escalator where a handsome guy directed us to a small man with a clipboard and an attitude. We approached him, and I offered a campaign smile. "Senator and Mrs. Brady." I said it as if it still meant something.

"*Mmhmm.*" The asshole had a pompous smirk that made me laugh. I wouldn't be able to use the title much longer in any official capacity, so I might as well use it while I could.

Vani and I watched him peruse the list, and then he fixed his gaze on us, offering a big grin. "Oh, you're *him*? Well, well, aren't you a tasty treat? Table eight. Have a great time." The guy even gave me a wink.

"So, is he your type?" Vani smirked as we walked into the ballroom to see a scene that should never have happened at any birthday party. The room was decorated with anything and everything black.

"Don't be a smartass, you know he's not, and is this a fortieth party? Jesus, did he agree to this or is it a roast of some sort?" We walked farther into the room and took our place on the peripheral as hors d'oeuvres were passed.

"Good evening, Senator. Mrs. Brady, it's a pleasure to meet you. You're quite lovely," Sean Fitzpatrick greeted as he worked the room. He was alone, but he seemed happy and relaxed. Maybe I could be that way too, someday?

Chapter Four
Nash Lincoln

I was behind the bar stocking wine and beer into the large chest when the hospitality crew showed up, all very eager to dress the room. I was grateful to be working at the party, even though it was a Monday night. I'd take every catering gig I could get over my *other* job.

I worked as an escort a few times a week—sometimes it involved sex, but it was always at my discretion—and sometimes, it was just acting as a companion for the socially elite men and women who procured my services in the nation's capital.

I preferred bartending a lot more than the escort gig, but the two jobs combined put a roof over my head and food in my gut. It paid for my membership to a gym down the street from my place, and I generally didn't have to be smart or witty because all anyone was interested in was my face and my ass.

The party that night was for a well-known lobbyist, Sean Fitzpatrick. I'd met the man six months ago at another fancy hotel downtown. I was there as the companion of a judge's widow, and part of my job was to allow my client to interact with her friends without my interference. I was patiently waiting on the peripheral of Mrs. Symington's group of friends and enjoying a club soda, when a strong hand touched my shoulder.

I turned to see a gorgeous man with a big grin. He was slighter in build and height than me, but he oozed confidence. "I'm Sean Fitzpatrick. You're quite handsome. Are you here with Georgia Symington?" I would later learn his ego was even bigger.

I nodded and allowed Mr. Fitzpatrick to lead me away from the group a few steps where the two of us talked about nothing in particular. I got the impression he wasn't in Mrs. Symington's circle of friends, but he was eager to be, so during a break in the action, I introduced the two of them.

It turned out that Mrs. Symington was on the trustee's board of a charity from which Sean was seeking support for one of his causes—I was shit with details—and Mrs. Symington was eager to jump on board with whatever Sean wanted.

Sean didn't seem any more comfortable with the guests at the party than me, so we had time to talk and get to know each other. I found him to be much more down-to-earth than I'd initially thought, and I gave him a little background into my life and escort job that I generally didn't share with strangers.

Later that night, Sean slipped me his business card as the party was breaking up. "I host a lot of events around town, and we always have issues finding bartenders who don't steal the liquor. If you're interested, call me. I'll put you in touch with my catering manager, Naomi Chu."

I called him the next week, and an hour after we hung up, I got a call from Miss Chu, a woman I would later come to respect very much. I was grateful to have more jobs as a waiter or bartender, which allowed me to turn down many of the lower paying escort jobs. I owed it all to Sean Fitzpatrick.

"Nash! Delivery!" I turned to see Naomi motioning in my direction.

I quickly closed the coolers and hurried toward the back of the venue, seeing boxes of liquor. "All of this?" I had no idea how big a party on a Monday night could be, but considering it was DC, there was no logical answer.

"Here's the order sheet. Can you do the inventory and sign off for the delivery driver? That means if anything is unaccounted for, you're on the hook—but you know that. I need to go deal with those decorator people."

The expression on her face told me she was pissed, so I took the paper and nodded, going to work. Head down, eyes focused straight ahead.

A young Hispanic guy I'd worked with before named Jorge walked from the back and grinned. "Hey, Nash. I wasn't sure if you'd be working tonight, but I'm glad you are. I almost ditched. The political parties Fitzpatrick hosts are one thing, but personal shit is another."

I chuckled. "What? You don't like the idea of a bunch of gay guys ogling your ass on a Monday night?" Of course, none of my catering coworkers knew I was bisexual, nor did they know what my other job entailed. I was grateful to Fitzpatrick for not fertilizing the grapevine.

"Hey, I'm not homophobic. Some of my buddies from the neighborhood were gay when I was growing up. A lot of the families were funny about it, so many of my friends left as soon as they were old enough, but I still see some of them from time to time."

"What's your beef, then?"

"No, I'm not worried about the ogling. It's the fact nobody tips, man. It's like they think because they're friends with Fitzpatrick, they ain't gotta tip us. I need the extra scratch. My girl told me she wants to get married, and I better be saving for a ring or no more *panocha*. I gotta have it, two, three times a day, man." Jorge's girlfriend withholding the candy made me want to laugh.

"Yeah, I feel ya. So, are you waiting tables or slingin' drinks?" That damn Texas twang was there in my voice, much to my surprise. Jorge must have heard it too, because he started to laugh and began pointing at me with both index fingers.

"Hey, what can I say? Grew up in southwest Texas, near the border. Creeps in from time to time." I shrugged. I didn't give a shit what anyone thought about me or my accent—or so I kept telling myself. I'd tried damn hard to rid myself of the telltale twang over my adult life. Sometimes it worked, but when I least expected it, it crept back in.

Jorge laughed. "Hey, man, I'm just bustin' on you. I ain't got room to talk. My parents immigrated from Juarez before I was born. I grew up in DC, but my abuela doesn't speak English, so we learned both languages at the same time. Comes in handy in this job. Somebody's an asshole? I pretend I don't speak English, and they usually leave me alone and stomp off, mumbling like a fool."

We both laughed at that one. Avoiding confrontation was a great way to keep my job, or so I'd learned, though, at six foot with a muscular build, I could intimidate my way out of a jam, having learned the technique growing up in foster care around southern Texas.

Jorge and I talked about football as we stocked the bar. He went to get supplies from the kitchen while I cut fruit for the garnish. The decorating crew was in full swing, and everywhere I looked, there was black, silver, and pearly white. There was a banner hung at the front of the room near where a band was setting up, and it read, *Happy 40th, Sean!* I wasn't sure if the man was going for classy or creepy, but both worked for the occasion.

An hour later, the guests started arriving, and we became invisible. A few of the power players in town I recognized from previous parties and events, where I'd been on the arm of a woman or a man, depending on the type of party and the guest list. Of course, they didn't recognize me because the *help* was generally faceless and nameless beings in the world of Washington society.

After six months in DC, I wasn't sure if I liked it yet, but I'd been subletting a place from the owner of the escort business, Caroline Bering, of Monumental Promotions, Inc. She was giving me a hell of a deal on the fully furnished apartment she kept in Georgetown, which I truly appreciated.

It was decorated in an eclectic style with lots of flowery, overstuffed chairs and shabby chic tables—or so Caroline told me when she showed me the place and offered it as a sublet. It was comfortable, and if I ever had time for a love life, I'd have a nice place to fuck somebody. As it stood, that was a pipe dream.

I had planned to give the town a year, so the clock was running, and since I had no idea what I wanted to do next, I was biding my time. I'd made a promise not to get involved with anyone until I knew what I wanted out of life. I damn well didn't need any sort of entanglement. I had too much shit to figure out on my own.

I had no skills beyond fucking or mixing drinks, but both got me where I needed to go. No attachments. No regrets. Those were words to live by that I'd learned from my only friend, Clint, who had been my roommate at the group home where I'd been placed until I phased out of the foster system and took control of my future at eighteen. Clint and

I took off together, and we had a good time until he went his way, and I went mine. It was a relief to have someone I could trust back then.

I'd been on my own for nine years, traveling the country and finding shit jobs along the way to keep me from starving and sleeping on the ground. I'd been homeless a few times, and I hated it, which prompted me to find new and different ways to make money.

Hustling was something I'd dabbled in after Clint and I separated, finding it provided a decent living, but I had to stick to my guns—no condom, no suck or fuck.

When I arrived in DC with my trade ready to be plied, a woman stopped me outside of the Hamilton Hotel, where I'd stopped to wash up after fucking a businessman in a nearby alley for a hundred bucks—he wanted me in his ass bad because he suffered from low self-esteem. He kept telling me he couldn't believe someone as gorgeous as me would fuck him, and he cried when he jizzed all over the dirty ground behind a dumpster. I felt bad for the guy, but then I decided maybe I was providing a public service. I still laughed at my naïvety.

Anyway, the lady said I was handsome and asked if I'd thought about modeling. As far as I knew, DC wasn't known for its modeling industry, so I suspected there was more to it. Caroline Bering bought me breakfast, and I signed up to be a member of her elite escorts. Fast forward a few months to when I met Sean Fitzpatrick, and that was me in a nutshell. Nothing more, nothing less.

The birthday party was in full swing as people milled around the room while appetizers were being passed. I'd tasted a few as a server with a less than full tray stopped by, and the food was damn good. Jorge was busy flirting with a gorgeous waitress with a big rack, when an equally gorgeous woman and a hot-as-fuck silver fox strolled up to the bar.

I grabbed two beverage napkins and placed them on the bar top. "Good evening. What can I get you to drink? The host's signature cocktail tonight is called an Irish Gold. It's made with Tullamore Dew, peach schnapps, and a hint of orange juice, finished with a splash of ginger ale," I repeated for the hundredth time that night.

I'd tasted it, and it wasn't my cup of tea, but I was a company man when necessary, so I offered it. Surprisingly, the lady stared at me, pointing a sharp nail at a bottle of wine. "I'll have a healthy pour of pinot grigio, and he'll have a double Glenlivet on the rocks." She was *not* playing around.

I nodded and prepared their drinks. They were a stunning couple, but the guy looked familiar. I hated the feeling I knew someone but couldn't place where or why. I was left with one conclusion—at some point, I might have had sex with him, and seeing his wife gave me an uneasy feeling in my gut.

I didn't run background checks on guys I fucked, or let fuck me on occasion, but I was good with faces. The handsome guy standing at the bar was familiar.

I placed their drinks on the bar, and thankfully, the guy tossed a twenty in the tip jar. I nodded as they left, taking in both of their asses. Not a bad view as far as I was concerned.

The couple went to mingle, but I couldn't help but keep trying to ferret out how I knew the guy. It niggled on my mind, and I was unable to take my eyes off them as they made their way around the room. The two of them seemed to move as one, and it was hypnotizing. I'd never seen a more beautiful man in my life, and the fact he was with an equally gorgeous woman reminded me the fucking universe wasn't always fair.

The night wore on, and between making small talk with Jorge, who kept trying to fix me up with his sister, his cousin, his girlfriend's sister, and even his mother, I was bored out of my skull. There were toasts for Sean Fitzpatrick, and thankfully, only the birthday boy enjoyed the signature cocktail.

When the handsome man I'd been eye stalking returned to the bar without the beautiful woman, I was determined to get to the bottom of why I thought I knew the guy.

"Another Glenlivet, sir?" The guy's hair was dark blond on top with grey at the temples, which made him look like a stock photo.

"I'll have a beer instead."

I held up two bottles, one a domestic and one an import. The man pointed to the domestic, so I opened it and offered him the bottle and a frosted glass. "Thanks," he responded before he lifted the bottle to his full lips, pushing the glass away.

"Can I get a glass of pinot for your wife?" I didn't see her anywhere nearby.

"She's in the ladies' room. Vani had a little too much to drink, so she went to freshen up. It never happens, you know, where she drinks too much, but all the pressure—" He drifted off as he continued to scan the room. It was then that I figured out why he looked familiar. I'd seen his face—and his ass—on the front page of the free paper for months.

He was a United States senator, and he'd gotten caught doing someone who wasn't his beautiful wife. He'd recently lost his re-election bid and had somewhat disappeared from public life. I was surprised he'd show up at such a high-profile event.

"Are you looking for someone?" I studied him closely before I realized he was staring back. I'd been bored, but now I'd found something, or someone, interesting to focus on. At least the man was smoking hot!

"I'm looking for a Judas. You know, you think you know someone, and then one day, you find out they sold you out for a bag of magic beans. I mean, come the fuck on? We've been friends since college, and now? Fucking *now* he decides to sell me out? The bastard didn't even have the decency to show up tonight so I could confront him like Sean promised."

Senator Blondie seemed to have an axe to grind, and I had no customers, so I ventured into the breach... I thought I wanted to be an actor for a week when I was in New York, so I tried out for a Shakespeare play. Not good at it. Another dream dashed to bits.

"So, your man did you wrong? How?" I quizzed, not meaning anything by the phrase.

"Fucker isn't my man, but he betrayed me. If I find him, I'm gonna beat his ass." Senator Blondie sloshed his beer. Just then, Sean Fitzpatrick came around the corner with the man's wife, who looked as if she'd been waging a war of her own.

Sean escorted the woman up to the bar—holding her upright—and took in the sight of the two of them. "New plan, Nash. I need you to see that the Brady's get somewhere out of sight. The Senator can't afford another scandal."

Brady? The cogs slowly turned and slid into place. I remembered the man's name was Spencer Brady, the junior senator from Virginia. "Oh, this is—?"

"Yep, and I need you to get them out of here without the press seeing them and causing more problems. I'll get someone else to clean up. I won't forget this." I could see Sean Fitzpatrick was completely serious.

Considering I wanted to get away from being an escort, which meant I'd lose my place to live, I needed cash, so maybe Sean had connections that could get me out of sex work? I couldn't pass up his offer. "Okay, uh, where do they live?" I quickly dried my hands.

"Oh, uh, I don't actually know, but I'll get a suite, and you can take them upstairs and make sure they get to bed. I don't think they sleep together, so I'll make sure it's a two bedroom. I'll be back." Sean rushed across the room toward the lobby, leaving me more than a little confused.

I walked around the bar and looked at the guy, seeing he was still fucking gorgeous, even if his eyes were red, and he wasn't steady on his feet. Of course, I knew all about the bullshit that had happened to the man, but I was sympathetic.

A person should be able to determine when they want to tell others about themselves—their real selves. Nobody had ever asked me about myself, so I'd never said it out loud.

People like Sean Fitzpatrick assumed a lot about me that I didn't bother to correct, but then again, it was *my* truth, wasn't it? Nobody had any business knowing anything intimate about me unless *I* chose to tell them.

Sean rushed back with an envelope in his hand. "Get them out of here. The guy who fucked him over—allegedly—just arrived, and with the amount of alcohol they've consumed, it'll be front-page news. Get them anything they want, on me, of course." Sean quickly shoved the envelope into my hands and hurried off to greet a dark-haired man who didn't look happy at all.

I turned to see the couple I'd been assigned were both nearly passed out on their feet, so I steadied the lady and motioned for the man to follow me out through the kitchen to the freight elevator. It had the potential to be a long night.

I woke up to someone puking, but then, it sounded as if it was in stereo, so I hopped up from the fancy, uncomfortable couch and went to one bedroom door and then the other, confirming they were both returning the liquor from the previous night.

Glancing out the sliding doors to the balcony, I noticed the sky was barely beginning to pale, so I went into the full kitchen, checking the clock on the microwave to see it was five in the morning. I grabbed two glasses from the cabinets and filled each with filtered water. There was a gift basket on the counter with packets of hangover remedies, so I retrieved two packages of ibuprofen and went to the room on the left where Mrs. Brady seemed to have finished emptying her stomach.

"Mrs. Brady, I have water and painkillers. May I come in?" I asked quietly. The door opened, and Mrs. Brady offered a sick smile, tightening the complimentary robe around her middle.

"What's your name, young man?" the woman whispered. She seemed classy to me, nothing like the foster moms I'd had when I was going through the system. This woman gave off a kind and gentle vibe, and I immediately liked her.

"I'm Nash, ma'am. I brought you some water and some pain relievers. It's awful early, so why don't you take them and lie back down? I'll order breakfast in a few hours if you tell me what you'd like."

Mrs. Brady grabbed the water and the pills, downing them in a few gulps. "I can't think about food right now. Where's Spencer?" She returned the glass to me.

"The Senator is in the room across the suite."

"Where are you sleeping, Nash, is it?"

I smiled at her kind nature. "I'm on the couch, ma'am. I'm fine."

We both heard a god-awful sound coming from the other room, which made Mrs. Brady laugh. "Oh, Lord, I can't remember the last time we both got shit-faced. Will you take him the water and pills? He's gonna need them."

With that, Mrs. Brady closed the door, and I heard another groan from the opposite side of the suite.

I hurried over and knocked on the door, "Senator Brady, sir, I have water and painkillers. May I come in?" Somewhere along the way, I'd learned some manners that got me by pretty well. If I'd had a mother, I'd have bet she would have been proud.

I heard a grunt and took it to mean it was okay, so I opened the door. The man was standing in his boxers and undershirt, holding a towel up to his mouth. "I, uh, here." I held out the water and the pills, which he took, popping the meds and chugging the water in a few seconds.

"Mrs. Brady went back to bed. It's quite early, so I suggest you do the same. I'll order breakfast in a little while, and then I'll get you out of here without anyone seeing you," I suggested.

"How'd we get up here in the first place, uh, what's your name?" The senator's voice was a whisper, likely from all the vomiting.

"It's Nash, sir."

"Ugh, please, call me Spencer or Spence. How'd we get up here?"

"Mr. Fitzpatrick suggested perhaps you and your wife might be more comfortable in this complimentary suite, and he asked that I escort you and make sure you were both okay. I crashed on the couch in case you needed anything."

"That's, uh, that was kind of you. I'll take it up with Sean but thank you for looking out for us since we both seem to have lost all common sense because of all this bullshit."

The man walked to the bed and sat, planting his elbows on his knees and burying his head into his hands. Never before had I seen a more downtrodden man in my life. What they must have been going through, I could only imagine.

Chapter Five
Spencer

I woke the second time to the smell of bacon and quickly realized I was ravenous. Vani and I had only eaten a few appetizers at the party the previous night, so it was no wonder we'd gotten completely wasted. The night was mostly a blur, but I remembered speaking to Sean at some point and then being snubbed by several of the attendees when we tried to say hello. If that was the new normal, I'd pack up the truck and move on down the road.

I dressed in my clothes from the previous night, knowing how mortified Vani would be at doing the walk of shame in her party dress, so I skipped the tie, shoving it in the pocket of my suit coat before I opened the door to the bedroom. I should have felt the need to call my office and check in, but I found I didn't give a shit. LDS—lame-duck syndrome—had taken hold, and I planned to fully embrace it.

As I headed down the hallway, I heard my wife chattering away. "...and really, it's nobody's business. We are consenting adults, and hell, I suggested they go away before campaign season officially kicked off because they weren't going to get to see each other until after the election."

Who the fuck is she spilling her guts to on a cloudy Tuesday morning?

"Until this morning, I didn't know it was Blaire Conner. How will the senator take it that the man's name was leaked?" It was the guy Fitzpatrick had assigned to take care of us—a guy we knew nothing about. Who knew if the guy was a reporter, and my wife was giving an exclusive in the dining room of the suite? When would the bleeding stop?

I walked in to see Vani dressed in a tracksuit with the local baseball team's logo on the front of the jacket. It looked stylish with her black stilettos, as I could see through the glass-topped dining table.

"Vani, why bore the young man with our *personal* business?" I raised an eyebrow in her direction. Her beautiful face flushed, which highlighted how well rested she appeared to be, unlike me, who looked as if I'd just been released from the drunk tank.

"Oh, Spence, you're so pessimistic. Nash is fine. He's not the enemy. Sit. He ordered lots of food, and it's all on Fitzpatrick." Vanessa released a quick giggle.

I wanted to laugh, because my wife loved food and had a hearty appetite, sometimes eating me under the table. She never gained a damn pound, god love her.

Nash, our new caretaker, grabbed a plate and began filling it for me. Once it was sufficiently piled up, he placed it in front of me before going to the cart to grab a coffee cup and saucer.

It all smelled delicious and looked tasty, but the food was no match for Nash's ass... assets... which were on display in the black chinos he was wearing. I glanced up to see Vanessa smirking at me before she took a delicate bite of toast and winked. I was more than a little leery of that look.

"So, Nash, tell me about yourself." He poured me a cup of coffee from the carafe resting on the table near Vani.

"Uh, well, I've got a vagabond heart. I don't like to stay in one place too long." He passed the sugar and creamer to me for my coffee.

"Spencer, Nash is new to town. He works part-time as an escort for the men and women in town when they attend events, and his other job is working for Naomi Chu when she has a catering job. Remember? Naomi catered Judge Dean and Rett Beaumont's wedding in New York. We were supposed to attend, but it snowed, and the airport closed. It was on Christmas Eve a couple of years ago. Anyway, Nash knows Georgia Symington." Vanessa spilled every one of the man's secrets and spilled them in a hot minute.

I glanced at Nash to see he was smiling at Vani, which made me wonder if he wanted in my wife's panties. "Where'd you get the tracksuit. Not your usual style," I pointed out.

"Nash went downstairs and picked it up for me from the gift shop, so I don't have to walk out in my cocktail dress. He brought you a sweatshirt and a baseball cap as well. Oh, NBS had no problem outing Blaire. His name was released early this morning. He was unable to be reached for comment. Have you been contacted?" Vani scrolled through her phone.

I reached for my shirt pocket to retrieve mine, only to find it dead. I flipped it around to show the blank screen to Vani just as her phone rang. She looked at it before handing it to Nash. "Answer it and say the Senator and his wife have no comment, please. Otherwise, they'll keep calling, and I don't want to turn it off in case Jay needs us."

I started to grab her ringing phone when Vani slapped my hand. "Leave it alone, Spence. Nash, go ahead, please."

The man cleared his throat. "Hello? Senator and Mrs. Brady have no comment. No, you can't have my name. Don't you people use *a source* or *a spokesperson* when you make shit up? You're welcome." Nash ended the call and handed the phone back to Vani with a sexy smirk.

"That should take care of things, at least for a while. So, Senator—"

I held up a hand to stop him. "Spencer, please."

He smiled. "Right. Spencer. So, we need to figure out how to sneak the two of you out of here and get you home, sir." Nash glanced between the two of us.

I nodded as I poured syrup over my hotcakes, not ready to face reality. We ate until the food was gone, and I was as stuffed as a tick.

Vani rose from the table and began to clear when Nash stopped her. "I've got it, Vani. Finish your coffee." He stacked the plates and platters before moving everything into the kitchen.

"*Vani*, what the fuck are you doing? He might be a reporter in disguise," I hissed at her.

Of course, she giggled, as she shook her head at my paranoia. When one lived in the shadows, it was hard not to jump to conclusions.

"Now, Spencer, he's not a reporter. He's a gorgeous young man who has a compassionate heart, I just know it. He mentioned he'd read about everything in the free paper they give out at the metro, and he asked if we were okay. We got to talking, and I find him quite charming." Vani smiled at me, which made me wonder if *she* was attracted to him.

I cocked my eyebrow again, and she rolled her eyes. "Not for me, Spence. For you. He's bisexual. I think the two of you would make a very attractive couple." Vani's mind was clearly made up on the matter.

"Oh, bullshit. He's, what? Twenty-three? You think he'd be interested in these crow's feet?" I pointed to the lines around my eyes that had become more prominent in the last three months.

Vanessa rose from her seat and walked around the table, pulling out the chair next to me before sitting and taking my hand. "I love you, Spencer. You have been my best friend since we met, and I have loved you like a brother for longer than I can remember not loving you. I've been very happy with the life we've built together, but it's got to feel good to finally have your truth out there, even if it wasn't the way you'd have preferred it to be told.

"For twenty years, you've been my rock, and you've sacrificed so much for Jay and me. We got through my PTSD, and all the counseling I had to endure because of the rape and the feelings I had surrounding the miscarriage. You were there for me, supporting me every step of the way, for which I will always be grateful. Hell, you married me to salvage my honor, Spencer. You've lived your life for everyone else, even down to running for the Senate."

I stared at Vani. "Vanessa, you don't owe me anything."

She smiled. "You're wrong, Spence. Running for office wasn't your choice, was it? Your parents, the bastards, they pushed you into it! Hell, I guess I pushed as well. I thought it would be glamorous to be a senator's wife, and you hated practicing real estate law, remember? I was selfish not to consider how much you denied yourself to help me find my happiness. I'm sorry I haven't thanked you before now."

"Now, here we are. We have the chance to start over and for both of us to find our happiness, not just me. Jay is going to come around, Spence. He's in shock right now, and it can't be easy to be the son of a tarnished senator on a large college campus, but he's making the best of it. How about you and I make the best of it as well?" Clearly, my wife was up on her soapbox.

As per usual, Vanessa hit the bullseye. No, I'd never wanted to be a lawyer, but my father, Ronald Brady, who was a retired circuit court judge in Norfolk, had insisted law school, and then Congress, was the right path for me.

It was the only way he and my mother, Hillary, would attempt to accept Vanessa, and back then, she needed that acceptance. Considering they'd abandoned us after I became front-page news, maybe Vanessa was right? Maybe we should worry about ourselves for a change?

"So, what? I should take him back in the bedroom and—"

"Aw, now. I'm not quite *that* easy unless I'm being paid five-hundred bucks an hour. Mr. Fitzpatrick called to say he's going to send a car for you. The driver will be on the third level of the parking garage next to the freight elevator. He'll be here in half an hour, hardly enough time for me to show *either* of you a good time." Nash had a sexy smirk and a healthy amount of humor in his voice.

Vani giggled. "Not me but thank you. I'm ace, which means I—"

"You're not sexually attracted to anyone. Yes, I know what it means." Nash glanced in my direction. "Based on the papers, I'd say you're a man's man all the way, huh? I swing either way. What a fine group we make."

The three of us chuckled at his comment. He was spot on.

"Anyway, I'll get you to the parking garage and leave you to it. I'll be back in fifteen minutes. I need to speak to my boss to see that I still have a job." Nash left the suite, phone in hand.

Vani hissed to get my attention, wagging a well-manicured finger at me. "At least get his number. If nothing else, he's not judgmental, and we really don't have any friends left. If they turned their backs on you, they're dead to me." Vani kissed my cheek and stood, pushing in the chair and heading toward the bedroom where she'd slept.

I sat at the table, trying to figure out what to do about the latest disaster, and I came to one conclusion—I wanted to corner Mario and force him to tell me what happened, and then Vani and I needed to get out of town for a while. I needed to check my calendar for the rest of the year to see if any important votes were coming up and begin to plan what was next for the two of us—if Vanessa still wanted to be a part of my life. That was a giant hurdle to jump.

I tossed a fifty over the front seat to the sedan driver as I hopped out of the car on our driveway. I reached in to pull Vani across the seat and help her out. There was patchy snow that must have fallen overnight, and she was wearing heels, so I didn't want her to fall. Out of the corner of my eye, I saw a news van roll up, blocking the driveway, which wasn't going to be a good thing. A woman hopped out with a cameraman in tow, shoving a microphone in my face before I could react.

"Senator Brady! Senator Brady! Would you follow up on your statement from earlier disclosing that Blaire Conner was your guest in Antigua. Will you comment on why you and Mr. Conner were engaging in sexual relations during the day on a public beach?" Yeah, it was time to get the hell out of Dodge.

I started to give the party line— "No comment!"—when Vani stopped dead in her tracks and wheeled on the reporter, Bree McCoy, who worked for the local NBS affiliate where Blaire had worked before he got promoted to the network.

"You! You have a lot of nerve coming to my home and attempting to humiliate a good man. Get off my property. You're trespassing, and I'll call Fairfax County Police and have you prosecuted to the fullest extent of the law if you don't get off my driveway immediately." The way Vani was pointing that finger, I knew it was a threat she would see through.

I grabbed her arm and pulled her along with me, hoping her sense of self-preservation kicked in. That would be something to look forward to on the five o'clock news, her losing her shit and dignity with a snippy up-and-comer in local media.

Once we were in the house, we both kicked off our shoes and headed for the kitchen. I plugged in my private cell and placed it on the counter, before sliding off the ball cap Nash had provided, though clearly, it didn't protect me from the vultures who were circling to pick at my carcass on my own driveway.

Vani let down the high ponytail she'd swept her long blonde mane into and flopped into a chair at the table, releasing a heavy sigh. "I'm sorry."

I walked over behind her and bent to kiss the top of her head. "You didn't do anything wrong, love.

You're frustrated with this situation, and that one deserved a dressing down."

My phone—the burner phone—began dinging with texts, so I walked over and picked it up from the counter, seeing messages from Blaire.

"Fuck." I was *not* ready for another battle to come my way.

"Blaire?"

"Yeah, and—" I trailed off before I opened the first of several messages from Blaire.

> **How the fuck could you? Call me!**

> **Spencer, you put out a *statement*? You bastard!**

> **I'll never forgive you for this!**

I ran upstairs to my office to retrieve my official cell, checking the messages to see a text from Mario.

> **Senator—In accordance with your instructions of yesterday afternoon, I have issued a statement on your behalf, confirming that Blaire Conner was the man in the picture you were having sex with on your vacation in Antigua. I agree, it's better to get everything out in the open. I'll be in touch—Mario**

I read the message three times and checked back through my emails and the other texts on my phone, seeing nothing from me instructing anyone to do anything of the sort. I called Mario's cell, and it went directly to voicemail. The fucking coward refused to talk to me? No fucking way was I letting that fly.

I hung up and called my director of communications, Mitchell Flora. Anything released from my office went through him first, and if he knew nothing about it, then someone was fucking with me, yet again.

The phone rang three times before it was answered. "Communications. This is Tammy," I heard.

"This is Senator Brady. Where's Mitch? I need to speak with him immediately." I shouldn't yell at her, but I couldn't help it. What a clusterfuck!

"Sir, he's in a meeting with Mr. Fernandez. Should I interrupt them? I was told not to, but for you, I will," the young woman offered.

"Transfer me to the conference room, but don't announce me. Just put the call through." I sounded so hateful, but something had to fucking give before I bashed my head against the nearest brick wall.

The phone rang four times before it was picked up. "I said we weren't to be disturbed!" It was Mario, and I was so beyond pissed I could barely hold my temper.

"Yes, well, you didn't answer when I called," I snapped in return.

"Oh, Senator, I'm sorry. My cell is charging in my office," was Mario's response. If not answering a call from me was all the fucker thought he should be sorry about, he was sadly mistaken.

"You need to come out to the house. We need to talk about the statement you and Flora released today. I didn't authorize it."

"Uh, what? I... I got a... got an..." Mario was stammering, which only served to piss me off worse.

"I don't know or care what you got, but you didn't get it from me. You need to come out to the house ASAP." I hung up.

I dialed Blaire's number, hearing the phone answered on the first ring. "*What?*"

"Blaire, it's me, Spence. I promise you, I didn't give permission for a press release, and I'm trying to get to the bottom of it right now. I'm so sorry this is happening to you. I never meant to hurt you."

The sniffle I heard was behind me. I turned to see Vanessa standing in the doorway. She stepped forward and reached out her hand, so I gave her the phone, not seeing that any further damage could be done.

"Blaire? This is Vanessa Brady. I'm so sorry this happened to you. I was the one who suggested

Spencer should take you away for a few days before the campaign kicked into overdrive. I've known the two of you had seen each other since that party in January where you met. I approved completely."

I couldn't hear what Blaire said, but I could hear Vani's response.

"It's not a game, Blaire. Your feelings matter. I'm guessing Spencer didn't tell you we have an open marriage, did he? We live separate lives together, which is what we've always done. I'm sorry you got caught in the crossfire. Goodbye."

Based on the turn of events—and the look on Vani's face—the relationship with Blaire was definitely over. I knew it in my gut, but it seemed as if my wonderful wife was trying to help me tie up loose ends. I would forever be grateful.

Chapter Six
Nash

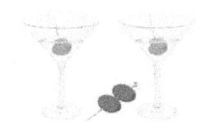

I was folding laundry in my sublet when my cheap cell phone chimed from the charger on the kitchen counter. I picked it up to see it was a text from Vani Brady, as she'd invited me to call her when she demanded my cell number and gave me hers in return. I still wasn't certain of that situation, but I did like the two of them. They seemed to have had a lot of shit thrown at them lately, and from what I'd learned, they were great people who didn't deserve any of it. Their business was exactly that—their business.

Vani was a sweet person, though I was sure there was a toughness under all the mascara, lipstick, and those big blue eyes. She was beautiful, but she'd made it clear she wasn't into me. I wasn't offended. I hadn't really considered a threesome with her and her husband, though the idea of it was intriguing. I was into him, but I wasn't making a move. Based on what I'd read and heard, the man had enough bullshit in his life to last a lifetime.

> **Please come to 16 Sunnybrook Lane, Great Falls. It might seem premature, but we need you. Be careful! The press is camped out. Vani**

For reasons I didn't know, I grabbed my laundry and went to my bedroom, pulling out a duffel bag I got as a gift when I went to an open house at a nearby gym. I couldn't afford to become a member, but the guy at the desk said I had a magical tongue and no gag reflex, so I worked out when he was working.

I called a cab after checking my cash stash and packed some clothes. I didn't have a credit card, so Uber wasn't an option, but I could get a cab from Bailey's Crossroads to Great Falls easily. What I needed clarified was why should I do it?

> **What's going on? Are you guys in danger? Nash**

It seemed a logical question to me, so I waited for a response before I inserted myself into an unknown situation with two virtual strangers. After a minute, a response came.

> **Danger? Not likely. Pain? Definitely. There's a lot to be said. Please come talk. There's a gate to the backyard on the right side of the house. Go through the woods. Vani**

As much as I wanted to ignore the text, something new tugged at my heart. *No attachments. No regrets.* Suddenly, those words seemed offensive, but I didn't know why. I realized I couldn't figure it out on my own, so I sent a response.

> **I'll be there in an hour. Nash**

It was surprising to watch my fingers tap out the text, but I was acting on instinct, not common sense. Why? I had no idea, but it seemed important that I go see Spence and Vani. When I received the return call from the Red Top Cab, I grabbed my things and went outside to wait under the shelter of the front door awning. *What the hell am I doing?*

The cab pulled away after I had my duffel out of the back seat, the driver happy to have been paid in cash. I understood his attitude completely, because getting paid under the table—as happened when I tricked—didn't suck. I didn't have a bank account, credit cards, or a credit score, as far as I knew. I lived on cash and lies, mostly to myself.

I was an independent contractor in both of my jobs, and I had the tax forms in confirmation, but I didn't pay taxes. Hell, I didn't make enough to owe taxes, but some government offices might disagree. I wasn't chancing it, regardless.

I'd asked the driver to let me off down the block, seeing the swarm of media vipers parked outside the prestigious brick home on the cozy cul-de-sac. I walked down the hill and into the woods, finding the gate Vani had mentioned. It was unlocked, so I let myself inside and trudged up to the back deck, knocking on the door while holding my duffel in my left hand.

Vani opened the door and held her finger to her lips. "Thank you for coming. Spencer's chief of staff is here, trying to explain why he issued a statement regarding the encounter in Antigua without Spence's consent."

I was confused. "Why did you need me?"

Vani took my hand and led me up a back staircase to the second floor. There was an open stairway from the first floor where we could hear the men speaking in the living room downstairs.

"Look, Spence, there was a note on my desk that said, 'Issue a statement and confirm it's Blaire in the pics. I need to be crystal clear about this and accept responsibility.' Here's a copy."

Vani leaned closer to me and whispered, "That's Mario Fernandez, Spence's chief of staff. The other man is Mitchell Flora, the director of communications for the Senate office."

"Does Spence know I'm here?" I was fucking confused by the entire situation. It wasn't easy piecing together their relationship, much less my part in it.

No attachments. No regrets.

When the shouting began, Vani and I stepped back into the shadows. "You left a note on my desk!" one of them yelled.

"I didn't write it. I put it there after it was left on *my* desk!" the other person yelled in return.

"*What fucking note?*" That was Spencer, and I was sure the neighbors heard him. When I looked at Vani, she took my hand and led me down the hallway to a bedroom.

"So, I think, but don't hold me to this, someone is out to completely decimate our lives. We're not sure why, yet, but we want to get out of town for a while. How strong are your ties to the area?" Vani asked, which completely surprised me. We'd only met about fifteen hours prior, and she was asking me to go away with them? It made no sense.

"Why? Why would you want me to go with you on a trip?" I asked, needing clarity.

Vani closed her big blue eyes before opening them and looking into mine. "You are a calming spirit, and right now, that's what we need. We also need someone to watch our backs as we attempt to maneuver through this minefield."

I was under her spell, but not because I wanted to fuck her. I wanted to make her feel safe, which was new for me. I wouldn't allow it to become an attachment, but it didn't seem right to leave the two of them alone when they were in such a bad place. Situations like the one where they found themselves tended to lead to bad decisions, and usually, there was no turning back from those.

Before I could answer, the front door slammed. "*Vanessa*!" Spencer's deep voice boomed through the cavernous rooms in the majestic house.

She turned to me, offering a tender smile. "We need you, Nash. I can feel it in my bones. Please, think about it?"

"Think about what, Vani?"

"Think about becoming a dear friend who will support us during this mess, and maybe become family when you're ready?"

I could only nod, not exactly sure what she meant by the odd statement, but not having the strength to tell her no. How in the hell could anyone tell her no?

I was in the kitchen while Vani and Spencer were upstairs with Spencer's chief of staff. Apparently, something Mario said had Spencer on alert, and he'd called Vani upstairs. I went through the fridge to find cold cuts for sandwiches, so I went to work. Idle hands and all that bullshit learned from one of my foster mothers, who was a religious fanatic.

I heard Vani and Spencer coming downstairs, but there was another set of footsteps following behind. When they walked into the kitchen with a handsome man sporting a worried face, I stopped and turned to the couple. "Should I make more food?" I asked, looking at Vani for confirmation.

"No!" Spencer's voice echoed off the walls.

"Spence, dear, don't be an ass. Mario, sit down and have a sandwich that Nash has been so kind to make for us. What do you think is going on?" Vani picked up the platter of sandwiches and placed it on the table where I'd already stacked napkins and a few paper plates I'd found in one of the cabinets. I sat down at the island and allowed the three of them to settle at the table.

The other man took a seat and looked at the two of them. He seemed to be assessing the situation, which was probably a good idea. "I went into the office early this morning, and I was in the middle of making calls to see if we had any allies left, when Mitch came into my office with a typed note he'd found on the printer beside his desk.

"It instructed us to issue a statement that Blaire Conner was with you in Antigua, and since I couldn't get you on the phone to confirm your directive, we went from the note, Spence. We'd have never done anything of the sort without your permission, I swear," the man informed.

One thing I'd learned over the years was how to judge people, and as I studied the man sitting with Vani and Spencer, I could see he was telling the truth. He showed a lot of sympathy for what the two of them were going through.

"Ah, shit. You think Mitch is up to something? How did he... who the hell besides you, me,

Vani, and Blaire knew we were going to Antigua?" Spencer asked.

Vani offered a giggle as she turned to Mario. "Sean Fitzpatrick seemed to know. He told us you were in Cock of the Walk one night looking for a hookup when you two ran into each other." Based on the man's face, she definitely caught him by surprise with her statement.

"I... I... Fuck! I forgot about that. It was months ago," Mario responded. "Can I get something to drink?" he asked, looking in my direction. I stood and went to the fridge, grabbing three bottles of water and placing them on the table. I was a bartender at heart. Nothing new.

"Thank you, Nash," Spencer offered. I winked at him and returned to my seat at the island.

"So, how come you never told me you're into guys?" Spencer asked his chief of staff.

"I didn't think it mattered to you one way or another," the man sniped back. It was then I saw it—attraction and jealousy. The guy was into Spence, probably had been for a long time, but he knew Spencer wouldn't be interested in him, and it pissed him off.

Spencer glanced at me before he turned to Mario. "You've known I was gay since we met in undergrad. It wouldn't have mattered to me, Mario. I thought you were one of my best friends, and I foolishly believed we told each other everything." The sound of the Senator's voice reflected how hurt he was by the man's comment, but I could tell Spence had taken it the wrong way.

"Spence, I don't think you're understanding him." The words were out of my mouth before I had the chance to bite my tongue. I was usually good about keeping my opinions to myself but something inside me pressed on.

"I think Mr. uh, your chief of staff has feelings he's sure you won't return," I clarified before biting into my own sandwich.

Vani looked at the man before taking his hand. "You love Spence, don't you? Oh, Mario, honey, I'm so sorry." She tried to comfort the man who must have been mortified.

"I just—I didn't want to fall in love with him, Vanessa. I'd never, ever do anything to hurt either of you. I couldn't help myself, and then, when Blaire came onto the scene, I knew nothing could ever make you look at me the way you looked at him. I saw you looking at him when we were in Newport News with the Governor. He's the type of guy you go for, not someone like me," Mario lamented.

Mario was a handsome guy. Slight of build, with pitch-black hair held perfectly in place by some sort of product. His Hispanic heritage did right by him, and I could tell he was a proud man. He'd been friends with the dark blond god named Spencer Brady for many years, and I could only imagine how heavy that torch must have been to carry alone for so long.

No, a man like Mario might have gotten a little too liquored up and said something out of school to someone like Sean Fitzpatrick, but I had my doubts he would ever betray Spencer, especially not about his sexuality. "I don't think Mr. uh—what's your name again?"

I could see I unnerved the man, so I was ready when he yelled, "Who the *fuck* are you?" And, just like that, the tension in the room evaporated.

I chuckled and stood from the island, walking over and extending my hand to the man. "Nashville Lincoln. You can call me Nash. Pleasure's all mine."

"Mario Fernandez. You look familiar." Mario had a puzzled look on his face.

Vanessa giggled. "He's very handsome, and he has a welcoming face. That's probably why you think he's familiar. We don't suspect you betrayed us, Mario. Help us find out who did. The only way to get Spence's name out of the papers is to put someone else's in its place. Will you do that?"

Fernandez nodded before he stood from the table, tossing his wadded-up napkin onto his empty plate. He turned to me and offered an odd smile. "I think we know each other from somewhere. I'll figure it out, but thanks for the sandwich."

I nodded as Vanessa stood and took the man's arm. "Come on, Mario, I'll show you out." She pointed to Spencer's untouched ham sandwich. "Eat."

The look on his face made me chuckle, but he picked up the sandwich and took a bite, winking at me. I sat in Vanessa's abandoned chair and placed a hand on his arm. "He knows me from the DNC fundraiser I attended with Mitzi Shaw in April. He hit up one of the busboys that night, and I walked in on the two of them fucking in the men's room," I answered, not pointing out that I could end up being more of a liability to him than Blaire Conner.

Spencer placed his hand over the top of mine, offering a gentle pat. "We weren't there that night because we took Jay to tour a couple of schools in Chicago. He decided he wanted to be away from home—because two-hundred-and-sixty miles isn't far enough," he answered, looking a little heartsick.

"Well, Spencer, you've got big shoes to fill. Ever think how much pressure that puts on a kid who's still trying to find his place in the world?" As if I knew anything about raising a family.

He chuckled. "I think my recent fuck up leveled the playing field, didn't it?"

Yeah. He made a good point.

Chapter Seven
Spencer

I found myself feeling completely comfortable with Nash as we sat at the kitchen table after I finished my sandwich. The only person I'd ever felt that way with was Vanessa. Somehow, I trusted Nash Lincoln, a man I barely knew. I trusted him much more than Blaire, which was strange because I'd known—and fucked—that man for nearly a year.

"So, who else will recognize you from escorting someone powerful?" He'd escorted Mitzi Shaw, the widow of the former Speaker of the House, Albert Shaw. Albert died from pancreatic cancer the first year I took office. He was a good man, but he bit like a rattlesnake if provoked.

Senators and staffers called him Copperhead behind his back, but it wasn't because his hair was dyed an unnatural rust color to cover the grey. Every party Vani and I attended at the Shaw's home was pleasant.

The couple was always kind and welcoming, introducing us to the power players in town as if we were family. I'd missed seeing Al's copper-penny hair in the chamber. He was a good man—until one crossed him.

"I usually just blend into the background. I fetch drinks when needed, and just like a fancy purse, I'm a shiny accessory. People don't know my name, and they don't care. You'd be better off not trying to be my friend. It'll cause you nothing but trouble." Nash's concern was written all over his face.

I touched his cheek where there was a short, scruffy beard I was craving to feel rubbed on every square inch of my body. I felt my cock beginning to swell in my jeans, but the sound of footsteps on the stairs reminded me that we weren't alone. We were in the home I shared with Vanessa, and doing anything with Nash would violate our sacred rule—I didn't fuck guys in our home.

I moved back from the gorgeous man and began clearing the table, glancing at the clock to see it was just after two in the afternoon. "I, uh, I guess I better..." My phone started ringing in my shirt pocket, so I retrieved it, seeing it was Jay.

"Hello? Jay? Son, are you okay?" After not hearing from him since the middle of August, even when he was at home, I prayed it was the beginning of the two of us rebuilding our relationship.

"I'm okay, Dad. I have a broken arm, but nothing that won't heal. I'm at Lewis Gale Hospital in town. My car was T-boned in an intersection near Walmart. I was going to get groceries with my roommate, Cole, and some asshole came out of nowhere. Cole has a broken arm and leg on his right side where the truck hit us. Can you get Mom to come down so we can straighten this out with the cops and the insurance? She didn't answer her phone."

While I was glad he was okay, my heart deflated a little at his explanation that he called because he couldn't get Vani on the phone. "Which arm?"

I headed out of the kitchen to find Vanessa, who was curled up on the couch in the den reading a book. I knelt in front of her and put the phone on speaker.

"My left. I held it up to keep the airbag from breaking my nose." Jay sounded exhausted.

"*What?*" Vanessa quickly sat up, tossing off the cashmere throw that usually rested along the back of the brown leather couch.

"He was in a car accident. He was on his way to Walmart to grocery shop, but now he's at the hospital in Blacksburg. His roommate, Cole, has a broken arm and a broken leg from a truck T-boning them at an intersection. We need to get down there." I was going along whether my son liked it or not.

"Just send Mom. You don't need to come." Jay was insistent, but I was done hiding, especially from him.

Vanessa nodded that she understood I was going. "We'll be there in a few hours. Stay put. Check on your roommate."

Just then, Nash, who I'd forgotten all about, came into the room and sat in my recliner. "What's wrong?" He silently mouthed the words to me.

I handed Vani the phone and walked over to him to whisper. "Our son was in a car accident in Blacksburg where he attends college. We need to go down there to check on him and straighten things out about his car. Goddamn, when it rains it pours." I stared off into space, wondering what the fuck could go wrong next.

"You, uh, you want me to drive you guys down? You can take advantage of the ride and start figuring out the car. I'd suggest you check to see if the other driver remained on the scene, or do you know?" Nash's question was insightful.

"I didn't even think to ask. If you'd drive us, I'd appreciate it. I'm not in the right frame of mind to drive right now, and Vanessa is a horrible driver, so you'd be doing us a favor. I'll go pack." I didn't wait for either Nash or Vani to answer before I left the room.

I was grateful Nash was there. He had a level head for such a young guy, and I was impressed. I was becoming more fascinated with Nash Lincoln the more I was around him.

"It was a clean break of the ulna, Senator, but the radius is intact. Jay will be fine in about eight weeks, but he'll need to keep the cast on. I don't anticipate any lasting effects, really, but physical therapy will help him regain his strength. Any questions?" The doctor at the small hospital in Blacksburg was named Dr. Farthing. She had a congenial bedside manner.

We were in the hospital room of Jay's college roommate, Cole Glennon. Cole was a shy young man, much like our Jay, but the two of them seemed to get along well, which was a relief. I was watching the two of them as they explained the accident to Vanessa and Cole's father, Caleb.

It reminded me too much of when I met Mario at UVA, and the two of us became best friends. I truly needed to clear the bad air between us. We'd been through too much shit to throw away a friendship over something he said he didn't do.

Caleb Glennon walked over to where Dr. Farthing and I had been discussing Jay's injuries. "Uh, how long before I can take Cole home?"

I'd heard Caleb tell Cole that his mother was at home with his brother and sisters. I had no idea where the family lived because Jay hadn't mentioned much about his roommate since everything went to hell after I lost the election.

"We haven't met, but I'm Spencer Brady, Jay's father. We, uh, we didn't accompany Jay when he moved in." I began what would have been a long rambling explanation that I was putting together as I spoke so as not to look like the shitty father I'd become.

Caleb Glennon chuckled. "Yeah, I read about it. No worries, Senator. We all have our ups and downs in life." He then turned to the doctor, waiting for her response to when he could take his son home.

"Oh, uh, yes. I'd like to keep him overnight because he has a slight concussion, but you can take him home tomorrow. He's quite lucky." The doctor explained Cole's injuries, so I walked away and joined Vani and Jay, seeing my son's neon-pink cast for the first time.

"Wow, people will be able to see you from a mile away." I looked at the spot where there was a small heart and the initials, "CG" before Jay jerked his arm away.

I glanced at Vani who subtly shook her head that I shouldn't mention it, so I turned to Cole. "I'll take care of your hospital bill, son. I'm sorry you were hurt, but I'm grateful it wasn't anything that time and rest won't cure."

"Thank you, sir. Jay tried to get out of the way of the car, but it ran a light and was speeding. We were in the far right lane, so we got hit first. It was coming right at us, and Jay tried to pull me to his side of the car to lessen the impact, but my seatbelt was buckled."

Cole sounded as though he was guilty of something. Jay touched his shoulder, offering comfort to his friend.

The boy—young man—was cute. He had platinum blond hair and big blue eyes. I glanced at my son, who was nearly my height with dark-brown hair and light-brown eyes, and I saw something I didn't expect to see. The two of them were more than friends. They were boyfriends, or close to becoming boyfriends. "Jay, son, can I talk to you outside, please?"

I glanced at Vani, and she winked and nodded, so the two of us excused ourselves and left the room. I directed us toward the elevators to go down to the cafeteria so we could get something to drink. Once the doors closed, I turned to look at the young man who had changed more than I'd bothered to notice.

The remorse over my lack of attention to my son, being caught up in my own life too much to worry about him and Vani, hit home like a speeding truck. What a selfish bastard I'd become!

"You okay?" I placed my hand on his shoulder. Based on the two black eyes that were blooming, and the cut over his nose, he hadn't tried to shelter his face as he'd said. He'd tried to shelter Cole. The kid had strong protective instincts, and I was proud of him.

"Eh? My body aches. The doctor said I could take over-the-counter meds for the aches and pains, and I'll be okay in a few days. I gotta wear the cast for two months, though," repeating what the doctor had just told me.

The doors opened, and we stepped off the elevator, heading toward the cafeteria. There, sitting at a table alone, was Nash. When he saw me, he started to get up, but when he noticed Jay was with me, he sat back down. It wasn't that I didn't want to introduce Jay to Nash, but it just wasn't the right time. Jay was the priority, not me or my bullshit.

We went through the serving line, and of course, my son, the bottomless pit, ordered a double cheeseburger and fries. I got a coffee and grabbed a yogurt for Vani in case she was hungry. I paid for our food, and we went to a table near where Nash was sitting with a bowl of fruit and a bottle of water.

"So, we need to talk." I stared into my son's eyes, feeling like a pissant staring into the face of the young man who had changed from the little boy who used to love tossing a ball or going for a bike ride with Dad. The little boy I'd lost without noticing, right before my very eyes.

My son was a man now, and I was the biggest fuckup he'd ever met. No wonder he wouldn't talk to me. He was disappointed in me because I'd let him down, and I couldn't blame him.

"I'm sorry, Jay—James. You know, I was the one who gave you the nickname, Jay. You were such a happy kid, full of energy, and I said to your mother that you needed a less stuffy name because there was nothing stuffy about you." I remembered how much he'd loved it when I asked him if he wanted a nickname. He was all for it.

"I hate that name. James, I mean. That old lady at the foster house used to yell it at me when I did anything at all. She hated me, saying I was unruly and disrespectful." Jay's past before he came to live with Vani and me was a bitter memory for all of us.

When he first came to live with us, Jay was always testing the waters. He was rambunctious—all boy. I used to laugh at how hard he tried to piss us off, but there was nothing he could do or say that would make us angry with him. We were too damn glad to have him as part of our family.

"Well, then you never have to use it. Hell, we can legally change it if you'd like. You let me know. You can change your last name if you want as well."

It hit me hard that he might not want to be known as my son. God only knew how long the scandal would be in the headlines, and he didn't need the stigma my name brought with it.

I glanced up from stirring my coffee to see Jay studying me. "Why wouldn't I want to be a Brady? Do you not *want* me to be a Brady anymore?" He looked upset, and that was the last thing I wanted.

"No, of course not, son. I just meant if you're too embarrassed to be affiliated with me, then I get it. Right now, not many people want me around."

Jay swallowed and placed his burger on the plate, wiping his mouth as he chewed. "Have you always been that way?"

"What way?"

Jay leaned forward. "Gay. Or were you just experimenting? You're a little old for that, aren't you?"

I chuckled. "Yeah, I'm old, and yeah, I've always been gay."

Jay nodded. "Did Mom know? She was mad when that picture was in the paper, but she didn't cry. I didn't ask her about it because I didn't know what to say. Your ass was on the front page of the paper, Dad."

I let out a bitter chuckle at the memory. "Yeah, it was, and not a very flattering angle either, was it? Son, your mother has known me since we were in high school, and her family moved to Portsmouth. We were best friends, and she knew all about my orientation before we got married." I wasn't sure how much to share with him at that point. How much would he want to know?

"How old were you guys when you got married?" Jay seemed to genuinely want to know.

"Mom was seventeen, and I was your age."

"Wow! Why so young?" His face showed surprise, and I had to wonder how we'd never had this discussion before today. Was it another way I'd let him down?

I swallowed the bile at remembering the horrific incident that led Vani and me to getting married. "I should let Mom explain it, but it's a painful memory for her. You see, Grandma Velma was dating a guy while Mom was in high school. I'd just left Portsmouth to go to college, but Mom and I kept in touch while I was at school.

"The guy, his name was Rick Langley, and he had been dating Velma for a few months. One night, he, uh, he came over to the house while Grandma was working late, and he attacked your mother. Hell, he raped her. She got pregnant, and Grandma didn't believe her when she said Rick had been the aggressive one. Grandma was angry with your mother, not Rick, for what he'd done, and your mother didn't feel safe at home."

As I said the words, I felt the same gut-wrenching pain as when Vanessa had told me the whole ugly story. "Your mom called me at school, telling me what had happened to her. I got in the shitty old Jeep I had at the time, and I drove to Portsmouth to get her."

"Oh, god! I had no idea that happened. Why didn't she ever tell me?"

I shrugged at his question. "I think she was worried you might think less of her if you knew the truth. After we moved her out of there, we got married. She'd already been through hell, and in a small town, it was better if we got married than for people to find out she was pregnant by her mother's boyfriend. I had no problem saying I was the father of her baby because I wasn't out to many people."

"That's so horrible. Did she move with you?"

"Yeah, Mom finished high school in Blacksburg while we snuck around, and she stayed with me in the dorms. I got us an apartment as soon as I could so we didn't have to live with Mario." I then waited for the inevitable question.

"What about the baby? Did she give it up like my mom gave me up?"

I could see the pain in his face, but his abandonment wasn't a new issue—we'd taken him to a therapist when he was thirteen or so, because he had questions we couldn't answer.

"No, son. Even though that baby would have been a product of rape, we were both excited to have it. We knew it would be tough not to associate the baby with the crime, but we were ready to tackle anything. Unfortunately, Mom had a miscarriage, and she had to have a hysterectomy, which means she couldn't have any babies. We were sad for a long time, but then we met you, and here we are." I touched his arm before I sat back in my chair.

We should have had the conversation with Jay years ago, but for whatever reason, we didn't. Now, I was in the position of having to hash it out, or we would lose our son. I wasn't about to let him get away from us so easily. I loved the kid too much.

"How is she able to go see Grandma and be nice to her?" Jay's question was the same one I'd asked myself many times over the years.

I gave the only answer I had. "Your mother is a special woman with a forgiving heart. That's the only way I can explain it. Look, I'm sorry we didn't have this discussion sooner, but your mother and me? We love you more than anything. I hate that all of this happened, but we can't turn back time. I should have told you about myself sooner. I'm gay, son. I should have explained it to you before it was on the front page of the fucking paper, and for that, I'm sorry."

Jay finished his meal without saying anything more. I knew he was thinking that he had the worst parents in the world, so I braced myself for his condemnation.

After finishing his soda, offering the requisite burp, Jay wiped his mouth and placed his trash on the tray. "I guess this apple didn't fall far from the tree."

I had an idea about what he meant, but I wanted to give him the chance to explain things to me when he was comfortable. I'd been that kid once upon a time.

"So, uh, Cole's nice. You guys seem to get along well." Would my comment be the prompt for him to fill in the blanks?

"We started chatting when we found out we'd be roommates. Both of us got early acceptance, and once we were paired, we reached out so we wouldn't be uncomfortable when we got to school. He's pretty shy, but once you get to know him, he's really sweet and kind, Dad. His parents have known he's gay since he was fifteen, and they support him."

My heart kicked up a bit. His next words hit their target.

"I didn't tell you about me, but Mom knows. I told her when I started high school. She kept telling me it was fine to talk to you about it, but I didn't know how you'd react, especially since you're a senator, so I didn't say anything."

I reached across the table and placed my hand on his broken arm, hoping my gesture of support was welcome. "I love you, Jay, and I'm proud of the man you've become. I'll support you in anything you ever do." I stood and pulled Jay up with me, hugging him.

"God, Dad. Stop." He might have protested, but he didn't let me go. I chuckled because it was the typical teenage response, and I was glad to hear it. We were a normal family, and having the confirmation of it from my son gave me a sense of relief.

I released him and stepped back. "I'm sorry, but I'm not sorry. How does that go?" It was something I'd seen online.

Jay laughed, and I heard Nash chuckle before he coughed, "Dumbass." Yeah, that one hit home.

I looked up to see the smirk on the handsome man's face, and I didn't know what to say. God, he was gorgeous, and I was falling under his spell.

Dumbass as charged.

Chapter Eight
Nash

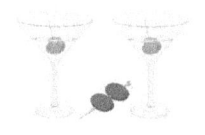

I'd tried not to get involved in the conversation between father and son, but hearing the story Spencer was telling about Vanessa struck something inside me unlike anything ever had. Hearing them discuss the kid's accident, and Spence trying to be as supportive as possible was amazing.

I could see the senator loved his son, and it seemed the kid loved him as well. I wished to hell I'd had that support at Jay's age.

I watched the two of them as they cleaned their mess and headed toward the cafeteria exit. When Spencer stopped, he said something to his son, who nodded before continuing out the door. Spencer strolled over to where I was seated at the table, dropping into the chair across from me.

He plopped a small yogurt onto the table and smiled. "You still hungry? Vani won't eat it because it's sugar-free."

I picked it up and looked at the label, seeing it was strawberry. "I'm allergic," I announced, not ready to be checked into the hospital for an epi shot.

It had been a dark day when I found out I was allergic to strawberries as a kid. I was at an adoption fair and had grabbed one of the homemade tarts the social worker offered, eager for any sort of treat.

I ended up in the emergency room because my throat closed due to an unknown allergy, which shot to hell any chance of meeting prospective parents that day. I didn't get adopted, but I never touched strawberry anything ever again.

"Oh, damn, I'm sorry. I, uh, I can get you something else," Spencer offered, looking seven kinds of guilt ridden.

I laughed. "I'm fine, Spencer. That was your son?"

"Yeah. He got T-boned at an intersection here in Blacksburg. I need to go find the goddamn police station because there are a lot of unanswered questions. Will you go with me? You might have to keep me out of jail." I wasn't sure if he was serious or not, but I was on board.

"Yeah, sure. Do you need to send Vani a text?" I wouldn't allow myself to forget he was a married man. I could have taken him to a hotel, motel, or a vacant field, and fucked him, but he wasn't mine. Neither was Vani, and I was still confused about their relationship.

Spencer dug his phone out of his jeans' pocket, pecking out a quick text. "Done. Let's go."

I pulled the large SUV into the parking lot of the Blacksburg Police Department. Spencer reached for the door handle, but I hit the locks to keep him inside. The anger I felt rolling off him would have the two of us sharing a cell in five minutes.

"Don't go in there half-cocked. You don't know what they know, and if it happens maybe your son ran a light and the accident was his fault, you don't want them to investigate it too much. Calm down, Senator. This isn't the Senate floor."

Spencer clenched his hands together and stared at me for a moment. Finally, he sighed. "Yeah, you're right. I need to be grateful he wasn't killed.

God, if this has anything to do with me..." He trailed off, getting lost in his thoughts.

I put my hand on his forearm and gave a gentle squeeze of understanding. "Let's not jump to conclusions. Kids have accidents all the time. If they walk away from it unhurt, it's just a hunk of metal that can usually be fixed." *When the fuck did I become Mr. Rogers with the advice?*

My hand was suddenly warm, so I glanced down to see Spencer had covered my hand with his own. My heart sped. I was quickly becoming obsessed, and it wasn't good for either of us.

"Thanks. You're right." He patted my hand and offered a nod.

I hit the locks and turned off the motor, taking the keys from the tray on the console and dropping them into the pocket of my jeans. I got out and walked around the front of the vehicle as the passenger door slammed. We met in front of the SUV.

"Please, please, don't let me run my stupid mouth. The last thing Jay or Vani needs is me making an ass of myself, yet again."

I was sure the man was right. He was in protective mode of his family, and from what I knew about them, he had every reason to be—Vanessa Brady was unlike any woman I'd ever met. She deserved the world on a platter, and it was easy to see Spencer had done his best to give it to her.

Jay seemed like a good kid who was doing his best to adapt to college life while his parents were in the middle of a scandal, and it sounded like the young man had some secrets of his own he hadn't shared, based on the conversation I'd overheard in the hospital cafeteria. The family seemed kind and loving. They deserved a second chance.

We walked up to the door of the small police department and went inside, seeing a woman at the desk on the phone. She held up a finger and quickly scribbled something onto a pad before ending the call.

"Good evening. I'm Officer Frye. How can I help you?" Of course, Spencer took command of the room, just as I'd expected he would.

"I'm Senator Spencer Brady, and my son and his friend were in a car accident this morning. Jay Brady and Cole Glennon. The accident was at the intersection by Walmart. Is there any word on the other driver involved?"

The woman quickly pecked on the keyboard before she looked up. "The officer who answered the emergency call isn't on duty right now, but you can call or come by in the morning, if you'd like. His name is..." She jotted the name onto a piece of paper before she slid it over to Spencer.

"Was the other person injured?" Spencer picked up the paper.

The woman looked at the screen again and smiled. "I *can't* tell you that the other person involved in the accident is in our jail for being intoxicated and running the light. They'll likely be charged with a DWI and reckless driving.

"I also *can't* tell you it's the driver's third offense, and she'll likely lose her license this time. So, when you talk to Officer Lewis in the morning, you don't know any of this information. How are those young men? I heard about the accident over the scanner earlier today. I have a son attending UVA, myself." She was sympathetic, that much I could tell, and it seemed to calm Spencer.

"Jay has a broken arm, and his roommate has a broken arm, leg, and a concussion. Will Officer Lewis be able to give me the identity of the other driver so I can explore taking civil action?"

Officer Frye stood, scanned the police station, and leaned close. Spencer and I mirrored her actions. "Of course, you can seek legal recourse for the accident, but her kids have been taken away, and as they say, you can't squeeze blood out of a turnip."

Obviously, she was telling him it was a lost cause. That information, in and of itself, was quite sad.

"Talk to Nelson Lewis about it, but I'd say be grateful if we can keep her off the streets." Officer Frye was vehement in her statement, poking her finger on the desk to emphasize her words.

Spencer nodded, so we turned to head out of the police station when a woman in a pair of grey sweatpants and an orange T-shirt stopped us. "Senator? I don't believe any of it. I'd say those pictures were photoshopped." In typical politician fashion, Spencer turned to her and grinned, giving her a thumbs up.

I laughed. "How long you gonna ride falsehood?"

He looked at me with a smirk. "Until I don't have a reason to do it any longer."

That was a surprising response, and I had no idea what to do with it, but I was enjoying spending time with the senator from Virginia. He had a quick wit; he was compassionate and loving; and the man was hot as fire. Who wouldn't want to spend time with Spencer Brady?

We returned to the hospital to check on Vani and Jay. Visiting hours were nearly over, but Jay had somehow talked the staff into allowing him to stay with Cole, and I stood outside the door of the room to see Spencer and Vanessa tell the two of them goodbye.

Cole's father had left earlier, according to what I'd heard Jay tell his parents as I waited outside the room. When they came out, I could see they were both upset, so I shepherded them out to the SUV and put them in the back seat. "Uh, where... Do you want to drive back to Great Falls?"

Vani laughed. "No, Nash. We'll find a motel for the night. We'll stay until Cole's dad takes him back to Roanoke in the morning. Jay's not going to be happy about Cole leaving him, so maybe we should stay for a few days, Spence? There's no reason to rush back to Great Falls."

She was damn well right on that one, so I started the SUV and looked in the rearview mirror. "So, uh, which motel?"

Vanessa played with her phone before offering a smile. "There's a Hyatt. I got us two rooms," she responded. She showed the phone to Spencer, who nodded.

"It's on University Boulevard. Make a right up here," Spencer directed.

Apparently, the two of them had been to Blacksburg before and knew where they wanted to stay, so I drove them to their hotel of choice.

I grabbed their bags from the back of the SUV and headed toward the sliding doors of the hotel, waiting for them to catch up. Vani walked by, winking at me as she walked through the doors and headed toward the desk.

Spencer stopped next to me. "Thank you for all of this. I'm not sure how we'd have gotten through it without you."

His low voice tickled against my ear before he followed his wife to the desk. My feelings were all over the place, and I wasn't sure how to respond, so I nodded. There was nothing wrong with a nod, right?

Spencer returned to where I was standing, a handsome smile on his face. "This might be a little strange, but they only had two rooms. Do you mind sharing?"

I raised my eyebrows. "Sharing with?"

"With me," the senator responded with a sexy smile.

"And why won't you be sharing with Vani?" I asked.

Spencer smirked. "Vani and I have never shared a bedroom. You're stuck with me."

I wanted to protest that it wasn't appropriate, but he looked damn vulnerable, so I simply nodded. The poor bastard had been through so much already. I didn't want to add anything more to his plate. It seemed full already.

Chapter Nine
Spencer

As I walked to the desk at the hotel to hear Vani asking for two king rooms, I stopped her when the clerk walked away. "What are you doing? We can have two queens and share a room. It will be fine."

"I'd like a room to myself, and come the fuck on, Spence. If you can look at Nash and tell me you'd rather share a room with me, then I'll back off." The sass in that woman made me smile.

"Vani, honey, he's not attracted to me." I was whispering because he was standing nearby, and I wasn't having the discussion in the hotel lobby.

"You're not stupid, and you're not blind, or so I thought. Use lube. I think he's hung." She handed me a key card and headed toward the elevator.

"Wait, Vanessa!" I called after her. My lovely wife turned to me and smiled. "You don't need to hide any longer, Spence. Go for it!" She disappeared down the hallway and stepped onto the elevator, laughing as the doors closed as she held her finger on the button.

I turned to see Nash standing to the side of the lobby, a concerned expression on his gorgeous face. God knew, the man was everything I ever dreamed of finding in a partner on a physical level, but under the circumstances, I wasn't sure what to do or say to him. The fact he was so young and handsome had me feeling guilty.

"So, Senator? We gonna stand here all night?" He grabbed the key card folio from me and looked at the number written across the bottom, before heading toward the elevator, motioning for me to move. I grabbed my suitcase and pulled it behind me as I stepped onto the car with him.

Nash hit the button for the third floor, and I kept my eyes planted on the illuminated rectangle where the floor numbers were displayed. When we arrived at our destination, Nash stepped off and reached for my suitcase, pulling it with him. "Come on. We have a big bed. I'm not going to touch you."

I wasn't worried about him—I worried about me.

I stepped from the car, suddenly unsure whether I liked his response. Oh, I wanted him to touch me everywhere, but I had a freight train full of bullshit that went everywhere with me, and Nash didn't deserve to have to help me pull it up hill.

Once inside the room, I felt like a virgin on prom night. I looked around, spotting a way to get a little space to organize my thoughts, so I went for it. "I, uh, I'll get us some ice." I grabbed the ice bucket.

There was one king bed that didn't seem to be big enough for the two of us and a separate sitting area with a television. I needed a minute to establish a plan.

His laughter echoed in the room as I allowed the door to close behind me. Why the fuck did I feel like I was doing something wrong?

Vani and I had been open about our relationship within our trusted circle, but not with outsiders. My job didn't afford us that luxury. Hell, she'd pushed me to share a room with him. I shouldn't feel bad about it because nothing was going to happen between us.

I walked down the hall to the alcove where the ice machine was located. There were three vending machines, so I reached into my pocket and grabbed some change.

"You are an adult. Hell, you're—well, you were—a United States Senator. You've argued with career politicians about healthcare, minority rights... He's a guy. You can just talk to him. Yeah, that's it. Just talk to the man." Thankfully, nobody else needed ice because they'd have thought me insane as I stood there talking out loud to the vending machine.

"Sure, we can talk." I was startled enough by the voice to drop the change I was holding. I turned to see Nash standing at the entrance to the ice machine alcove.

"Fuck!" I stooped to pick up the coins and felt a presence next to me, turning to see Nash right there reaching for coins next to me.

"Spence, I'm not a guy you need to worry about. I mean, if you want to pay for my services, then we can talk price and requests, but I'd bet you've got enough shit going on that you need a friend more than anything."

Nash knelt next to me. He took my left hand and put change into it, offering a reassuring smile.

"You want a soda?" I felt like a lecherous old fool, not for the first time in my life.

"Diet Coke, please. I'm watching my weight." I gave him an assessing look that I was sure said, "Why?" but I nodded and started to stand, my right knee not supporting me at all, which was embarrassing as hell.

Nash reached out a hand to help me. I was sure my face was blood red, but I took it to stand. "It's an old football injury from high school."

One day I'd need knee replacement surgery, but I wasn't ready to admit it yet. I wore my stubbornness like a badge of honor.

Nash helped me up, and I turned to the vending machine, getting the two of us soft drinks. I glanced at Nash, who was fitting the plastic bag inside the ice bucket with a smirk on his face. Yeah, I was in a bit of a hurry to get out of the room and had forgotten the bag. Shoot me.

"So, uh, where are you from?" My voice was loud so I could be heard over the clatter of the ice dropping into the bucket.

Nash chuckled. "Texas. You're from down around here somewhere, right?"

"Yes. Our hometown is southeast. Norfolk is the big city down here. Actually, Vani and I lived near there for years. Our families still live in the area."

"What did you do before you became a Senator?" We walked to our room, with Nash opening the door he'd left unlocked by moving the dead bolt latch to keep the door from closing. It was good he'd thought to do it. The key was inside.

After we settled, I slid off my sneakers and sat on one side of the bed while Nash took the other, both of us leaning against the headboard. Nash's bag was on the bench at the end of the bed next to mine.

"I practiced real estate law in my father's firm. I hated it, but I'd gone to law school to study it at my father's insistence, so it was what I knew."

"Sounds kind of dull." One size of his sexy mouth tilted in a half-smile.

"Dull doesn't begin to cover it. Once I graduated UVA Law, Vani and I moved to Hampton Roads. Vani had been taking night classes and was studying to get her real estate license. I guess all those nights helping me study real estate law rubbed off on her. Anyway, she got a job working at a realty office in Norfolk, and we had a little house not far from my parents.

"I got assigned to a complicated eminent domain case against the Commonwealth because the government wanted to seize ten acres of a family farm to put in an access road for a new public works warehouse. They chose the land because it was closer to the railyard which would cut off miles of delivery—" I could see I was losing him.

"Anyway, I won. That was when the party knocked on my door. I've always thought it was strange that I was even noticed, but I later found out it was one of my father's cronies who brought me to the attention of the higher ups in state politics, and the rest, as they say, is history. Now, your turn." I was rambling, but it was an occupational hazard of being a politician.

"Okay. Cycled through eight foster homes before I was put in a teen boys' group home. I was kicked out when I turned eighteen, and I've been making my own way for as long as I can remember." There was no emotion attached to the story at all.

My first thought was that Jay could have ended up like Nash—nobody looking out for him and nobody loving him—and the idea of it made my stomach turn. "Do you know anything about your parents?"

Nash offered a steely expression before he responded. "Nope. And I don't want to. That's the past."

The comment hit home. I had parents, and I wished I didn't know anything about them. "Okay, uh, how'd you end up in DC?"

Nash took a swig of his soda before settling onto the bed, his head at the foot. He'd stacked a bunch of pillows behind him, and he looked comfortable. Myself, I was a squirming mess.

"I've done everything from washing dishes to roughnecking on an oil rig. I had to learn to survive on the streets, so I did what I had to do. It's a tough world out there, Senator. Not for the weak of will or the faint of heart. In polite company, I'm considered a man of the world, but when it comes down to it, I'm a whore and an opportunist just tryin' to get by."

I watched Nash settle into the pillows, folding his hands behind his head, likely waiting for judgment from me. In a way, we were similar, but he faced his demons head on. Of the two of us, I was the coward.

"Of all of those jobs, which ones did you enjoy the most?" I was genuinely interested in his response.

Nash looked at the ceiling for a minute before he glanced in my direction. I took a drink of my soda and placed the glass of ice on the nightstand on my side of the bed.

The light was fading outside, so I reached over and turned on the lamp. I took in the long sight of him, seeing a handsome man who was more comfortable in the shadows than in the spotlight. That used to be me. Two terms as a senator had cured me of that notion.

"I like bartending at fancy parties. The society elite are a special breed all unto themselves."

I nodded. He had that right. "I'm going to sound like a snobby bastard, but your incredibly well spoken for a guy who didn't go to college."

Again, he offered that sexy chuckle from deep in his broad chest. "I learn quick. I learned that dropping consonants and speaking like I had a mouth full of marbles didn't get me respect from anyone, which is why I watched a lot of old movies where everyone had perfect diction. I also picked up things from people I met along the way. I am truly a product of my environment."

And, by his logic, I was clearly a product of mine. A man in the closet with a wife who looked like she just jumped off a wedding cake, and an adopted son who was smart as a whip, with no help from me at all. Jay had the guts to come out of the closet, while I cowered in the corner of my self-imposed prison. Well, until someone decided to shove me out of it with a kick in the naked ass.

"Why would someone want to hurt me? Why did they feel it was necessary to humiliate me and my friend? To what end? What did they gain?" I was thinking out loud again.

Nash moved closer to me, sitting up and staring at me. "Who are your enemies? Who are your friends? Usually, the guilty party comes from one of those camps."

I looked at him for a moment as his words sunk in. I still wasn't entirely satisfied that Mario had nothing to do with it. If he was, as had been alleged, in love with me, was that motive enough for him to ruin me and Blaire in the process? Was his jealousy so blinding he thought he could sweep in and save me after destroying my life?

"I went to the party to confront him. I don't know Fitzpatrick well enough to be invited to his birthday party, really. He was more of an acquaintance than a friend, but now, I'm indebted to him. Wonder if that was his ploy?"

"My boss at the escort service says nobody does anything in DC without calculating the pros and cons. If your friend outed you, what was he looking to gain, and if Sean set you up, wouldn't that make him look like a big fucking slimeball in the LGBTQ community he claims to fight for? Outing people is a big no-no, isn't it?" Nash had a point there.

"Your boss is a smart person. Nobody does a damn thing in DC without there being a price. What's yours?" If he knew the law of the concrete jungle, then he was angling for something. Better to know the price upfront.

Nash laughed loudly, tossing his head back in the process. "Oh, you wanna talk money now?" It was a challenge, and as much as I wanted to accept it, my head was too jumbled to do anything justice.

"No. Look, you don't have to stay. I mean, I can pay you for your time. I'd imagine your boss wants his cut anyway."

"My boss is a woman, and you're not a trick. You and Vani are my friends, and I always look out for friends. I don't have that many."

"A woman? Wow. There was a woman back in the seventies or eighties who operated an escort service in Manhattan. Her family prided itself on being blue bloods who claimed to be able to trace her lineage all the way back to the Mayflower. Her escort service made money hand over fist, from what the gossip mill churned out. I've heard the story of how all the power brokers on Wall Street and Capitol Hill were scared shitless that their names would be released as clients. The woman was arrested, if the story is true, and ended up writing a book about her experiences in the business."

I had no idea why that story stuck with me, but I vaguely remembered my mother asking my father if she should be worried about hearing his name as the trial progressed. Dad made a lot of trips to New York for cases. I had to wonder if he'd cheated on my mom. Was that the part of my scandal that hit home the most for her? Could that be the reason my parents turned their backs on me?

"Well, I'm not sure about her genealogy, but she let it slip once that she's married to a power player in DC. She used it as a threat against another escort that if he didn't fall in line and do as his john asked, she'd make sure he got blackballed in town, and he'd never get a job working on the Hill. I overheard her take the call when she was showing me the apartment I sublet from her." Of course, Nash's comments intrigued the hell out of me.

"Can I ask her name? I've never had anyone take me into the inner circle where names are passed around." I was joking but it was true. I hadn't been *around* long enough to be trusted by the senior senators. That club was elite. I wouldn't have been invited until John Buford, the senior senator for the Commonwealth, retired, died, or was defeated. Instead, it was me who was defeated.

"Caroline Bering is the name on my paycheck, but she has another name tacked on the end that she doesn't use for business," Nash answered, eyes closed as if in thought.

I racked my brain, but I knew no one named Bering who would be a power player in town. It didn't mean they didn't exist. It just meant I didn't know them.

"Well, anyway, I don't know her. I'm gonna take a shower unless you want to go first." I got up and opened my duffel bag to pull out some pajamas and a toiletry kit.

"No, go ahead. Mind if I check the tube?" Nash picked up the television remote from the table. I nodded before I headed for the bathroom.

"Oh, Spence? Caroline's last name is hyphenated. I forgot about that. Turner. Caroline Bering-Turner," he added, stopping me in my tracks.

Chapter Ten
Nash

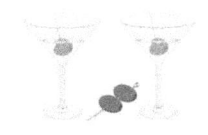

The name was barely out of my mouth before Spencer stomped back from the bathroom to my side of the bed, stubbing his toe on the bed frame. He jumped around, cursing for a minute, before sitting next to me. "Are you joking?"

I dropped the remote onto the mattress. "Why would I joke about that?" Seemed like a trivial detail to me.

"Caroline Bering-Turner is married to Senator Frank Turner. He's the senior senator from Georgia. I have a history with him." Spencer's announcement had me cocking an eyebrow at him.

"Not like that. I went against him during a vote a few months ago, and he's not one to forget. I wonder if he's behind all this bullshit?" I knew he wasn't asking me. Nevertheless, I wanted to help him.

"Uh, I could do some poking around with Caroline. If I get a few cocktails in her, she gets loose lips—and her lips want to wrap around my cock. She's been with most of the guys and some of the girls who work for her, but not me. I don't believe in mixing business with pleasure."

"Wait, you wouldn't— No, I can't ask you to sleep with her to get any information. That's unethical." Spencer's outburst made me want to laugh.

Ethics? He was worried about ethics? Someone had totally fucked him over and torpedoed his career, and he was worried about me doing something unethical to get information for him? Could he be for real?

"I don't know shit about ethics, okay? I know street justice, and if someone fucks with someone I c-c... Someone who doesn't deserve it, then they have earned whatever retribution is headed their way."

Was I going to say I cared about him? How the fuck could I care about him when I didn't know him.

No attachments. No regrets.

Getting involved in Spencer Brady's clusterfuck wasn't on my radar, so why was I putting myself out there to do something for him that I wouldn't even do for myself?

What the hell was going on with me?

Spencer was pacing the room as he furiously pecked into his phone. Suddenly, there was a knock on the door. When he didn't move to answer it, I walked over and looked out of the peephole to see Vani standing at the door, fist cocked to knock again.

I unlocked and opened the door for her to come inside. I pulled on my shoes to give them privacy and took the elevator to the lobby to get fresh air. I walked out through the sliding doors, feeling the bite of cold on my cheeks. It was November in the mid-Atlantic, and as I was coming to learn, the weather could turn on a dime.

I saw a convenience store across the parking lot and decided beer sounded good, so I took the walk. I was still spinning as I considered the idea that I was not only attracted to Spencer Brady, but I genuinely cared about what happened to him and Vani.

Vanessa had explained to me earlier that they didn't have a typical marriage. She said they'd never had sex, which I found hard to believe, initially.

They were both gorgeous, but when she explained her sexual identity to me, I understood. While it was clear they loved each other, and they'd been together for a long time, which created an intimacy between them I'd never had with another soul, they weren't physically attracted to each other.

I couldn't say I was jealous of their relationship, but I was a little green-eyed when it came to his former lover, the news guy. It seemed like the reporter cut and ran when things got tough.

I pulled out my phone and scrolled through my contacts, finding a number I never thought I'd use. The offer—"If you ever need anything, make me your first call,"—would surely apply under the current situation.

"Hey, Nash. What's up?"

"You told me if I needed anything, I should call you. That still stand?" There was silence over the line.

I heard a car horn in the distance before his throat was cleared. "Yep. Where are you?"

"I'm in Blacksburg, Virginia. I'm with Senator and Mrs. Spencer Brady. They're my friends, and they're in a bind." I believed it only right to give him the option to say no.

"So, it's not for you? What's in it for me?"

Whatever it takes. "Whatever you want." The words came out easily. I never knew I had the ability to be self-sacrificing. I'd just learned something new about myself.

★★★ ★★★

Wednesday morning, I took Vani and Spencer to campus so they could check on Jay. I waited outside on a bench in front of the dorm to give the family their privacy. The deep rumbling sound caught my attention before I saw the bike.

A sleek Road King glided into the parking lot adjacent to the dorm. Denver Wilkes stood from the huge bike looking in my direction. He took off the helmet, stashing it into the saddlebag, before striding to where I was sitting. The grin on his handsome face made me happy to see him.

"How'd you get away by yourself?" As the Road Captain for The Devil's Volunteers, a motorcycle club out of Sparta, Tennessee, he usually traveled with a large crew. It was a surprise to see him alone.

My time with the club was relatively short, but when I left for something else, I left a piece of my heart there with Clinton Barr—my best friend and mentor in the group home who had already phased out of the system.

Clint came back for me when I was fresh out of the system at eighteen, helping me survive the streets as we left Texas to start a new life anywhere but the Lone Star State.

We ended up doing some handyman work for the Volunteers that summer when we stopped in Sparta, and unlike me, Clint had taken to club life like a duck to water. Sadly, he was killed in an accident a few years earlier. Denver and Clint had been in a relationship at the time, and I knew Denver took it hard. I went back to Sparta for the funeral, and I'd hung with the guys for a few days to ensure Denver was okay. I rarely heard from him, but as he'd promised when I left after Clint's funeral, he was there if I ever needed him. And he'd kept his word.

Denver brushed his hand over the black leather jacket he was wearing, which contained no club markings. "Incognito, man. Not my first time around the block. How've you been, little brother?"

I hugged him, clapping him on the back a few times in return, hoping he knew how grateful I was that he'd come. "I've been fine, really. I sort of stumbled into this problem..."

Denver laughed. "What's her name? She the senator's daughter?"

Oh, shit. "Uh, no. See..." I mumbled, not sure how to explain things to him when he was looking right at me.

"Nash, dear, is this man giving you trouble?" Vani asked as she sidled up next to me and gave Denver a withering stare.

"Vanessa Brady, this is Denver Wilkes, an old friend of mine. He's, uh, passing through and stopped by to see me. Where's Spence?" I heard the nerves in my voice.

"He's talking to Jay. They had some air clearing to do. So, Mr. Wilkes, it's a pleasure to meet you. Nash is a wonderful guy. He was kind enough to drive us down from Northern Virginia. Our son was in an accident yesterday, and we were too upset to drive, so Nash, here, agreed to bring us. Would you like to go over to the food court to get a cup of coffee?" Vani gave us the up and down. I wasn't surprised she was suspicious. Denver was an intimidating guy at six seven. He was a bear of a man, who looked like he could snap me with two fingers.

Denver looked at me for guidance, so I nodded. "Yeah, let's go. Vani, send Spence a text where he can find us." Once she was finished, the three of us strolled across campus, Vani interrogating Denver like he was under a hot light in a police holding cell.

We went into a large building where, not surprisingly, tons of college kids were milling around a dozen food and drink options, finally taking a seat near a gourmet coffee cart. "I, uh, what can I get everyone?"

I worried about leaving Vani and Denver alone at the table. I wasn't afraid he'd say something to offend her. I was worried about what she'd do to him.

"I'll have a cappuccino with extra foam and brown sugar. Two lumps." Vani gave me a smile and batted her lashes.

I turned to Denver, seeing a smirk I didn't expect. "I'll have what the lady's having," he announced, bold as balls, the bastard. I shook my head and walked away, hoping Vani hadn't gutted him by the time I returned.

I ordered two cappuccinos and two regular coffees, preparing Spencer's the way I knew he liked. The young barista handed me a cardboard holder for the drinks, so I handed over a ten-dollar tip.

As I started to return to the table, I saw Spencer standing next to Vani's chair, looking none-to-happy at the sight of the massive man who was sitting next to his wife. Again, another red flag. Maybe he was less gay than he thought?

I hurried over, placing the cardboard carrier on the Formica to get everyone's attention. "Spence, this is an old friend of mine, Denver Wilkes. Denver, this is Senator Spencer Brady." I was sure Vanessa had already dispensed with the pleasantries, but I hoped my introduction would cut the tension I sensed, based on the expression on Spencer's face.

"Yes, so I've been told. It's nice that your friend stopped to see you. How did he know where to find you?" Spencer's question came out through clenched teeth.

"Tracking software. Little brother didn't even know I had it installed in his phone, but I wanted to be able to find him if he needed me," Denver answered. I knew that was bullshit because I'd bought a cheap piece-of-crap phone when I went to work for Caroline so she could get in touch with me when I had a job. I seriously doubted Denver knew how to work a smartphone, much less track me from it.

Spencer stared at me for confirmation, so I nodded. I wanted Spence to trust Denver because I knew he'd be able to help us out. He didn't know shit about technology, but Denver had told me the club had a new member—okay, he said *geek*—who could work miracles. I just needed to know who sent those pictures to the media back in August that led to the scandal, and then, who followed up by sending the rest of the photos to NBS which cost Blaire Conner his job.

We all sat at the table in the food court, making small talk for about an hour. Spencer cleared his throat. "So, uh, I guess we better get on the road, team, huh? It'll be late when we get home."

I felt Denver grab my arm. "Didn't you tell them you're going with me?" I nearly did a spit-take as I tried to swallow my coffee. It was news to me that I was going anywhere with Denver.

Before I could say anything, Denver took my hand. "We have some things to discuss. He'll be in touch." He glared at me. "Let's get your stuff and head out. It's a five-hour ride." Denver's announcement was for the benefit of our companions, I was sure.

"Oh, uh, yeah. We'll walk with you. Here are the keys." I handed Spence the keys to the SUV. We walked out to the vehicle, and I grabbed my duffel, slipping the strap over my torso. I was going to be riding the bitch seat for five hours to Sparta and not thrilled about it at all—especially in November.

Vani wrapped her slender arms around my neck. "You stay in touch, Nash. I don't like this one bit, but you're an adult. Please, don't ghost us." I nodded and broke the hug.

I turned to face Spencer, seeing him side-eyeing Denver. Of course, the larger man was fighting a smile, seeming to pick up on the sexual tension between Spencer and me. I couldn't wait to hear what he had to say about it.

"I'll call you. I owe Denver a debt, and I'm going to pay it." I sounded cryptic, but if he knew what I was going to do to get the information I wanted, he probably wouldn't be happy.

"Be safe. Stay in touch with Vani." Spencer's response was more of a demand, though he seemed to try to distance himself from me.

It wasn't what I expected, and not what I wanted to hear from him. The previous night after I returned with a twelve-pack, the three of us played cards and drank beer, gossiping about people we knew in DC.

I had walked Vani back to her room, and she'd told me she thought I was good for Spencer. It made my heart beat a little faster but hearing Spence tell me to stay in touch with his wife had me wondering if I'd mistaken any attraction between us.

"Yeah. You guys okay to get back?" I shook his hand, feeling a tingle up my arm at the contact.

"We'll be fine. You stay safe on the back of that rolling casket." Spencer glanced to where Denver was waiting for me by his bike.

"It's no more dangerous than..." I started, remembering how Clint had died. A trucker hauling a load of sheep fell asleep behind the wheel and ran Clint off the road on I-81. It was late at night and there was fog, according to Denver, but my friend was just as dead.

"We'll be careful. I'll be back to DC in a few days." I meant it from the depths of my heart.

Spence pulled me in and hugged me. "We just started getting to know each other. I feel like things are unfinished, but you do what you must. Take care." He kissed my temple and stepped back, waving to Denver as he walked to the passenger's side of the vehicle, helping Vani inside.

I headed across the parking lot where Denver was waiting. He handed me a helmet and a set of black leather fringed gauntlets. "Here. It's gonna be cold as fuck. Hang on and remember to lean with me. We're not going far." I had no idea what Denver meant, but he pulled his helmet on, and we were on the road before I could ask.

I was surprised when we drove about fifteen miles down the highway and pulled into the parking lot of a Best Western. There were three other bikes on the lot, and a couple of guys sitting outside the rooms in chairs on the sidewalk, smoking and drinking in the frigid afternoon air. "I thought you said you came alone." There was a mic in my helmet, which surprised me. The fact Denver had Bluetooth blew my mind. I'd never call any of The Volunteers tech savvy.

"Well, you needed to track down information, and you needed it faster than we used to be able to get it in the old days, so come say hello. You and I will talk later." His response echoed in the helmet.

I had no idea what was going to happen, but I'd set things in motion. If I wanted to help Spencer, I had to commit to the task completely.

Chapter Eleven
Spencer

I seethed the whole ride back from Blacksburg, and Vanessa decided it was a great time to rapid-fire questions at me for which I had no answers. By the time we got home, my head was pounding, and I saw no way I'd fall asleep anytime soon.

After helping Vani get her suitcase up to the master bedroom, I went to my room and changed into running clothes. I'd heard the weather report for the rest of the week, and it was supposed to rain the next day and freeze overnight. I grabbed my reflective vest so I didn't get run down, and I took off down the driveway, heading toward the trail.

Talking to Jay had been a salve. He told me about Caleb picking up Cole, his roommate, that morning to take him home early. He was going to attend virtual classes until the Thanksgiving break, and Jay was coming home. I was relieved I didn't have to beg to get him to come back for the holiday.

Jay said he could get a ride with another friend as far as Stafford, and I said I'd come pick him up. We made plans to get him a new car since his was totaled, and the police had electronically sent the insurance report to our insurer. The insurance company would fight the other driver to recoup the cost of Jay's vehicle, and our family was on better footing, for which I was grateful.

My mind kept circling around to Frank Turner, whose wife turned out to be Nash's pimp... Madame? I wasn't sure of the proper terminology, but I didn't like it.

I wished to hell he didn't have that job, but it wasn't my place to say anything about it. Just like it wasn't my place to stop him from going off with that motorcycle gang member with the tattoos on his neck.

I'd wanted to push for the story of how they knew each other, but there was no time to say anything when it was announced, unceremoniously, that Nash wasn't returning to Northern Virginia with us. I was fuming because it didn't appear as if Nash was in the know, either. I wasn't sure what the guy's play was, but I didn't like it at all.

I ran for an hour, and I went in through the mudroom because my shoes were dirty, and I stripped off my sweats, tossing them into the washer. I kept a clean pair of lounge pants in a drawer under the folding counter, so I pulled them on and walked into the kitchen to find Mario sitting at the table, drinking my Scotch.

"Vani's been trying to call you. Where've you been?" He was pissed off, and the alcohol wouldn't help.

From the cabinet, I pulled down a glass, dropping a large ice ball inside—which reminded me of Blaire. After I poured three fingers into my glass, I walked to the table and sat down. "I went for a run. My phone's on the charger upstairs. What's could you possibly want?"

The simmering anger seeped out through my cold voice. I wasn't convinced Mario didn't have a hand in the shitstorm that started after I made a *very* poor decision to go away with a fuck buddy. I decided it was time to ask some questions.

I studied Mario, seeing his scowl, so I pressed him. "What's wrong? Have there been any developments?"

Mario cleared his throat and glanced at me. "Could you put a shirt on?"

I looked down, remembering mine had been wet, so I'd tossed it into the laundry basket. I nodded before running upstairs to my room to grab an old UVA T-shirt from my dresser.

Vani was on the phone in her room, so I headed downstairs to grill my friend—or my former friend. It remained to be seen where he landed at the end of our talk.

"Okay, so, I'm adequately covered. What's going on?"

"Well, uh, Vani was partially right when we talked after Blaire was outed. I did have feelings for you, and I couldn't understand why you didn't see me." His admission was quiet as if he wasn't comfortable admitting it.

"So, you had me followed to Antigua and had someone take those pictures?" I prayed I was wrong. He'd been my best friend for more than twenty years, and it would rip out my heart if he'd been a vindictive dick about it.

Mario held up his hands in surrender. "No, Spence. No, I would never do that. I was content to be by your side and support you in any way I could, and that would never include me hurting you like that. I've been going to counseling, and I see things a lot clearer now. I know you love me, just not the way I wanted you to love me. I took the attention you gave me as your friend for the affection I've been looking for all my life."

God, this is going to be brutal.

"Your being in the closet allowed me to stay in the closet as well. I guess, in some way, I thought we could just live in the closet together, and I was fine with Vani being in our lives, but I see that was unrealistic."

I nodded because he was at least being honest. I knew the man. If he'd been lying, I'd have been able to tell.

"Spence, I don't want to live in the closet anymore. Fuck, Spence, I'm forty-five, and I've never been in a relationship—a real one—because I was content to believe what we had was enough. It's not. I realize that now, but I swear on my mother's life, I would never out you." Based on the look on Mario's face, I believed him.

I stood and pulled him up, offering a heartfelt hug. I was happy and relieved to know I still had my partner in crime by my side. We patted each other on the back and took our seats again. "So, I learned something. Caroline Bering-Turner runs an escort service."

Mario laughed. "Yes, and your sexy bartender friend is one of her studs. I recognized him from a party he worked at a few months back. Good taste, Spence, but it's not new news."

My eyes had to be wide as saucers. "Bullshit! You mean you knew it and didn't tell me? I suspect Frank Turner had me followed in retaliation. You can't tell me he's not a vindictive son of a bitch."

Mario took a sip of his drink. "Yes, he is, but his bill wasn't going to pass whether you voted with him or not. Seems he's got himself a situation, Spence."

"Oh, and what's that?" I quickly took a drink and swallowed it so I didn't spit liquor everywhere if it was shocking.

"A love child. I've heard rumors about a guy showing up at his home in the Palisades. Apparently, the guy came to work for Caroline as an escort, and he was able to find out the logistics of when Turner would have impregnated his mother. The kid's threatening to file a lawsuit against Turner for back child support." *Color me shocked!*

"The GOP is scrambling behind the scenes to keep it quiet, but Frank has a few disgruntled staffers who found out about his son, and they're giving interviews to the Post. You'll be off the front page within a matter of days, but I don't think Frank

Turner was the one who had someone follow you. There's gotta be someone else."

"When in the fuck did you find out about this, and when were you going to tell me?" A weight had been lifted from my shoulders for an entire minute at hearing Frank Turner had his dick in a ringer, but then I remembered, if he wasn't the bastard who outed me, then who was?

★★★ ★★★

Friday morning, I woke up before daylight. I checked my messages on my work phone—which I needed to turn in soon—and my personal phone, sad to see nothing from Nash. I wondered what he was doing, and who he was doing it with. Vani hadn't heard from him either—as far as she was telling me—and I was starting to worry.

Had a crazy biker gang kidnapped Nash, and if so, for what purpose? How in the hell did Nash even know a biker gang? Was he a member who'd left without permission?

God, would they hurt him? Did he have a tattoo of the club logo on his body somewhere, and they planned to cut it out or burn it off like I'd seen in a show on television? My mind had nothing to occupy it, so it wandered, and it wandered in dark directions.

I really, *really*, liked Nash Lincoln. He had sparkling eyes, brown hair that looked inviting to my fingers, and lush lips I'd longed to kiss. I cursed myself for not pressing things with him on Tuesday night when we shared a room. Something about the encounter seemed seedy, me paying him for sex. I didn't want it to go that way. I wanted Nash to want me because of me. Was that a stupid pipe dream?

Finally, deciding I'd never go back to sleep, I went downstairs to make coffee and toast. I turned on the television in the kitchen, catching the local news station. "Breaking news this morning. In a statement released overnight, Senator Frank Turner has been hospitalized. The statement reads..." The newscaster continued, but all I could do was smile.

I didn't think the mean old bastard would die, but I could smell a crisis diversion tactic like the next politician. Maybe I would go into the office and finish cleaning out my things. It could be fun to find out the gossip regarding recent events.

The Thanksgiving break would start on the following Monday, so why not go into the office? I'd been removed from all committees I'd sat on during my terms in office. I wanted to show them, all the naysayers, that I wasn't down for the count. I wasn't sure what the next chapter held from me, but I was going to face it with eyes wide open and a big fucking smile.

I called a car service to take me to the Hill that Friday morning. Vani had agreed to come meet me for lunch, and as I read the Congressional newspaper on my phone, I wasn't surprised to see anything more than a brief statement that Frank Turner was in the hospital, not disclosing any diagnosis or possible reason for his sudden illness.

The driver let me out at the members' entrance, and I thanked him and dropped a hundred over the seat, hurrying through the side entrance of the Hart Office Building where most of the Senate offices were located. I scanned my card, surprised when the door opened, and went through security, happy the guards greeted me kindly. I'd always tried to be respectful of them, and I was grateful they returned the sentiment when I needed it most.

I took the stairs to the seventh floor, sometimes my only exercise for the day, and when I came out of the stairwell, I was surprised to see Mario standing with Mitch Flora, both seeming to wait for me.

"What?"

"The guard called like usual. You forget we have protocols for these things, Senator. Here's your schedule." Mitch handed me the familiar typed index card. I glanced down the list, surprised to see so many people wanting to speak with me.

"Why are there so many meetings?"

Mario placed a hand on my shoulder and ushered me into the office, which erupted in shouts and applause upon my entrance. The cheer was shocking. There were still loyal people on my staff, and I was grateful for them. "I took the liberty of telling the staff today would be your last day in the office. They wanted to have a party, but I told them not until after three. Make the rounds and then meet me in your office." I nodded to my chief of staff and handed him my briefcase.

Once I was safely tucked into my office with coffee and the morning's news blurbs on my desk, I looked to Mario for information and was relieved when he smiled and sat in his regular spot.

"Okay, so all the meetings?"

"Seems Sean Fitzpatrick has leaked that he wants to hire you as soon as your cooling-off period expires in six months. These people want to get in your good graces before you leave. You didn't mention you'd discussed anything of the sort with Fitzpatrick." Mario seemed a little put out, which reminded me of something Fitzpatrick had said recently.

"Yes, well, you didn't tell me you were cruising Cock of the Walk and ran into him, telling him I was in Antigua with Blaire, now, did you?"

I saw the blood drain from his face, but I kept my mouth shut. "I'm sorry, Spence. I was hurting, and Sean seemed like a nice guy. He asked where you were, and I just blurted it out. I called him the next day, and he promised he wouldn't mention it to anyone. Do you think he told someone who isn't a friend?" He appeared to be terrified.

I chuckled and put my feet on the desk, loafers and all. "Why do you think I went to his birthday party? He invited me so I could confront you. What's going on with you?" God help me, I was skeptical of his involvement in the scandal. Maybe he vented to someone he trusted, and they betrayed him?

"This has been difficult for me as well, Spence. Everything isn't about you." Mario stood and stormed out, slamming the door.

Clearly, something was going on with him, though I had no idea if I'd figure him out. Besides,

I had other worries on my mind. Where the fuck was Nash Lincoln, and why wasn't he returning my texts? I'd sent several, basically begging to hear from him, but I'd received no responses. It was driving me insane.

Chapter Twelve
Nash

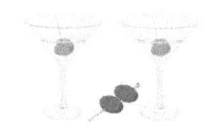

After I told Denver and the three other Volunteers what I knew about the pictures of Spencer and Blaire on vacation in Antigua and the circumstances under which they were taken, Pacman—a guy I'd never met before but could guess was the geek—began rapidly typing into his keyboards. Yes, he had two laptops and a desktop with two screens, and he was going to town like his life depended on it.

Stan Harry—the Heretic, as I remembered he was called—laughed. "Don't worry about Pacman. He's got it. So, little brother, tell us what you've been up to." Stan was the club treasurer, and a protective sort, or at least that's how I remembered him.

I glanced at Denver, seeing a smile and a nod. "Well, I live in DC. I work as a, uh, a walker for wealthy widows who attend fancy parties, and I tend bar for parties now and then."

Blue—Blue Moon, as in he told the truth once in a blue moon—laughed. "I like that title, *walker*. I used to walk right up to whores and give them cash to blow me. You do that?"

The tension in the room escalated but I wasn't offended. It was what it was. "Hey, when you get paid five bills an hour for your company and your cock, you get a little less particular about who wants what."

Heretic stared at me for a solid fifteen seconds before he cracked up, slapping my hand and offering me another beer. "Dude, you speak the truth." Hell yeah, I did.

I hung out with The Volunteers for the weekend, and Packard, the geek, was still sorting through a mountain of miscues and bullshit. Whoever was responsible had covered their tracks well.

Denver got me a room while we were all in a holding pattern, and we hung out in the evenings. It was nice, being back in their company, and I wondered if I hadn't had such a restless spirit, could I have patched in? I'd been a prospect, as had Clint, but he'd stayed. I had to keep moving back then.

On Sunday, The Volunteers decided to break camp and head back to Sparta—everyone except Denver. "I'll be home tomorrow. I'm gonna take Nash to Roanoke where he can rent a car tomorrow to head home. I'll see y'all."

I thanked all of them for coming and waved good-bye as two of them roared out of the parking lot while Pacman followed in a tricked-out cage.

I turned to Denver. "I'm ready." He smiled and took my hand, leading me to my room and closing the door.

"I checked out of my room. Is it okay if I stay here with you?"

I could see the man was vulnerable, and I had worried about calling him, knowing the memories it would bring back, but a debt was a debt.

I woke up first on Monday morning and slid out of the bed. I made my way to the bathroom and got into the shower, trying to make sense of the previous night.

It wasn't what I expected it to be, and I'd done my best to give him what he'd asked for. When I stepped out of the shower, I quickly dried off and dressed in my last set of clean clothes.

When I walked out of the bathroom, Denver was sitting on the side of the bed, blanket over his lap.

"You okay?"

I walked to the bed and sat next to him, wrapping an arm around his broad shoulders. I kissed his cheek. "I'm fine, Denny. Are you okay?" I whispered as he leaned his head against my shoulder. I felt a quiet sob break free, and my heart broke for the gentle giant.

I held him for a few minutes until he rushed into the bathroom. I pulled my phone from the charger on the nightstand, prepared to send a text to Spencer, but then I remembered him saying I should keep in touch with Vani, so I pecked out a text to her.

> **Vani—On my way back to town. Let's catch up this week. If you want. Whatever you want. Nash**

When I read it back, it didn't smack of confidence. I got three laughing emojis back, which made me smile. Vani wasn't one to fool, that was for sure.

Denver came out of the bathroom, fully dressed and looking like he had his shit together. "Thank you, Nashville. I can't tell you how much last night meant to me. It's been so fucking long. Well, there's been nobody since I lost Clinton." I stood up and wrapped my arms around his waist, giving him a hug he was reluctant to return.

Finally, I felt a kiss to the top of my head, and I pulled back, reaching up to pull on the beard. "I like this. You know, Clint would have loved it."

Denver nodded and pulled away. "Your man seems to have the potential for a great beard. Maybe if you tell the senator that you like it, he'll grow it." Denver was cutting to the chase. He wasn't one to mince words.

"How did you know it was him and not her?" I felt my cheeks flush.

Denver chuckled. "I remember when you and Clint ended up at the clubhouse. Hand's little sister thought you were right up her alley."

I laughed. Hand, as the club president was called, had a baby sister who was a gusher—as in, she was clingy and needy, and if one didn't give her all their attention, she'd tell her brother, and he'd beat the hell out of you. He beat my ass once over that idiot, and that was one of the reasons I decided to leave.

"Yeah, well, she needed more than I was prepared to give. Whatever happened to her?" We grabbed our things and headed out of the room.

Denver chuckled. "She found herself a younger guy, and she's pregnant. He's a prospect, and if Hand doesn't kill him, I'll be the first one in line to throw the Prez a parade. They guy's name? Seymour."

I looked at Denver to see he wasn't laughing. I couldn't hold it after that. Pansy, her actual name, loved the movie, "Little Shop of Horrors." It would figure she'd find a guy named Seymour.

We headed downstairs and hopped on Denver's Road King. Once we had the helmets on and our shit in the saddlebags, I wrapped my arms around Denver's muscled abs to hold on, my thoughts settled on the events of the previous night. They were nothing like I'd expected.

I exited the rental office with the keys to a Mustang that Denver had insisted on renting for me. "I'd have been fine with the Nissan."

We'd had an argument in the line because I wanted to pay him for the car. I didn't have a credit card, so that was a problem, but Denver had insisted he was going to cover it. After I assured the agent I could drop the car at the rental office in Crystal City, the deal was done.

"Yeah, but you remember what Clint wanted to do before you left, and you guys never got to do it?" Denver grinned, taking me back to the conversation.

"I wanna take a road trip with you and little brother in a Mustang. You think we can do that someday, Daddy?"

I nodded, feeling the tears swelling again. "I miss him every day, Denver. I'm so glad he met you. You made him very happy." I couldn't help the sob.

Denver kissed my forehead and walked away without looking back. I hoped and prayed the man found peace, and maybe he could find another boy someday. He deserved the best.

I pulled into the driveway of 16 Sunnybrook Lane, parking in the driveway instead of sneaking through the woods like the last time. It was daylight, not midnight, and the trees had lost their leaves, redecorating the once-immaculate yard into colorful chaos. It was comforting to see that everything on Sunnybrook Lane wasn't perfect.

I walked onto the porch and rang the bell, hearing the heavy *Bong... Bong... Bong.* It reminded me of an old television show I remembered watching in one of the better foster homes from my youth.

I was there temporarily because the house was full, and I had to sleep on a pallet on the floor of the bedroom the biological boys shared, but it was a glimpse of what a real home could be like.

The foster mom always had a snack ready for us when we got home from school, and we were allowed to watch *The Adams Family*, while we ate before it was homework time. The main house where the television show took place had a doorbell like the one at the Brady home.

When the door opened, I saw Vani with a welcoming smile. She stepped out and I folded her small frame into my arms. "Is everything okay?"

"He's out for a run. He's been worried about you, Nash." Her tone was that of a chastising older sister, which I appreciated.

I pulled back and offered a smile. "There's no need for anyone to worry about me, Vani. I've been taking care of myself for a long time."

"Yes, but it's a whole different animal when someone loves you." She stepped out of my arms and pulled me into the house. I saw some boxes in the grand dining room, and I was immediately on alert.

"What's up with this?" I saw fancy dishes, squares of foam, and brown paper spread on the large dining table.

Vani offered a glowing smile—that I took as fake. "We're going to paint, so I'm emptying out the hutch. This is the anniversary china that Spence bought me. I show—or used to show—these fancy houses, and they all had china on display.

"Spence never wanted me to feel like I didn't have the same opportunities or options as others, so one year, he kept coming up with odd scenarios where a staffer was trying to pick out china patterns and asked for the group's opinion. He'd come home with these pictures of patterns and ask me which one I liked the best, and I told him this one. Imagine how unsurprised I was when I got a beautiful china service for eight on our fifteenth wedding anniversary. He's sweet, but he's not very subtle." She had a bright smile as she told the story.

I swallowed the lump in my throat. It was as though I'd lost something I never had in the first place, and the feeling settled low in my belly. How could I have been so fucking stupid to think someone as kind, loving, and classy as Spencer Brady could find a hood rat like me worth his time?

"Well, I just stopped by to see if you made it home okay, and ask if you've found out anything more about the pictures? Did Frank Turner send them?" I definitely wanted to talk to Caroline about her husband, but one step at a time.

"Oh, you haven't heard the latest. Come sit and have some coffee, or..." she glanced at the grandfather clock near the door and turned back to me with a smile. "How about a cocktail? It's five o'clock somewhere." She giggled as she headed toward the kitchen.

"I wish I could, but I need to take the rental to the airport to turn it in so it doesn't cost Denver another day. Call me sometime. If I hear anything from my friends, I'll let you know." I headed toward the door.

When I opened it, I was met with the sight and smell of Senator Spencer Brady. The combination nearly knocked me on my ass.

"Where are you going?" Spencer seemed excited to see me, and he asked a great question. All my plans for my life had flown out the window the night I took him and Vani up to a room at a swanky hotel so they could sleep it off without making more headlines. I didn't know what the hell to say to him in response to his question because all I could think was that I wanted to go with him—anywhere.

"I need to go home, but first I gotta drop off the rental. I, uh, is Jay home from school for the break yet? How's his arm?" I was trying to deflect his attention about what I was doing in hopes of giving myself some time to get my shit together.

"Okay. Let me shower, and I'll take you to... Where do you need to turn in the car?"

"No, I mean, it's just Crystal City, and then I can get the metro to my apartment in Foggy Bottom." I was fighting like hell to keep from taking him into my arms and kissing him like he was giving me life.

Spencer stepped closer, and I could smell the sweaty, musky deliciousness of him, which made my heart pound faster. It was intoxicating, and I couldn't stop myself from huffing at him.

"I'm going to shower, and then I'm going to take you to turn in your rental car. I don't know if you've heard, but things have taken a turn for the worse in the Turner family. I have it in good authority that Caroline is lying low. She might be out of business for a while."

THE SENATOR 161

That was news to me. Maybe it was the night I'd spent with Denver and how I felt after, but in that moment, I wanted the Senator to claim me and ask me to be his lover. It wasn't anything I'd ever wanted before, but the power in his voice had my insides melting.

Spencer touched a hand to my cheek before he turned and ran upstairs, leaving me in a puddle at the bottom of the winding staircase. I felt a gentle touch on my back and turned to see Vanessa with a bright smile on her pretty face. "Come talk to me, Nash."

I followed the petite woman into the kitchen and took a seat while she prepared drinks for us. "So, you've missed the town gossip, I guess? Senator Frank Turner is in the hospital for undisclosed reasons. I guess if a sixteen-year-old girl showed up at my door and called me *Mommy*, I'd probably have a medical episode."

"Wait, the Senator has a daughter who's not Caroline's?" I had to wonder how Caroline was taking *that* news.

"That's the story. I heard Caroline is moving out of their home and taking him for every penny he has. They had an agreement that if he ever cheated, she gets everything." Vani had a smile on her face that was a little vindictive but under the circumstances, I loved seeing it there.

Not knowing Caroline's husband was also a Senator, I'd have never suspected she mixed with society's elite, but it certainly made more sense how she had access to all the power players.

I'd escorted many widows to fancy parties in town, and I'd spent quality, *expensive* time with lawyers, judges, doctors, and politicians, sometimes at a function, but more often in a bed, against a wall, or on the floor. The money rolled from one person to another, and I'd taken my part of it along the way because those people who paid for my time? They were all jobs for me—not real with any feelings at all.

Of course, my opinion of the Washington upper crust changed when I met Spencer and Vanessa Brady. Suddenly, something else occurred to me.

"Damn! She's gonna want the apartment back, I bet. I gotta find somewhere to live." *Now, is it all about me? Fucking hell.*

Vani giggled. "Well, we have room here if you need it."

I stared at her, taking in her demeanor. She meant it, and I couldn't understand why. "You and Spencer have a life and a son. There's no reason for me to get in the middle of all of that. Hell, Vani, we've only known each other for a week. Why would you give a shit about me?"

Vanessa placed a glass on the counter in front of me, slowly pushing it to me. "I don't know what you drink, and I'm not a bartender, so it's Glenlivet. It's Spence's favorite."

I nodded and took a healthy swig, slowly swallowing down the liquor to help ease the nerves in my belly. It felt as though I was at a crossroads, and in the past, I hadn't made the best decisions under those circumstances. I glanced in Vani's direction to see she was sipping a glass of white wine and studying me carefully.

"I—I'm not—" I was trying to put the words together in a way that made sense instead of the jumbled mess in my head.

Vani nodded and placed her wine on the marble counter. She took my hand and offered a comforting smile. "You do what's best for you. Spencer won't commit to you because of me, but I'm moving out. We're selling the house, and I'll give him a divorce when he asks, but he needs to do it for himself—not for me and not for you."

I swallowed the lump in my throat. She was spot on, though I wasn't sure why it hit me so hard.

"That man is loyal to a fault, but I believe he's also twisted up. Let him take you to drop off the car at the airport, and then have him take you home. You've got some things to consider as well, Nash. Yes, it's fast, but that doesn't make it wrong." Vani was so sweet as she reached for her glass.

I slugged the rest of my drink, realizing she was dead on. Each of us had to do what was right for him or her. I had more than a little thinking to do.

Chapter Thirteen
Spencer

"I'll be in touch. I gotta track down Caroline about my job and the apartment. You should think about what's next for you, Spence. We've done nothing to be ashamed of, and I'd rather we keep it that way. You're a good man, and Vanessa is a wonderful woman. I know you love each other, but it's time to decide what kind of love you two have." Nash was in preacher mode. I could hear a sermon from a mile away.

I started to jump in, but he wasn't finished yet. "I won't be another Blaire Conner. I don't roll that way, and I don't think you're comfortable having another down-low relationship either. We're all adults here. It's time we made adult decisions."

My SUV idled at the curb of his apartment building near George Washington University's campus. He reached over and squeezed my right hand that was resting on the console before he opened the door and hopped out. He hauled out his duffel, giving me a sexy wink before he closed the door.

Stunned was a word to describe my current mood. I thought we were making headway, Nash and I, but it sounded to me as if he was pulling away.

Why, though? I had to know what Vani said to him before I returned from showering, so I shifted my SUV into drive and headed back over the river and out the GW Parkway toward home.

Just as I was about call Vani, my Bluetooth buzzed through the speakers. I glanced at the dash to see it was Mario, so I accepted the call. "Hey, Mario. What's up?"

"Guess who called you? Give up? Frank Turner. He's out of the hospital, and he wants to see you," Mario informed.

Another revelation wasn't what I needed. "He wants to—? Why?"

"Wouldn't say. He only wants to talk with *you*. Should I call him back and schedule a time?" Mario didn't give away his thoughts on the matter. He was careful that way.

I almost said that I should talk to Vani first—that was usually my go-to answer, but maybe it was time I started handling things by myself? Maybe that was the direction my life was headed? Vani needed a chance at happiness, and the life we were trying to live was a huge lie, which now, everyone knew. She'd been loyal to me through the chaos, but was that good for her?

"Tell him I'm in the area and can drop by now. What's his address?" I knew the Turners lived in Potomac, but I didn't know where.

Mario rattled off an address, and I pulled over to plug it into my GPS. After we ended the call, I exited the Parkway and headed toward the Beltway to find the large colonial hidden in a gated community where the Turners called home.

After I showed my identification to the guard, I was allowed to enter through the massive iron gates. I wound my way through the exclusive neighborhood that made Great Falls look like a trailer park. I found 3 Patriot Way, which seemed aptly named, considering the neighborhood probably gave off a red-white-and-blue glow at night, what with all the flags flying from large poles outside the mansions.

Don't get me wrong, if someone were to cut me, I would bleed red-white-and blue because I loved my country—or the ideal of what my country could be. What I didn't love were dishonest politicians, which, I supposed now included me in many people's eyes.

I parked on the circle drive of the huge brick colonial with four large columns across the front porch. There was a massive brass light fixture hanging from the ceiling that could kill someone if it fell, and the mat at the front door didn't say welcome.

I rang the bell, and about a minute later, a woman in a grey uniform with a white apron opened the door. "Good evening," she greeted with an accent unfamiliar to me.

"Hello, I'm Spencer Brady. I believe the Senator is expecting me."

She nodded and opened the large door, sweeping her hand to invite me inside. The house was quite formal, which was expected. I was surprised to see some fall decorations on display, along with a grand pumpkin on the octagonal marble table in the entrance.

"May I take your coat, Senator?"

Glancing down, I saw the leather bomber and the jeans I'd pulled on when I was rushing to get to Nash. I was so fucked up over what happened when Nash was getting out of the SUV that I doubted I should have gone to see Turner, but I needed answers, and something in the back of my mind told me he was the key.

The beginning of an idea formed in my mind about what I wanted my future to look like as I attempted to rebuild my life. Of course, I couldn't begin to pursue any of it until I knew who was responsible for exposing my folly. Turner likely knew who, which was why I was there.

I took off my jacket and handed it to the woman who smiled pleasantly. "The Senator is waiting in his study. Right this way." She gently laid my jacket on a bench and led me down a hallway. She knocked on the door, and we both heard the familiar bark, "*In!*"

The woman rolled her eyes, and I chuckled in solidarity that the man was an insufferable bag of wind. The woman slid the pocket doors open, and I walked inside, hearing them slide closed behind me. I had no idea how long she'd worked for the Turners, but I wished her the best of fucking luck.

I glanced around the room as I waited for the Senator to turn the large leather chair to face me.

He was sorting through a leather folio as best I could tell, so I stood like a good boy and waited to be invited to sit.

The leather book slammed shut, and Turner spun in his chair to face me, tossing the volume on his desk, which made a booming echo in the room. "Sit, Brady, Sit, sit, sit." Turner wasn't known for his patience.

I took a seat in the honey-colored, leather chair across from the desk, staring into the bulldog-like face of Frank Turner. His wire-framed glasses were low on his bulbous nose, and his perma-scowl was solidly in place. "Good to see you up and around. My chief-of-staff said you wanted to see me."

I crossed a loafer-clad foot over my knee. He made me nervous, but I'd learned a long time ago never to show it. The old bastard thrived on fear.

"Yes, Brady, uhhh?" Turner opened the folio again and flopped three pictures across the desk to me. I picked them up, seeing my white ass as it had been on the front of numerous newspapers and online rags, though this time, it wasn't blurred. I had to admit, it wasn't a bad ass, as middle-aged asses went. The running and weight training helped a lot.

"Yes, Senator, I'm familiar with these photos. Are you going to confess you were the one to send someone to Antigua to photograph me with someone who wasn't my wife? Oh, congratulations. I heard it's a *girl.*" I bit out the words, adding as much sarcasm to my voice as he'd used the day he tried to dress me down for voting against him. Two could play that fucking game.

"Yes, uh-hum. We all have our skeletons, don't we? Anyway, how do you know, uhhhh, oh, here it is. Gregor Jablonowski? Do you know this person?" Turner's thick eyebrows were raised as he questioned me.

I thought for a minute, but nothing pinged in my grey matter. "No, I don't. Who is he?" Never heard the name before in my life.

"A freelance photographer who was dispatched to Antigua to follow you. He told my man he was tipped off by someone in your office who wanted proof of your infidelity to show your wife in hopes it would end your career.

"It wasn't me, but I've never been above using information that came my way to cast doubt on an adversary. In this particular situation, I wasn't involved in this blatant act of potential blackmail. My question for you is, who in your office would give information to someone regarding your schedule such that a photographer would know exactly where you'd be staying in Antigua and who you'd be with during your stay?" Turner questioned me in that condescending way that he always addressed junior senators.

The fact he'd put such a fine point on things was unsettling. I wouldn't allow my mind to wander in Mario's direction again. How many times could I accuse the poor bastard of something that even I couldn't believe he'd do? It had to be someone else.

"And how do you know this?" I needed any breadcrumbs he might have to track down that Jablow-whoever person. I didn't know a private investigator, but I remembered Nash saying he could check things out for me.

Maybe he had connections? That biker guy looked like he knew his way around the underbelly of society. It was worth a call. Honestly, it was a *reason* to call.

I got home to find a note from Vani that she went to bed early because of a headache, so I went into the family room and sat in my recliner to think things through.

Unsure of exactly what Nash meant when he said we had some decisions to make, I tried to see things from his perspective. I concluded that if I stayed on the sidelines, the handsome young man would decide I was too much trouble and run away. I really needed to consider why I'd become so attached to a guy I had met a week before.

In my mind, I should have been worried about that attachment, but those weren't the thoughts that went through my mind when thoughts of Nash Lincoln danced through my head. Those images were more of a lascivious nature.

I went to the kitchen to make a drink and grabbed a pad of paper and a pen from the junk drawer before sitting by the island to consider my options. Dating back to high school, I'd always been a better learner with visual aids. In law school, the small apartment Vani and I shared was filled with dry-erase boards so I could parse through case law to learn the way our justice system worked, and when I took the bar exam, I knew the law inside and out.

Part of me urged to let shit go regarding the defeat I'd suffered due to the involuntary outing and those fucking pictures. What would I gain by tracking down the people or persons who ruined my life?

The likelihood there would be any form of justice won was next to nothing. Hadn't enough damage been done already?

The other part of me shouted that someone had to pay for the pain and suffering of my family. My son walked around camps wearing a baseball hat and sunglasses, so nobody recognized him. My wife had been told not to come to work until her personal life was sorted, which meant until she'd filed for divorce. It was a fucking mess and someone should be held accountable, right?

My phone buzzed on the table—the burner phone I'd started using since I'd turned in my government phone. I picked it up to see it was an unexpected text from Nash.

> I hope I didn't upset you earlier, but I want to do the right thing here. You and Vani are amazing people, and you've both been through so much already. I don't want to contribute to the chaos surrounding your lives. NL

I thought about how to respond because I didn't want him to blame himself for anything. I'd already acted like a jealous asshole when he introduced us to his friend, the biker. I was learning that when it came to Nash, I had a hard time acting rationally.

Instead of texting him something that could be misconstrued, I decided to call. It barely rang before it was answered.

"Hi, Spence." Nash's voice was soft and a bit groggy sounding.

"I didn't wake you, did I? It's only... Oh!" I looked at my watch to see it was nearly eleven. I'd been sitting in the kitchen, nursing a double scotch for a lot longer than I thought.

"I'm sorry. I didn't realize it was so late. I can call you tomorrow." I prayed he didn't hang up.

There was a rustling through the line and then a quiet sigh. "No, I was having a hard time falling asleep. I thought you'd get my text in the morning. What did you do after you let me out? I didn't even thank you for the ride. I'm so sorry, Spence. It was nice of you to follow me out to the airport and bring me home. I wanted to ask you up, but I thought, under the circumstances, it was a bad idea. I don't want someone getting the wrong idea, you know?"

It was my turn to sigh. "At this point, I don't think there's a wrong idea to get. Look, I realize things are fucked up right now, but I want to get to know you, Nash. I know you don't like to talk about your past, but I promise, I won't judge you. If it's too painful to tell me, I understand, but I want us to get to know each other." I hoped my desperation for more contact with him wasn't obvious in my voice.

If he was worried about being seen with me in public, then we could slow things down and do it the old-fashioned way. I had no problem with taking our time if it meant there might be something at the end of the rainbow.

"Okay, so what's your favorite way to relax?" Nash sounded more awake.

I chuckled as I stood from the table and turned off the light in the kitchen, untucking my shirt as I walked down the hallway to the den and spread out on the couch. It was cool in the house, so I turned on the gas logs in the fireplace and pulled down the throw from the back of the chair.

"Uh, plop my ass on the couch in the den with the fireplace on and a blanket over me. In the summer, I love to sit outside as the sun goes down. I used to like to read, but it's been so long since I really got to read for fun, I almost don't remember how." My mind spun to think of my own questions to ask.

Thankfully, Nash spoke without me asking anything. "I have dyslexia, so learning to read was a struggle for me, and I still dislike it. I like to listen to podcasts to learn about different things." Nash's voice sounded thoughtful and younger than usual. He carried himself with such maturity I often forgot how young he really was—though, I didn't really know the number for sure.

"How old are you?"

"Twenty-seven. You're forty-five, right?" I was surprised at his response. I'd thought he was at least thirty. That was something I should have been worried about, but I couldn't find it in myself to care.

"Yes, I am. Does the age thing bother you?"

I heard that deep chuckle that got my blood running, and I returned it, feeling like a giddy teen talking to his crush. I'd had many of them back in high school, but of course, I never acted on them. I probably wouldn't be alive if I had.

"Naw. I'm generally attracted to older people anyway. More interesting stories to tell. Guys my age are usually limited to who they fucked, how many times they fucked, and how fast they were able to get away after the last time they fucked.

"Women want commitment and exclusivity on the first date. I can't operate that way, usually," Nash explained.

That caught my attention. I didn't know he was bisexual, and then I wondered if maybe he was interested in Vani, not me. "I, uh, I guess I didn't know you were bi. Do you prefer dating one gender over the other?" I struggled to get my goddamn libido under control.

If he was more interested in Vani, I'd back off. She was asexual, but that didn't mean she couldn't have a relationship. Of course, I'd take my leave to give them a chance. I loved her—not romantically—so I knew firsthand how easy she was to love.

Nash cleared his throat, and I braced myself for his response, which would probably break my heart. "Vani and I have discussed sexuality, but I guess she didn't tell you. I'm bi, and I don't really prefer sex with one gender over the other. It's got more to do with the person than it does with the parts."

Relief flooded my body at first, but then I realized his answer didn't give away whether he was attracted to me. "Have you dated a lot since you've come to town?"

Nash chuckled. "Not at all. I've been working two jobs. Why don't you ask the question you really want to ask?"

"That guy, Denver? Did you date him?" Apparently, it was bothering me more than I was willing to admit to even myself.

Nash flat-out laughed. "Denver is a great guy, but he's definitely not my type. He and my best friend were involved. I wasn't cut out for life in a motorcycle club, but my best friend, Clint, loved it, and he and Denver were attracted to each other at first sight. I never believed falling in love could happen like that until I saw the two of them together. Man, were there sparks when they met. I was happy for

Clint because he deserved every good thing coming his way." The nostalgia in his voice was sweet.

"Did they date for a while?"

Nash snorted. "I went with them on their first date—I didn't know it was a date at the time—and we were eating barbecue at an outdoor beer garden when an old country song played over the speakers. Denny stood and walked around the picnic table, bowing to Clint. The whole place went silent.

"Clint was extremely shy, and he asked me what the hell Denny was doing. Before I could respond, Denver said, 'I wanted to ask if you'd be kind enough to give me this dance.' Later that night, Clint and I were sharing a room at the clubhouse, and he said, 'Denver told me he loved me. I think that's just about perfect.' It was the most beautiful thing I'd ever heard." I could hear the memory was still important to him. It touched me as well.

"Are they still together?" I asked, caught up in the sweetness of the story. I could relate to that biker guy if my heart and my head could ever come to terms.

I heard a sniffle, which alerted me I wouldn't like the answer. "No. Clint patched into the club after I moved on. Denny called me one night to let me know he'd been killed in an accident. Driver of a semi fell asleep behind the wheel. Clint was riding the new Harley that Denver had custom made for his birthday. He was killed instantly, from what Denver told me." Nash sniffled again.

Hell, I had tears in my eyes, and I longed to hold him and let him cry on my shoulder until he was all cried out. After, I'd wrap him in my arms while he slept.

That fantasy was so real I could almost reach out for it. "Oh, sweetheart, I'm so sorry to hear that you lost your friend. Is it an anniversary time, or something? Is it why that guy came to see you?" I had to know why the guy turned up when he did.

Nash cleared his throat. "Actually, he's doing a favor for me. He's one of those people I don't have to talk to all the time. If I ever need him to do something, he's there in a heartbeat. Everyone in the club is like that."

"What... Uh, what's the club, if you can tell me?" I knew zilch about motorcycle clubs, but I'd at least search for it to see if they were criminals. Hell, I had a few friends in certain organizations who could run a check on them.

That might be the best way to handle it. If they were bad news, then I'd just look out for Nash as best I could. I didn't want anything to happen to him. He was becoming too important to me.

Chapter Fourteen
Nash

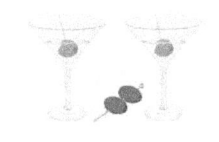

"Yes! Take it to the root, Senator." I pumped my cock in and out of his luscious mouth. His tongue was like suede as it swirled around the head and under the rim of my rigid shaft, driving me out of my mind.

His slick finger was circling my hole, sending sparks up my spine as his mouth worked me over, pushing his head down such that the swollen crown of my cock was in his velvet throat, making him gag.

I tried to pull back, but his finger in my ass tugged me forward, which gagged him again.

It was a beautiful sound, but something annoying kept blaring in the background, no matter how hard I concentrated on the feeling of Spencer's mouth, throat, and probing finger, I couldn't ignore the horn blasting in my ears.

I woke from the delicious dream and anger engulfed me immediately. I sat up and grabbed for my damn phone, which was blowing up. I saw ten missed calls from the same number, and after a minute, I recognized it. Denver.

It had been ten days since I'd returned from southern Virginia, leaving Denver and the crew investigating Spencer's situation. I'd texted Denny a few times since then, but all I got in return were complaints about my lack of patience.

Every night since I sent Spence that first text, we'd been spending time either talking or texting, depending on whether I was working. I'd taken a few escort jobs—no sex involved—since it was the holiday season, and I'd even worked a gig as a waiter on Thanksgiving for Naomi Chu.

Sean Fitzpatrick was holding an open house at a homeless shelter in Northeast, so I worked it, and then donated my pay back to the shelter. It was a gratifying day for me, and after the masses were fed,

Sean bought us pizzas. It was preferred by those working the event, because after serving turkey and the fixings all day, the last thing I wanted to eat was a Thanksgiving dinner.

Later that night, I found out Spence spent the night alone because Vani and their son, Jay, went to see Vani's family for the holiday. I felt horribly guilty for not inviting the Senator to spend the day with me. When I told him what I'd done and apologized for not inviting him, he was gracious about it. "My being there would have taken the focus off the necessity to have the open house in the first place. I'm proud of you for doing it. I wish I could have done something similar."

I coughed and swallowed, brought from my warm memories by my phone blowing up, yet again. "Yeah, Denny. What the hell, man?"

"It's fuckin' ten in the morning, kid. You still in bed? Oh, am I interrupting something? You and the Senator, dot, dot, dot?" I laughed at the fucking nosiness that permeated The Volunteers. It would always make me laugh.

"Hardly, and you know why. So, what's so important that you're ruining my beauty sleep." If I didn't press him, Denver would talk forever.

"Well, uh, I was able to find that photographer. He lives in Woodbridge. He works freelance, and it seems he worked on the Senator's campaign. Also, his sister works in Brady's Senate office, so that could be your leak. We're still trying to backtrack who gave the order for the pictures in the first place. We're looking through bank records right now."

That made sense. I wondered why they didn't go legit and become private investigators. With their tech guy, it sounded as if they could run the world.

Denny continued. "Hey, you know your guy has a lot of money to lose if he gets divorced. He was a good lawyer, and since he became a senator, he's gained a lot of supporters, who like to give him money."

That wasn't something I expected to hear. "You think he's dirty?" I blocked out the part where they were violating Spencer's privacy by checking him out too.

"Not at all. He gives a lot to charity, and he had an inheritance from his grandparents. His kid has a college fund, and the wife's apparently a great real estate agent because the woman made some bank last year. Just highlighting some points of interest that you might want to know," Denver responded.

"I sent you a check for the rental car. I pay my own way, Denver." I didn't like that he thought I was interested in Spencer and Vani's money.

People seemed to think because I was a sex worker on occasion, I was a gold digger as well. I worked two jobs. I paid my own way. I wasn't a charity case.

"Little brother, hop off that high horse before you break your neck. I'm tearing up the check, so don't send another. I meant nothing by it, so knock that chip off your shoulder. I'm just giving you the information you need to make an informed decision. Anyway, as soon we dig up something more, I'll call you. Take care of yourself." Denver ended the call.

I lay down on my back, ready to doze off again. I had nothing going on that day, which was a fucking relief. The banging on the door a few minutes later wasn't appreciated at all.

I rose from the bed, pulling on pajama pants and a T-shirt to go to the door. Shoot me—I liked to be comfortable and sleeping naked afforded me room to move around.

I went to the door and looked through the peephole, not surprised to see Vani standing there. I unlocked the door and pulled it open, watching her thoroughly appraising my appearance. "Where've you been?" Her tone wasn't appreciated. Neither was her barging her way into my apartment without invitation.

She was dressed to the nines. She looked beautiful, but her eyes showed a weariness that gave away her actual level of stress. "I've been here and working. How've you been? Want some coffee?" I walked toward the galley kitchen, hearing her heels clicking on the hardwoods.

"I didn't wake you, did I?" She didn't sound like she cared if she did as she placed her handbag on the counter before leaning against it.

"No. Denver took delight in doing it earlier. What's going on?"

She was dressed in a navy suit with a taupe-colored silk blouse beneath. She looked like Real Estate Barbie with her long blonde hair draped over her shoulders.

I started a pot of regular coffee and pulled down mugs, sugar, and flavored creamers. One was mocha, which I'd seen at the Brady's home. I'd never tried it, but it looked interesting, so I bought it.

Out of the corner of my eye, I noticed that Vani was looking around the kitchen, and then her gaze settled on my ass. She smirked and bit her lip before stepping out of the room to take a seat at the small dining table between the kitchen and the sitting area. That smirk had me a little worried.

"What's brought you by?" I poured two cups of coffee and put everything on a random tray Caroline kept in the cabinet, carrying it into the dining area and placing it on the table. I sat across from Vanessa to await her response.

She picked up the creamer and squeezed in a helping before she stirred and took a sip. "Mmmm. Delish." I knew that was bullshit because it was nothing extraordinary.

I glanced at her and cocked an eyebrow, seeing her glowing smile. "Okay, I was worried about you. Spence seems on edge, and he's not really talking much, so I thought I'd check in with you."

I chuckled. "Why don't the two of you stay together? So what if it's not a conventional marriage. Many aren't. It just seems like you guys belong with each other." It wasn't a lie.

I didn't expect the laugh at all. It started as a cackle before it faded to a snicker, lasting about ninety seconds. I sat and waited, taking in her beautiful face to see she actually seemed happy. I wanted to know why.

Finally, she composed herself, took another sip of her coffee, and blotted her lips with the paper napkin I'd given her. It wasn't because I bought things of the sort. Caroline had someone who stocked the place for me.

"I thought Caroline was going to want this place back. Have you talked to her recently?"

"I worked a few nights last week. She's not booking clients herself any longer. She's hired an assistant." Vani's expression alerted me that something was wrong.

"You worked for her? Who did you spend time with? Did you tell Spence?" The bite in her voice showed she didn't like the idea of me working escort gigs again.

I took a sip of my coffee, wishing I'd have added more sugar before it got cold. "Spence is a friend, just like you. I didn't tell anyone I was going on calls because it was truly nobody's business," I answered, trying like hell to keep my temper in check. In my life, I'd never answered to anyone, and I wasn't about to start at the age of twenty-seven.

"Okay, I get it. What's your relationship with Denver? He seemed awfully excited to get you alone."

I chuckled. "We're good friends. Denver was the partner of my best friend, Clint." It was the same information I'd shared with Spence.

Vani seemed to be racking her brain to try to find another way to ask her question, so I held up my hand. "See, this is another reason I think you and Spencer should give it another go. You're too far into each other's business, but you're not getting into mine. I don't know what kind of head games you two like to play but leave me out of them. Not my scene." It was clear by the snap in my voice that I wasn't participating in her little fact-finding mission.

I started to get up to shower when Vani grabbed my hand. "Please, Nash. I'm sorry if I'm out of line, but I'm planning to move. I want to move to New York, and I don't want Spencer to come with me. He has a better shot at finding a job he loves if he stays here."

I had to wonder if that was fact or wishful thinking on her part. A disgraced senator didn't seem like a good line item on a resume.

Vani gave a weary sigh. "Trust me when I say I love that man with everything inside me, but not the way you love him, and not the way he loves you. When I ask about you, he glows, Nash. I can tell you care about him very much. If you didn't, you wouldn't encourage me to give our marriage another chance."

Those weren't words I could dispute. I cared about Spencer a lot more than I knew was smart.

"I've used Spence as a crutch, and he made it easy because his job kept him from being who he really needs to be. I want a chance at a life that will make me happy as well, and I have a job offer from a realty company in New York. I want the job, but Spence will become overprotective if I tell him. I don't think he believes I can survive on my own, but that's my fault because for so long, I couldn't. I want you to help me break the news to him. If he knows you're here with him, then I think he'll let me go a little easier."

The news was unsettling, as I stared at the small but mighty powerhouse who looked so determined to strike out on her own. It seemed as if, whether I liked it or not, I was in the middle of their marriage. I was likely in love with Spencer Brady or falling, at least. I loved his wife, but not in the same way I was coming to love him.

An unlikely friendship had developed between Vani and me, and I'd always tried to do whatever I could for the few people I cared about. Vanessa Brady had become one of those people.

"Okay, I'll help you, but why were you staring at my ass?" I was perplexed by her interest.

Vani giggled. "Spencer has a picture of you on his phone, or should I say your ass in a pair of black chinos, from the night we met you. I catch him looking at it a lot. I'm not one to notice a man's ass, but you do have a nice one. I might not be attracted to your physical appearance, but I can't deny it's incredible. The man I know on the inside is the person I love, and I mean it in the most innocent way in the world."

I was touched. It was likely one of the kindest things anyone had ever said to me.

Vani touched my hand. "Do you have plans today? Can you come over for dinner? I want to tell him tonight because I'm planning to move to New York after Christmas. Jay's coming home for the main holiday, but he's going to spend New Year's and the time before classes start again in January with his boyfriend, Cole."

"Yeah, uh, I'm free."

"Good. You know, I hate the idea of leaving Spence in that big house by himself. I'm almost to the point that if he won't ask me for a divorce, I'm going to ask him. It's past time, but I just can't hurt him like that. He's a kind soul."

I nodded in agreement. "Okay, I'll, uh, I'll come out this evening. What time?"

It was the first week of December, and I had scheduled a few escort gigs and bartending a couple of holiday parties, but I'd find the time to check on him if that was what she was asking. Spence's well-being was much more important to me than work.

"I'll leave my car for you to drive out. I'm going to take a car service home. They'll be here in fifteen minutes. I went to meet with my ex-boss and clean out my desk. I'm so excited for my new job."

Twenty minutes later, my head was swimming with the quick information dump she'd given. She seemed genuinely excited about the prospects facing her. I just hoped Spencer would be as well.

Chapter Fifteen
Spencer

The first week of December, I went to my Senate suite to finish cleaning out my office and files. The space where I'd spent twelve years of my legislative life no longer felt like mine, and the realization of it brought an unsettled feeling. It seemed as if my future was becoming less and less certain, and I had no idea what to do about it.

Hell, I wasn't even fifty yet, so retirement was out of the question. Finding another position within the government wouldn't come easy, but I wasn't about to dip into my inheritance. I was keeping that money for Vani and Jay in case something ever happened to me.

A government worker's salary, no matter what anyone thought, wasn't great, and the DMV—DC-Maryland-Virginia—area was far from a low-cost area of the country. My grandparents had left me a nest egg, and I'd invested it and added to it when I was practicing law.

It was finally something I could be proud to leave behind for those I loved, so I wasn't about to dip into it to support Vani and me. I was perfectly able to go back to private practice, especially since she was currently out of a job. I could take care of us.

I was cleaning out the bookcase in my office when Mario barreled inside without invitation. I didn't really care, but he'd never done it before, so why now?

"Hey, Mario. What's up?" I paged through the various law books and copies of the Federal Register belonging to the Senate library that I'd kept in my office, ensuring I hadn't inadvertently left any handwritten notes inside as I prepared to return them.

"I got a call from a man named Denver Wallace. He said he's a friend of yours, and he has evidence pointing to a mole in our camp. He's downstairs, unable to come up because of security, but he wants us to meet him across the street. I'm perplexed."

I looked up to see Mario was, indeed, puzzled. "Did he give you any hints about who it is?"

"No, but he said not to bring anyone with us—just you and me."

I nodded and stood from my desk, pulling on my jacket. It was nearly lunchtime anyway, so I was at a good point to take a break.

"I'm starving, and after I leave this building for the last time, I damn well won't come back here, so can you ask someone to call over to O'Toole's to see if we can get the private room?"

Mario rolled his eyes but grabbed his cell, speaking on the phone as I tightened my tie and checked my hair in the mirror behind the door. I glanced out the window to see it was spitting snow, so I retrieved my overcoat and turned to Mario. "You coming with me?"

He finished his conversation requesting the private room, glancing in my direction with the exasperating look I'd grown accustomed to over time. "Give me a damn minute." He left my office and stomped through the bullpen, bringing a chuckle from me.

I scanned the room outside my office where my loyal staffers worked, having stuck with me after the scandal broke. I was grateful to each one of them.

Mitchell Flora had the desk phone receiver to his ear in his office. He was staring out of the glass wall at the young woman who sat at the desk outside his door, unhappiness evident on his face.

I glanced at her to see she was pregnant, and I didn't remember any of my staffers being pregnant, but that was when I saw she wasn't the same assistant Mitch had a few weeks earlier. The old one was named Lori Warren. The pregnant young woman sitting at the desk wasn't the blonde who used to walk around the office talking to herself.

I walked out of my office and into Mario's. "Who's the girl at Lori's desk?"

Mario looked out as he logged off his laptop and closed the lid. "Uh, she's from the assistant's pool. Lori quit just before Thanksgiving. She and Mitch had a falling out, or so the rumor mill churned out. Anyway, I got the room at O'Toole's, so let's go get your friend and get a move on. I need a drink." I chuckled and followed him out of the office.

We took the elevator to the lobby and walked out into the December sunshine to find the large man leaning against a pillar at the base of the stairs, smoking a cigar. I glanced at the people walking by to see their faces screwed up in disgust.

Based on the way Denver Wallace was blowing smoke in their faces, it was quite evident he didn't give a flying fuck if they liked it or not. I laughed, liking the guy for his "fuck you" attitude to the snobs on the Hill.

I glanced in Mario's direction, seeing his face was screwed up into a scowl before he turned to look at me for an explanation. "He's a new acquaintance, so don't piss him off. I'm sure he could take the two of us apart with his bare hands," I whispered as we approached.

When Denver saw us, he smiled and lifted his boot-clad foot, knocking off the ember from the end of the cigar. I saw him touch his thumb to the tip before depositing it into a long plastic cylinder and returning it to the pocket of his leather coat.

"Is he from the Matrix?" Mario joked as we made our way down the stairs.

"You better hope not, or he heard that and he's going to kill us both. Play nice." We stepped over to where the man was waiting patiently.

Denver gave Mario a stern look. "You think I look like Sam Jackson? Morpheus, I'm not. So, where are you going to buy me lunch, Senator?"

"Across the street." I pointed to the green pub with the stained-glass windows.

"Looks inviting. Shall we?" Denver responded as he headed toward the crosswalk and pressed the button for the light.

"So, uh, Mr. Wallace, how do you know the Senator?" Mario was as transparent as a pane of glass. I smirked, waiting for how Denver would answer the question.

Wallace chuckled. "He's got the hots for someone important to me, and I'm here to save his ass." It was concise, but not quite accurate. The fact I was probably in love with Nash wasn't anything I was about to share with my two guests. Those words were something I needed to consider, and eventually share with the man, himself, before I put it out there for public consumption. I also had Vani's feelings to consider. We were still married, after all.

My companions and I walked into the pub, and Erin was waiting for us with a sweet smile on her round, freckled face. "Gents, we've missed ye. This way." She took us around the bar and into one of the private booth areas, standing aside so the three of us could take a seat.

She handed out menus. "Today's entree special is shepherd's pie. We have Welsh rarebit for the daily appetizer, and for dessert, we have an Irish cream pie. What can I bring ye to drink?"

Not surprisingly, Denver was the first to respond. "I'll have a stout and a shot of Jameson."

I sighed. "I'll have a Glenlivet on the rocks, and Mario will have a Crown neat," I ordered. Erin nodded and left the room, pulling the pocket doors closed behind her.

I turned my gaze to Denver Wallace. "So, what's new since the last time you terrorized me?" I made a quasi-joke, while giving him the full force of my penetrating stare.

The big man didn't even flinch, instead laughing at my futile attempt at exuding authority over him. "Does that *ever* work?"

I chuckled with him, and finally, Mario loosened up enough to laugh with us, seeming eager to embarrass me. "It actually does sometimes, but not often enough that it's a trademark for him. So, please, Mr. Wallace, I'm dying to know how you and Spence know each other."

"Little brother asked me to look into your issue. We've been tracking the transaction for almost a month, and I'm afraid I have some very bad news for you, Senator." Denver stared at the two of us as the door opened and Erin popped in with our drinks.

The young woman's timing was perfect, because I wasn't ready to hear about one of my trusted staff members spying on me and reporting it to the press. After I took a sip of my scotch, I exhaled as the liquor made its way to my gut, loosening my nerves.

I hoped it helped me *not* have a shouting fit right there in the pub, especially since I'd seen several reporters sitting in the main dining room.

"Okay, I'm ready. Shoot."

Denver nodded and pulled out a tablet from the inside pocket of his leather jacket. After pecking it a few times, he tapped on something, and when he was satisfied with what he had, he handed the device to me.

I glanced at the screen to see a bank statement dated March 1 of that year. I scrolled up to see it was for an account owned by Mitch Flora, and I noticed there were regular deposits into his account for five-thousand dollars a week, starting around the same time I'd announced my intent to run for a third term.

"Okay, uh, do we know who made the deposits?" I handed the tablet back to Denver. He flipped the cover closed and shoved it back into the pocket of his coat.

"We're working on it. I thought maybe you'd want to deal with a traitor before you leave office. We're tracking the deposits, but they don't originate in the US, so that becomes a little trickier. I wanted you to know I wouldn't do this for any other lying bastard in any office of the government. I think you're all pieces of shit, but my good friend thinks you're a good man, so I'll follow through on this because of him." Wallace didn't beat around the bush.

I was shocked at his comments, but really, I shouldn't have been. He was a no-nonsense kind of guy, and that, I could appreciate in any man. I didn't like being dicked around either. Life was too short for that bullshit.

I needed to talk to Nash, and not just through text or on the phone. I wanted to see him in person because I wanted to hug him for asking his friend to help me out. My phone buzzed in my pocket, so I pulled it out to see a text from Vani.

> Come home soon, please. We're having company for dinner. I'm thawing a tenderloin for you to put on the grill.

I noticed Wallace looking at my phone and smirking at the message on the screen, likely wondering what the hell was my deal. I'd leave it to Nash to explain it if we ever got together.

Just then, the doors opened and a food runner accompanying Erin stood with a large tray outside the pocket doors. Before she could put the plate down in front of me, Denver looked at Erin and grinned. "I believe the Senator needs to leave us. Could you put his lunch into a box to go?"

Wallace shot back his Jameson's and winked. "I believe Mario and I will eat here. Get to know each other."

I glanced at my friend and saw his face flush before he nodded enthusiastically. I held the laugh, and I left the two of them in the private room, following Erin to the bar where she boxed up my food.

I paid the check for our lunch and gave her a healthy tip. "I'd knock before I went in there, if I were you." I laughed as I signed the check and grabbed the bag with my lunch.

It was a surprising turn of events, and I hoped to hell Mario enjoyed himself, the lucky bastard. I was so damn horny I was about to pop.

★★★ ★★★

After I arrived home, I let myself into the house through the front door. "Vani!"

The idea that Mitch Flora had betrayed me—and his NDA—clung to me like cheap cologne. I needed to talk it out with Vanessa, and I desperately wanted to talk to Nash.

I hoped he would agree to meet me somewhere after Vani's unknown dinner guests left, but I wouldn't ask him yet. I had no idea what the evening had in store.

Vani waltzed into the kitchen where I was sorting the mail, a mischievous smile on her pretty face. I could see she was dressed casually, which was a relief. "How was your day?"

I opened the electric bill, perused the amount owed, and cursed the state, county, and local taxes included before stacking it with the rest of the bills to go into the queue for payment.

"Good. Cleaned out my desk at the office and told Tom Parks to fuck himself. How about you?" Tom had been her boss at Parks Realty located in Tyson's Corner.

"I found my leak—it's Mitch." I tore up a few catalogues and some junk mail before turning to see my wife staring at me, a concerned smile taking the place of her previous happy one.

"Oh, Spence! That's horrible. Do you think he was behind the photographer showing up in Antigua?"

Vani articulated what had been running through my mind since I'd heard the news earlier. We'd discussed the situation in depth—and to death—trying to figure out who the leaker could be. Mitch had never crossed my mind.

Why would he do that? What would Mitch have to gain by leaking my personal business? What the hell had I done to him that would push him to take the step of betraying me? How the fuck did he even find out I was gay?

Mitchell Flora had worked his way around Capitol Hill since he'd arrived in DC. He'd graduated from The Ohio State University with honors, and he had held several positions in various offices on the Hill before he came to work for me after one of my father's former college friends from UVA recommended him when my previous communications director left me to have a baby.

Tina Hinson was a real pro at her job, and she'd asked around about Mitch, only hearing great things through the grapevine.

I'd hired Mitch based on Judge Blackwell's recommendation—and a background check, other than what was required to confirm the security clearance he already held.

Yet again, I was a naïve dumbass who trusted people to treat me the way I always tried to treat others. How much of a fucking country bumpkin could I be?

"What are you going to do?" Vani asked as she made us drinks, pulling a third glass from the cabinet. I noticed a stack of collapsed boxes in the corner of the kitchen, leaning against the wall.

We were planning to paint the house, but I didn't think we'd need that many boxes to pack up things to make room for painters. Eventually, we'd move somewhere else so we could sell the house, but we hadn't discussed it in detail because everything was still a mess in both of our heads.

"I'll call Mario tomorrow. I think he has a date tonight with Denver, Nash's friend."

The garage door began churning open, so I looked at Vani to see she seemed nervous. "Is that Jay?" I hoped my son had come home for an impromptu visit. I missed him.

"No. It's Nash. I, uh, I need to talk to you, Spence, and I asked him to come out for dinner. I think we both need his support, especially now." Vani's clarification had me totally confused.

The back door opened as the garage door closed, and I turned to see Nash Lincoln, the beautiful man I'd missed more than my own heart. He had a bottle of wine in his hand, and his scent took up space in the room like a new kind of air.

Without thought, I walked over to him and took him in my arms, feeling him return the hug. I inhaled deeply and felt myself relaxing for the first time in days, thanking whatever circumstance that brought him to our home. It was a blessing.

I pulled away and smiled at him before the sound of a sniffle caught my attention. I stepped away from Nash and saw the happy smile on Vani's face had returned as the tears fell down her cheeks.

Whatever was going on with her had me worried, but when Nash put his arm around my shoulder and settled his large hand on my neck, the tension in my body released. With his support, I was ready for whatever was coming my way.

I turned back to Nash and kissed the end of his nose. "How've you been? I've missed you." Thankfully, the gorgeous man leaned forward and brushed a kiss against my lips.

"I'm here if you need me. Vani invited me for dinner." Nash's comment made me wonder what he knew that clearly I didn't.

"Yes, uh, Nash, dear, let me make you a drink. What can I get for you?" Vani gave him a big smile.

"Bourbon neat." I helped him take off his leather jacket and took it to the hallway. Before I hung it up, I took a strong sniff of it. It carried his intoxicating scent, which had my dick thickening quickly in my unforgiving slacks.

"I'm gonna run upstairs to change. I'll be back." I rushed up the staircase to my room, closing the door before I hurried into the bathroom to splash cold water on my face so I could calm down—and hopefully, get my dick to follow suit.

I wasn't sure why Vani had called Nash to come over, but it must have been for a good reason. No matter what, I was fucking glad he was there. I quickly changed into jeans and a long-sleeved Henley before I slid on a pair of loafers and started for the stairs.

"Have you told him yet?" Nash's voice carried enough that I heard him from my spot on the stairs.

I crept down to the bottom in time to hear Vanessa giggle. "No way. I was waiting for you."

"What difference does it make if I'm here? It won't change the fact you're leaving town, will it?" Nash's comment hit me like a slap in the face.

My gut dropped to my feet. Vani was leaving town? Where the fuck was she going? Was Nash going with her?

"Nash, seriously, he loves you. It's going to be an adjustment for all of us, but it's time we untangled our lives. I'm so happy he'll have you to count on," Vani responded.

There was a lot packed into that comment, but there was a kernel of truth, so I stomped down the hallway and joined them in the kitchen, ready to make my declaration.

If Vani was ready to strike out on her own, I wouldn't stop her. I loved her and only wanted the best for her. I stepped toward Nash, keeping a bit of distance between us so he knew I was serious.

"She's not wrong, you know. I do love you." Vani's soft laugh made me grin.

My insides were on fire for the man, but everything had to happen in the correct order. I couldn't bear it if either of them were tainted by my previous mistakes.

Nash seemed flustered at my honesty, so I quickly added, "It's okay if you don't feel the same way. I think it's important that all the cards are on the table. If you want to walk away, I won't stop you."

I then turned to my best friend. "So, Vani, where are you going, love?"

I didn't expect Nash to take my hand and lead me to the table, pulling out a chair for me before standing behind me with his large hands—which I was dying to have wrapped around my cock—resting on my shoulders.

Vani was staring at him, and after a minute, Nash's fingers began massaging me. My wife nodded before she sat at the table and took my hand, both of their behaviors making me nervous.

"I love you, Spence. You've been so amazing to me in all the years we've been together, and you'll *always* be my best friend. I think it's time we went our separate ways." Her voice held the air of finality. I admired her guts to pull the trigger first.

For me, there was no need to argue, but I was curious what she expected me to say. I'd told her back in August to get in touch with Bertram Lloyd, a friend of my parents who was a top-notch divorce attorney. "Um, okay?" I responded, unsure why she was being so dramatic.

"She's moving to New York," Nash whispered before he kissed the top of my head.

It didn't make sense. I turned to look at him, "How'd you know it before me?"

I saw the guilty look on Nash's face, so I glanced at Vani. "Really? You couldn't tell me this without backup?"

"I was worried you'd overreact to the news I was leaving, and I know you're holding back on making plans because of me. I want you to move forward with your life as well, Spencer."

I stood, turning to Nash. "I'm glad you're here. Could you start the grill?" He nodded and walked out of the house without looking back.

"So, you called Nash to come here to soften the blow? Why? I love you, and I only want the best for you, Vani. I'm so sorry I can't be what you need." I was hurt she didn't think I'd support her decision.

We'd been through so much over the years, and I knew I was never going to be the person she needed, but I kept trying, clearly never succeeding. The fact she didn't feel she could talk to me without someone there for backup hurt a lot more than I wanted to admit.

Vani hugged me. "Spencer, you've been an incredible friend and husband. It's not that you didn't do everything right, dear one. We needed each other until we figured out we needed someone else."

I took a deep breath, exhaling before I asked the question. "Did you find someone else?"

Vani stepped back, sniffling before she totally pulled away, her beautiful eyes full of tears. "Yes, I did. Spence, I found *me*! I've only ever needed *me*, but I've just figured it out for myself. You gave me the time and space to work through all my issues, and for that, I'll always love you. You're a wonderful man, and I think you've finally found what you need." She pointed to where Nash stood on the deck trying to figure out how to light the grill.

"Right now, he's worrying about how you'll feel when I move, and I'm a little worried myself. We're codependent, Spence, and it's time for us to choose other paths. Go help him figure out the grill. He wants to make you happy. It's beautiful." Vani handed me the fire wand and pushed me outside.

I walked out onto the deck, not sure how I felt about the turn of events. Maybe Vanessa expected me to be much more upset, but since I'd met Nash Lincoln, he'd filled my thoughts day and night.

I sensed Vani understood it—maybe better than me. I had to learn how to adjust to her striking out on her own.

"Here. You need this." I offered him the blue wand to light the fire.

The autoignition had stopped working the previous summer, and I should have probably had someone come out to look at the grill, but I'd been busy doing the people's work. Now? I had nobody's work to do but my own.

"Oh, was I doing it wrong?" Nash stepped back from the grill; his expression worried.

I exhaled. "No, sweetheart, I don't think you could ever do anything wrong. The automatic starter broke last summer, and I didn't get it fixed. Now, you just turn on the gas and use this thing to light the pilot."

Nash nodded as I turned off the gas and handed him the wand. He mimicked my movements, and when the pilot caught, he looked at me with a triumphant grin. "I've never used a grill before. Do you use it a lot?"

I laughed. "I've been out here in rain and snow grilling stuff. Stick with me, kid. I'll show you all the tricks." I leaned forward and kissed his temple. He didn't move away, and my heart grew wings.

"So, uh, what are we cooking?" Nash asked, watching me close the lid to allow the grill to heat.

I wanted to haul him upstairs and show him the fire my soul felt for him, but I respected his boundary—nothing until I wasn't married any longer.

Would Vani's filing for divorce count? I had no doubt Vanessa and I would remain the best of friends, but would Nash stick around to see it through? That was the bigger question.

Chapter Sixteen
Nash

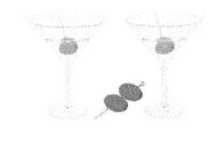

I stood from the table to clear the dishes. Vani and Spence were discussing the way to divide their assets, and I felt like a fucking third wheel. I had no business being in the middle of such discussions between a married couple, regardless of the circumstances.

I reached for Spence's empty plate, surprised when he touched my hand to stop me. "Sit down, please. We're not going to fight about this stuff, I promise."

"Oh, I was trying to give you some privacy. I don't mind doing the dishes," I offered as I walked back to the kitchen sink, dipping the plates I'd collected into the lavender smelling suds. I'd done every job in food service, and I didn't hate any of them. Washing dishes was like meditation.

The fact Spence and Vani were trying to sort out their separation made me uncomfortable. I didn't want to be the cause, and Vani had never made me feel as if it was my fault, but that didn't make it okay with me. From every vibe I got from the two of them, they were being honest about their desire to end their marriage, but not their friendship. I was the one who was having a hard time with it, and I really needed to consider why.

Spence stood from his seat at the kitchen table and walked to the sink, touching my cheek to gently turn me to look at him. "Please, sit with us. It's important to both of us that you realize how much we appreciate having you in our lives, but for very different reasons. I'm sure this is a more unique situation than any you've encountered in your life, but we're not gaslighting you. This isn't some setup to fuck you over or play you for a fool. Vanessa and me, we've been headed in this direction since Jay was in high school, but neither of us were ready to uncouple until we had Jay in college, and now, well, I think we're both ready."

I glanced at Vani to see she nodded with a sweet smile on her face. I guessed their minds were made up.

My stomach turned before I pulled my hands out of the dishwater. I couldn't begin to understand why they'd want me to sit with them, but it seemed important, so I dried my hands.

I followed him to the table and took a seat between them, taking both of their hands for a moment to get their attention. "Spencer, you are a United States Senator from Virginia. I realize you lost the election, but I don't want..."

I was prepared to talk him out of whatever relationship he was trying to create between him and me. His reputation was damaged, but not decimated. Any hint that he and I were together would annihilate any chances he had for recovering from the scandal to move on in his life.

I was an escort. If the press got wind he was with me in a romantic way, he might as well resign himself to pumping gas for the rest of his life.

"No! Stop that shit right now. I lost the election through my own fault and choices, but it set me free. For the first time in too long, I have hope for the future because I'm finally doing something I want to do."

He glanced at Vani and smiled. "No offense, love." Seeing his love for her through his kind words dialed up the guilt I was feeling even more.

Spence stood from his seat, walking around me to pull out Vani's chair. She stood and kissed his cheek before leaving the two of us. I heard her on the stairs and turned to Spencer, seeing his hand extended to me. "How about we go to the other room and talk?"

I nodded, taking his hand and following him into the family room in their grand home. I could see Vani had packed boxes in that room as well. "You weren't suspicious that more was going on than painting?" I asked as I took a seat in the corner of the lush sectional, pointing to the half-empty bookcase.

Spence walked over to the wet bar in the corner, opening the small fridge and pulling out two bottles of Bud Light. He held one up, and I nodded, so he carried them over to the table and placed the bottles on coasters after he opened them.

Spence took a seat next to me and looked around, seeing what I'd pointed out. "Fuck, I've been in a goddamn fog since the stupid election. I was coasting through life, afraid to really make any decisions about anything. Thank heaven, Vani took the step we both needed to take." He reached for his beer and took a swig, resting his head on the back cushion of the sectional. I could see the exhaustion on his handsome face, and I wanted to take him in my arms, but I kept both hands on my beer, still uncertain of my place in *their* relationship.

"I remember the first time I *finally* accepted I was gay and wanted to act on my attraction for another guy. I was in the locker room at school, which is a fucking awful place to have a sexual awakening, I'll tell ya. We'd finished baseball practice. Oh! I had big dreams back then that I could be a major league baseball player, but my father quickly squashed that idea, telling me no Brady was going to be anything but a member of the judiciary or the President of the United States.

"Anyway, there was this new guy. He'd transferred to our school district over the Christmas break, and he was gorgeous but very standoffish. His name was, uh—"

He was racking his brain when we both heard, "Lanny Fisher" yelled from down the hallway.

Spencer rolled his eyes and chuckled. "She has the hearing of a bat. The eyesight as well."

"Fuck you." Vani clomped up the stairs without waiting for a response.

"She's worried about you. About how you'll be when she leaves town," I offered before taking another swig of my beer.

Spence sat up and took another drink. "She's always worried about me. She feels like I sacrificed too much for her, but honestly, I knew my parents career ambitions for me required a wife, kids, dog, picket fence. Oh, that's not why we adopted Jay, but I'm sure that's what my folks think. He's a great kid, really. I'm worried about him, but he's stronger than I'll ever be. I'll stick around town, so I can be here for him, and of course, once Vani is settled, Jay will probably go see her on breaks. I hope to fuck I can make up for lost time with him."

I sucked down the rest of my beer, prepared to leave him. The poor man had a mountain of shit to stew over. "I, uh, I better go." I started to get up from the couch when Spence grabbed my hand.

"I know you have your rules, and I respect them, but please, please don't leave tonight. Please stay. Nothing—nothing has to happen between us..."

I couldn't take it any longer. I took his beer bottle and placed it on the coaster, climbing to straddle him.

There were a lot of things that needed to be worked out before anything serious could happen between us, but I'd knowingly been with married men before, getting paid for what happened between us. I had no care or concern for those men, or their wives at the time.

Was the current circumstance so different? Yes, I knew the players involved much better than my johns, but I also cared about Vani and Spence. She'd made it clear she wanted something to happen between Spencer and me, so was there something wrong with pursuing it, even if it was just a blow job?

I made a promise to myself, as my tongue entered his mouth tasting the hops from the beer on his tongue. I swore I wouldn't get in the middle of his divorce. However, there was a force drawing us together, and maybe, if we acted on it, he could get over whatever he felt about me and begin putting his life back together.

Spence succumbed to me, and I felt the thrill of power surge through my body. I pulled away, biting his bottom lip before I opened my eyes and released it, soothing the sting with my tongue.

"Oh, fuck, Nash. Please stay with me. I swear, I won't take advantage of you, but I need to feel you in my arms." Spencer's pleading voice was quiet, and it broke my resolve.

I scurried off his lap and onto the floor, kneeling between his long legs. I opened the button and zipper of his jeans, seeing white briefs trying to contain his hard cock. My mouth watered for it. "Lift."

He did so without question.

His hard shaft sprung free, looking angry and purple. I glanced up at Spence, waiting for consent. He nodded, and I kissed the head of his cock, tasting the salty tang of his pre-come on my tongue.

It was like a shot of Spanish Fly to my libido, so I bobbed down, deep throating that thick dick and swallowing around him. I usually made a mint from my oral skills, but it was a pleasure to suck Spencer Brady's cock. I wanted him to feel pleasure. He deserved it.

"Oh, fuck, Nash." He moaned as I slowly released him before pulling off his pants and briefs so I could get to his heavy balls. I quickly pulled his muscular thighs over my shoulders, pulling his ass closer so I could get to him. I sucked one of his balls into my mouth swirling my tongue over the hairless orbs before nipping at the skin.

I moved to the left one and offered it the same love I'd shown to the right. I glanced up to see Spencer beginning to stroke his cock as I slid my tongue behind his taint to nip at his pink hole.

"Please, please, fuck me." Spencer's begging had my cock so hard I had to reach down and pinch the base.

THE SENATOR

God knew I wanted to rail the guy, but that was more than a blow job, which was all I'd let myself enjoy. This encounter involved feelings, and if I fucked him or he fucked me, the feelings would go out of control on my end. I couldn't let that happen.

Without responding, I took his shaft back into my mouth and sunk down on his impressive length. My own dick was threatening to bust through my zipper, so as I continued to go down on Spencer, I pulled mine out and stroked myself.

I edged him to prolong his pleasure as I took my own from his moans while he gently ran his fingers through my hair. I felt his nails scrape my scalp, and I choked on his cock because I wanted to offer a moan of my own.

Spence stopped moving and tried to pull away, but I refused to stop. I continued sucking him as I used my own juice as lube to push a finger inside him enough to find his P-spot. He thrust into my mouth again, and suddenly, he flooded my throat with his release.

I swallowed around his thick, hard cock, feeling proud at what I'd accomplished. As he continued to throb in my mouth, I quickly shoved my hard dick back into my pants, deciding to take care of myself later.

I'd accomplished my goal of getting him off, and when he fell asleep, I planned to slip out of the house and leave Spencer Brady to the rest of his life.

Chapter Seventeen
Nash

My cell woke me the next Tuesday morning, which was the second week of December. I was scheduled to bartend at a holiday party that night for a big law firm in DC, and when I saw who the text was from, I wasn't sure if I should answer.

I'd left the Brady's home after I'd helped Spence upstairs to his bed, tucking him in after assisting him with removing the rest of his clothes. I fought the temptation to crawl in with him, instead, kissing his forehead and covering him with the soft blankets on his bed.

I picked up his phone from the nightstand and removed my contact information, feeling my heart crack as I did. It was best for all of us. Unfortunately, I couldn't get to Vani's phone to do the same.

The note I left for my dear friend on the counter thanked her for dinner and apologized for spending the night in their home. I knew it was off limits for them to have someone over for sex, and I'd crossed the line by blowing Spencer before I left. Make no mistake, the man needed it, and I needed to get him out of my system. Case closed.

I sat up on my shitty mattress in the weekly rental motel I'd found in Southeast DC after I'd moved out of Caroline Turner's fancy condo to avoid whatever debt she'd try to accuse me of needing to pay. Her assistant had called about several escort jobs, but I'd turned them down. I needed to separate myself from that life.

If I decided to have sex for money again, I damn well wasn't going to pay a middleman to set it up. It was my ass, mouth, and cock that provided the service, and I was keeping every fucking penny I made. I earned it fair and square.

I had the feeling it was time to pull up stakes and move on from DC—maybe head to Baltimore for a while to make plans for my future. I knew there were tons of bars, sports venues, and a few casinos in the area, so I felt certain I could easily find work as a bartender or a server, which was fine.

My phone buzzed again, reminding me of why I was awake so early. I picked it up, swiping the screen to see a message from Denver.

> I'm coming to get you, Little Brother. I heard you've cut ties with the Senator, so I'm guessing you're in a rough way. Come spend Christmas with the club. You always have a home with The Volunteers, you know.

I felt my eyes sting at Denver's kind words, but I wasn't his problem. I wasn't anyone's problem but my own.

> Denny, thanks man. I appreciate your offer, but I've got a full book until after Christmas. Maybe I'll come down for New Year's? Wish all the guys a Merry Christmas for me.

I tossed the phone on the nightstand and lay back against the shitty pillows, glad I had stopped at the superstore for a set of clean sheets and pillowcases as I walked back to the motel after the cab let me off six blocks away. The driver refused to go into the neighborhood, which was definitely a sign it wasn't on the social register. Unfortunately, I had to stretch my cash on hand, and the Four Seasons wasn't in the budget.

There was a banging on the door that wasn't appreciated, but the motel manager was a drug-slinging son of a bitch, and he liked to try to hit up the residents for extra cash if they were in the mood for some pharmaceutical recreation. I wasn't, and I was about to beat his ass for bothering me, yet again.

I pulled on my shorts and stalked to the door, pitying the fucking asshole on the other side. I slid the chain off and ripped the cheap thing open, seeing Vani Brady standing there in all her glory—stiletto-covered foot tapping a mile a minute, and an angry scowl in place.

"What are you doing here? No, wait—how the hell did you find me?" I snapped as I walked away, leaving the door open because I was damn sure she wasn't going to leave without a fight.

"Bullshit! You don't get to be the aggrieved party in this situation, Nashville Lincoln. You don't leave a 'Dear Vani' note on the counter and just disappear. Spencer is beside himself. You deleted your contact information from his phone, and he's pissed at me because I won't give him the number I have in mine. If you weren't so damn tall, I'd turn you over my knee and spank some sense into you," she ranted.

I was fighting to keep from laughing. She looked like a pissed-off chihuahua, bouncing from foot to foot in the run-down room I was now calling home.

"Vani, it's for the best. You and Spence are getting ready to divorce, and if he's going to have a chance at salvaging his reputation, he needs to steer clear of the likes of me and my fucked-up life."

Hell, my life was in the shitter as much as Spencer's. The difference between us—nobody gave a tinker's damn about me, and the former Senator's fuckups made front page of every newspaper across the country.

I heard a noise on the walkway outside my room and rushed to the open door, seeing a homeless guy checking the knobs to the rooms, likely in hopes of finding one that was open and empty. I pulled Vani further into the room and slammed the door, engaging the chain just to be safe.

"How did you find me?" My phone buzzed again on the bed, but I ignored it.

"I have people. Now, what are you doing here?" Vani didn't remove her leather gloves before sitting on a plastic chair in the corner. Hell, remembering their home in Great Falls, I couldn't blame her. The place where I was staying was worse than the Bates Motel.

"Well, I decided I don't wanna sell my ass to make money for someone else, so I had to move out of Caroline Turner's place into something cheaper. Welcome to my winter villa." My response was sarcastic. I went so far as to extend my arm in spokesmodel fashion.

Vani scoffed and glared at me, her irritation evident. "Why did you leave the other night? Spencer said he asked you to stay, and you agreed."

As if I could forget that night. It played behind my eyeballs every time I closed my eyes. I had resorted to using body wash as lube in my shower because I couldn't help but jack off to the memories of giving Spencer pleasure. I was a lovesick fool for the man.

"I never agreed to stay because I know you two have a rule against it, even if he forgot it that night. I left because I'm no good for him, and we both know it, even if he won't acknowledge it."

Hell, she was an adult. Surely, she could see it for herself.

Suddenly, something dawned on me. "Do you want me there to nurse him through his heartbreak when you leave, is that it?"

It came out as an accusation, but I couldn't understand why she was pushing us together. It made no sense.

Vani sat up on the edge of her seat, her face pinched in anger as she studied me. "I want Spencer to have as much happiness as he can, Nash. I love him like a brother, and he's sacrificed too much for me as it is. I could tell the morning after Sean Fitzpatrick's birthday party that Spence was drawn to you a hell of a lot more than he was ever drawn to Blaire Conner."

I was flattered, but I couldn't let her sway me. I was no good for Spence, and she had to see it.

Vani's expression was thoughtful. "I still think Blaire wasn't completely innocent in that whole Antigua debacle. I know Denver Wallace said Mitch Flora is the leak in the office, but I wonder if there's more to it? Spence mentioned he'd never given anyone the exact number of the villa where they were staying. Someone knew their precise location to get those pictures."

"Do you think Blaire set it up and implicated himself in this shit? He lost his job, right? Wasn't he just transferred to the NBS network? What was he getting out of it that was better than the job he'd just scored?"

Vani's reasoning had merit, but I wondered if there was something nobody knew happening behind the scenes. None of it made sense to me, and based on her gaze into nothingness, the senator's wife was having a hard time reasoning it out as well.

Vani reached into the pocket of her cashmere coat and retrieved her phone, swiping over the screen before she handed the device to me. I glanced at what she'd pulled up, seeing a story from a news website.

FORMER NBS RISING STAR REPORTER, BLAIRE CONNER, NAMED AS PRESS SECRETARY FOR VIRGINIA GOVERNOR BENNETT'S PRESS SECRETARY AS EXPLORATORY TEAM IS FORMED FOR FUTURE PRESIDENTIAL RUN

I glanced up to see Vani's cocked eyebrow. "I'm not sure what this means," I responded.

"Andy Bennett was a staunch supporter of Spencer's, the two of them having known each other for years. Andy was like a mentor to Spence and campaigned with us the first year Spencer ran for the Senate, also stumping for Spence when he was running for reelection. Spence campaigned with Andy during Andy's run for governor two years ago. Fast forward after so many years of friendship, and Andy hasn't called one time to check on Spence since the shit hit the fan." Vani seemed to be getting more upset as she sat there.

"So, what does that mean?" I was totally out of my element.

"There's something more behind this, and it's up to us to find out what it is. Spencer's heartsick, so he doesn't care, but someone is out to destroy him, and as a person who loves him, I'd think that would matter to you as well."

The compassion in Vani's eyes had me feeling embarrassed for treating Spencer callously and abandoning him when he was vulnerable. What kind of a person does that to someone they claim to love?

"Damn. Of course, you're right. Let me shower and change, and I'll... Wait, how did you get here?" I asked.

"I have a driver waiting for us outside on that shady parking lot. I'll pack your stuff while you get ready." The woman was headstrong for sure.

"I'm not..." I had no plans to leave the Shit Hotel.

"Oh, yes you are!"

"It's a bad idea!" I was shouting, hoping the volume in my voice would emphasize my decision.

"Stop arguing and get dressed. Am I going to find anything embarrassing in these drawers?" Vani grabbed the duffel I'd finally bought, tired of trash bags as luggage. They reminded me too much of my days in foster care.

"No. There's a bag of laundry in the closet, but everything else is clean."

Vani Brady wasn't one to take no for an answer. Besides, how much longer could I live without my heart? I knew beyond the shadow of a doubt I'd left it with Spencer.

★★ ★★

"So, you contacted Denver to find me?" I questioned as I sat in the back seat of a Town Car next to Vani, who had a smug smile of satisfaction on her face. Of course, she had gotten her way!

"Denver and I are cut out to be friends. We see eye to eye on many issues, especially when it comes to you. That gentle giant thinks of you as a member of his family, and there is nobody on the face of the earth he wouldn't fight on your behalf. He had his friend, uh, Pax? I think that was his name. Anyway, he had his friend track your cell, and Denver was kind enough to tell me where to find you. He tasked me with getting you the hell out of there before you got your gorgeous head blown off."

That sounded exactly like Denver, and he'd get a piece of my mind when I had a minute. "I was perfectly fine. Look, I'm supposed to work at a catering gig tonight for Naomi Chu. It's at the Mandarin Oriental in the city."

I hadn't consented to staying with her and Spencer, but I had agreed to get the fuck out of that slum hole where I'd been hiding out. Denny was probably right about me getting my head blown off.

"Well, hoity-toity! Whose throwing it?" Vani asked as we took the exit toward Great Falls.

Instead of answering, I turned to her. "Are you going to New York before Christmas?"

If I was going headfirst into their personal business, I deserved to know some facts, and if I walked into that house and held Spencer in my arms, the fight was over, and I'd be right where I didn't want to be—in the middle of a divorce.

Vanessa glanced at me and then shifted her eyes toward the driver, giving a shake of her head that had me relieved. We shouldn't be speaking in front of a stranger, and I respected her decision not to answer. "So, whose party is it?" she asked again.

I retrieved my phone, finding the message from Naomi Chu that included the details I needed for the night. I handed the phone to Vanessa, looking out the window of the back seat to see snow was beginning to swirl in the cloudy sky. There had been the smell of it in the air, but I hadn't paid any attention to the weather before I was whisked away by Vani.

She handed the phone back to me and made a call of her own. "Hello. I'd like to reserve a room for the night."

Vani quickly gave her credit card information and requested an email confirmation before turning to me with a triumphant smile. "I'll get you an Uber downtown in a few hours, and I'll have Spencer use the car service. I've already checked you in, so you'll just need to stop at the front desk and pick up a key they're holding for you."

"Why? I have to work. I'm not a guest." I was finding the woman to be ten kinds of dangerous.

"I know, and I got you a room at the Mandarin for the night so you don't have to trek out to the house when you finish. You'll have company. I trust you'll be satisfied with it." I glanced in her direction to see she was dead serious.

"I don't know if that's a good..."

Vanessa held up her hand to stop me from talking, her eyes shifting toward the driver again.

I glanced toward the tall man in the front seat to see he had wireless earbuds in his ears, and he appeared to be paying less than any attention to us. I looked back at my companion and laughed.

"You're just doing that to stop me from disagreeing with you."

The car pulled into the driveway of the incredible two-story home where Spencer was outside with a rake in the front yard. He stopped what he was doing and stared at the car, leaning on the rake until I got out of the black vehicle.

The surprise on Spence's face was instant, and I wanted to kick my own ass as I noticed the dark circles under his eyes. I'd done that to him, and I hated myself.

Spencer didn't move from his spot under the large maple tree, so I walked over to him, my duffel in tow. "I'm sorry. I don't seem to know what the right thing is to do with you."

The sexy man smirked and stepped forward, taking my duffel. "Yeah, you do. Come inside, please?"

I was completely under his spell, and I couldn't love it—or him—anymore.

Chapter Eighteen
Spencer

The bellman wheeled in the luggage cart and unloaded our bags, looking around suspiciously at the king-sized bed, the silver ice bucket holding a bottle of champagne, and the small unlit votives around the room. I was surprised to see them myself, if I was being honest. Vanessa had pulled out all the stops, and I'd have to give her a big hug.

The man left after I tipped him, and after he pulled the door closed, I looked at Nash standing silently near the wall. "Why do I feel like a virgin bride on her honeymoon?" His joke surprised me.

I chuckled. "Hey, I think I'm the virgin bride!"

Leading him toward the sitting area, I grabbed us each a bottle of water from the minibar and sat down.

I couldn't go through another week like the one I'd just endured. I'd thought losing the election had been the biggest hit to my psyche but losing Nash Lincoln had been a fatal blow to my heart, and my body simply refused to lay down and die. I knew I couldn't take another.

After swallowing a drink from the water bottle, I cleared my throat, staring at Nash to judge his reaction. He reached for my bottle and took a swig before handing it back, placing his bottle on the table.

"Those damn things are like ten bucks a pop. I'll share yours." He smirked and winked at me, lighting up my soul.

"You're worth ten bucks a pop if you want a water of your own, or you can share mine. Or you can have *me*. I need to know that Vanessa didn't bully you into doing this out of pity because I've had a shitty week." I put it out there because I wanted him, but not against *his* better judgment.

I knew Nash had boundaries about being with a married man, and I respected the hell out of him for it. I also knew that Vani thought his logic was bullshit because she and I had reached an agreement years ago about our marriage. At the end of the day, Nash had to live with his conscience, and I wouldn't be his biggest mistake.

The handsome man stared into my eyes, obviously seeking a truthful answer, and I was prepared to give it to him, regardless of the cost to me. "Ask."

"Are you still in love with Blaire?"

That was easy. "I was never in love with Blaire. Lust? Yeah, sure. Love? No, never. You, though, you're the first man I've ever loved. Like I said, I don't expect..."

"I'm in love with you as well, but..."

"I like *your* butt, but not *that* but. The fact you're in love with me is enough. Now, why did Vani book us this room, not that I'm complaining." A sweet smile bloomed on his face.

"I'm working the Christmas party tonight for Peters and Glass. Vani made the reservation for you to be here when I finish up, so I didn't have to take a car out to Great Falls. I guess she thinks she's moved me from my motel. I don't think it's a good idea for anyone to track me to your house." Nash's voice was laced with concern.

I leaned forward and captured his soft lips in a passionate kiss, teasing the seam of his lips with my tongue until he opened for me. He showed me the passion he had inside him by sucking on my tongue, just as he'd shown my cock the last time I'd seen him.

As our hands caressed the terrain of each other's body, I pulled Nash on top of me to continue the exquisite kisses. Every inch of the man was like a dream, especially those inches trapped in his jeans. I hoped to hell my dad bod could keep his interest and excite him enough so he'd want me the way I wanted him.

Nash pulled away and looked into my eyes. "You wanna flip for it?"

"No, I want to feel you inside me," I answered honestly. I hadn't bottomed for anyone in years, but for Nash? I'd turn myself inside out if it was what he wanted.

Nash glanced at his phone, turning back to me with a smile. "I have a few hours. How about we take a shower? My last residence had shitty water pressure."

It wasn't exactly what I wanted to do at that moment, but I wanted to be with him. If he wanted to get into the shower, hell, why not?

I had the privilege of peeling off Nash's jeans, a skimpy pair of briefs I was happy to find, and a thermal shirt that fit the man exquisitely. For a moment, I seriously considered keeping him in it. Of course, when I slid it off and saw his gorgeous naked body, I knew I'd made the right decision.

Nash took equal time peeling my clothes off before leading me to the large bathroom, turning on the shower to warm before he looked at me, an eyebrow raised in question. "Was this what you had in mind?"

I chuckled, trying at the same time to hold in my gut. My lack of breath alerted Nash to what I was trying to do, and he laughed as he began tickling my ribs. I finally released the held breath and giggled, something I hadn't done in years, squirming away from him enough to grab his hands. "Stop before I pee!"

We both laughed before Nash pulled me into the large, marble stall with him and held me in his arms. "You are sexy as hell, Spence. Don't think I'm not totally attracted to you, okay? I love every inch of you."

He kissed me and pushed me under the warm spray that surrounded us in the exquisite stall. There were at least ten jets and a rainfall showerhead over us. Kissing him under that deluge was like a dream come true.

I reached for the dispenser affixed to the marble to get shampoo, turning us so Nash was under the spray to wet his beautiful brown hair, intent on washing it. "So, this party, who's hosting it?"

Nash chuckled. "Well, I think the official host is Elouise Peters, the wife of the managing partner, but she used all of Sean Fitzpatrick's usual planners and staff, so it might as well be Sean hosting. He's the only person Naomi works for—or those who he approves—and I work for Naomi, so here I am."

I refused to judge him for his choice of vocation, but I believed he deserved to have a better job than just a catering server. But, then again, I'd damn sure rather have him tending bar or waiting tables at a private party than escorting anyone around town. That escort shit was far beneath him.

"Ah. Well, I'll be here when you're done." I was prepared to order room service, buy a movie, and relax in the room until Nash finished his job. Then, I planned to have him all to myself. That was my prize for patience.

Nash washed my hair, and after I rinsed it, he filled his hands with body wash, rubbing it over my less-than-impressive chest and down my body, stopping at my cock, which was jutting between us, seeking his attention.

"Looks like someone wants some love," Nash teased as he slid a slick hand over my erection, taking my breath away at the same time. I'd missed his touch, though I'd only felt it sparingly. It felt righter than my own.

"*Gah*!" I gasped as he continued to run his strong hand over my length before he filled his right hand with conditioner, not rubbing it into either of our hair. He slid it over my cock, and then he stepped forward and added his own hardness to the mix, nearly making my eyes roll back in my head at the sensation. If I died at that moment, my life would have been perfect.

Nash pulled me forward by my dick and I rested my arms on his shoulders. We were about the same height. He was more muscular, and younger—I couldn't forget he was younger.

His handsome face left me breathless as he continued to stroke us in tandem. My mind went numb at the sensation, and I shifted to use him for balance.

"Come for me, Spence," he whispered, the breathiness in his voice causing me to bite his lower lip because it was so fucking enticing.

"Not without you." I was finally able to groan as he sped up his ministrations which nearly had me on my knees. He applied the perfect amount of pressure, and my balls were aching to release in his hands, but I wanted him to come with me.

I reached out and placed my hands over his, the two of us stroking our joined pricks to the rhythm of our heartbeats. "I'm almost..." I gasped as I was overcome with sensations I'd never experienced in my life.

"Yesss!" He hissed as we both shot off between us.

I couldn't tell if he was holding me up or I was holding him, but as our mouths met under the rainfall showerhead, I knew in my heart if the man left me, I'd be broken. As crazy as it seemed, I sensed that he was where I was always supposed to end up.

The fact Vani knew it before me sort of pissed me off. Of course, I always thought the woman had a bit of an angel inside her, especially considering the shit that had happened to her over her life. Yes, she was definitely special, and the fact she brought Nash back to me was nothing short of a miracle.

I was reclining on the luxurious king-sized bed, watching a crime show while munching on room service popcorn while sipping a cold beer when my cell buzzed on the nightstand. I paused to dust off my hand with the napkin, feeling like I was on a mini vacation, and who the fuck would dare interrupt it? I picked it up to see a text from Nash.

> You should come down for a drink. Your friend, Senator Turner is here with a young brunette who is definitely not Caroline—and he's hammered. XOXO

That information was enough to get me off my ass. I pulled on my jeans and a sweater I'd brought along, and I grabbed the open beer I'd been drinking, heading to the elevator. If Turner was fucked up, hell yeah, I wanted to see it.

I punched the button for the mezzanine level where the party was held in the large ballroom, skirting around the folks loitering in the hallway where a makeshift bar was serving cocktails to the guests.

I strolled over to the bar to trade my empty bottle for a full one, tossing a twenty at the pretty young lady who asked no questions. I skirted around the perimeter of the room to find Nash at the main bar.

There was a line of people in front of Nash and a young man I recognized from Sean's birthday party. The two of them worked easily together. I leaned against the wall to watch the two of them moving like a choreographed dance duo.

A live band played some standards, and there were a lot of people on the dance floor, but I could see Sean Fitzpatrick near the front of the room, and he was definitely unhappy. The target of his rancor—Frank Turner. Things were about to get a whole lot better in my life.

I watched the two men argue for a few minutes before Sean shook his head and walked away, heading toward where I was standing on the sidelines sipping a pilsner. When he spotted me, Sean smirked and walked straight in my direction, seemingly on a mission.

When he arrived where I was trying to hide, he laughed. "You're welcome to come in, Senator. I invited you and your lovely wife, but your aid called to give regrets."

A month ago, I'd have been pissed, but I found I didn't give one fuck about it. "I no longer have aids, Sean. What's that asshole's problem?"

I pointed the neck of my bottle in the direction of where Turner seemed to be losing his mind as a young woman tried to calm him down. It was comical to watch.

"Seems Caroline has fled the coop, and she's taken all the money with her. He's in a tailspin, and when I tried to remind him that he was in public with a sex worker who he was openly fingering at the table, he got pissed at me. I've always hated the prick anyway. Come have a drink at the bar with me?" Sean asked.

I glanced toward the bar where Nash was mixing drinks, seeing he was busy. "He's not going anywhere. We need to talk," Sean suggested.

I retrieved my phone from my pocket and sent Nash a text that I'd be at the bar downstairs. I followed Sean Fitzpatrick to the elevator, seeing him press the button to take us to the first floor.

"So, what's new in your world? I'm sure you know all about what's new in mine." The door opened and several people exited the car, greeting Sean. He vowed to return in a moment after getting some air, and the door closed.

"Spence, you and I would make very strange bedfellows to most people, but I think we're the perfect pair." I stepped back from him, surprised when he laughed.

"Not that way, you narcissist. I know you're in love with Nash, and please, keep him out of the widows' beds. He's too good for that shit. No, I mean, I want you to come work for me. You could talk a dog off a meat wagon, and that's what I need.

"Even with this scandal, which will die down as soon as word hits that Caroline Bering-Turner was a madam in DC and she's taken all of Turner's assets with her to wherever the fuck she ended up, you're off the front page and not even a footnote in the obituary section. Believe it or not, this current disaster trumps your shit in spades. How's Vani?"

I chuckled. "She's moving to New York after Christmas. She has a job for a large real estate management company waiting for her. The split will be amicable. Why would you want to hire me?" It was out of left fucking field, to be sure.

We settled at a small table in the back corner of the lobby bar, and Sean ordered two beers for us. The bartender nodded and a minute later, the cold bottles were delivered, and my empty was whisked away.

Sean held up his beer in a toast, so I touched mine to his before we both took a swig. After he swallowed, Sean smiled at me. "You were like fucking Captain America before those pictures hit the papers, you know? Young, good-looking, Mr. Boy-Next-Door. A country boy who worked his way up the political ladder and ended up in the Senate.

I bet the Judge wanted you to become President, didn't he?" Sean was referring to my father.

I chuckled. "You've done your homework."

"I happened to come across an opposition paper on you from your opponent. She commissioned lots of research on you, Spence. She didn't use it—blatantly—but she knew all about your past."

My opponent, Shirlene Biggins, was an up-and-comer in the Republican party. She was thirty-six and married to a doctor. They had one child, and Shirlene rode the moral high ground on a large white steed—no abortion rights, no gay rights, no civil rights. She was exactly what the former president wanted in a woman, and sadly, with the scandal I'd brought on myself, she beat me handily when my colleagues turned their backs on me—especially the Democratic Governor. That was a hard pill to swallow.

"So, again, I ask why you'd be interested in having me work for you?"

A man like Sean always had an ulterior motive for doing anything. He was too fucking successful not to.

Sean chuckled. "Shirlene Biggins had an affair with Andrew Bennett when they both worked for the Attorney General in Virginia. She blackmailed him into not coming to your defense during this scandal, Senator. She's got a big hand behind her, and I don't know who it is, but it was enough to scare the fuck out of Bennett.

"Come work for me, and we'll figure it out together. Get back to me after the first of the year, and please, don't dick Nash around anymore. He's a good kid, and he's an honest bartender, which is hard to find."

Sean finished his beer and left me at the table alone. He walked to the bar and spoke to the bartender as he pointed to me. The guy nodded and Sean left with a wave and a smile.

I wasn't exactly sure what happened, but I had a job offer I hadn't expected. Maybe things were looking up? I could only hope so.

Chapter Nineteen
Nash

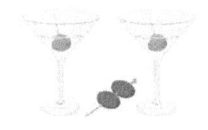

I found Spencer in the hotel bar after Jorge, my friend with whom I'd worked catered gigs several times, offered to take over closing the bar to get the bonus from Naomi. I wasn't about to fight him over it. I desperately wanted to get to Spencer.

"You ready?" I found Spencer in a booth in the back after I checked with the bartender. I offered to pay the tab, but the guy said Sean had covered it. Spence sat at a table alone, nursing a beer that felt warm to the touch. He looked up at me when I sat down across from him, and he seemed dazed for a second before the fog cleared. "You're finished? You're done for the night?"

I nodded.

Spence chuckled. "Let's go up. I'm just getting started with you." I seconded that notion.

We left the bar, Spence grabbing two beers for us before we got onto the elevator. Once we got into the room, the two pilsners were long forgotten. I kissed and sucked every inch of his body, and when I had edged the two of us to the point we were about to lose it, I slid on a condom and gently pushed my way into his gorgeous ass after rolling him onto his side.

"You okay?" I'd never do anything to hurt him. I was sure he felt the same about me. The look in his eyes as I pistoned in and out of his hole was beautiful.

It was like a fucking dream come true for me. I was home... Spencer Brady had become my home.

"I'm gonna come," Spence gasped.

"I'm right there with you." I reached down and jacked his shaft twice before the warm cum covered my hand. It wasn't a violent coupling, but it did the job for both of us. For a first time, it wasn't my best work, but I'd been nervous. It was a line I thought

I wouldn't cross, but looking into Spencer's eyes, how could I not?

I flopped onto my back, having drained myself inside the condom as I tried to catch my breath. His grip on my length was firm, and the condom was thin, so it was almost like there wasn't anything between us. That was a step I hoped we got to because I'd never gone bareback.

"Son of a... I think I'm stupefied." Spence tried to catch his breath as well. He was on his side, and his left leg was crooked up to give me access to him from behind, which had been incredible.

I hopped up from the bed and went into the luxurious bathroom to toss the condom, turning on the water in the huge tub. I knew it had been a while since he'd bottomed, and a hot bath might help loosen up his muscles so he wouldn't be so sore the next... later that morning.

I walked back into the bedroom and sat down on the bed next to Spencer, taking his hand in mine before I kissed his soft lips. "You okay? How about a soak?"

Spencer smirked at me, "Wait till it's my turn, baby. I'll take care of you, I swear." Oh, I couldn't wait for that thick cock.

"Yeah, yeah, let's get you comfortable." I pulled him from the bed and led him into the bathroom where the huge tub was filling.

I helped him into the hot water and took a seat behind him, pulling the sexy man to sit in front of me. I squirted some body wash under the faucet and watched as the tub filled with bubbles.

Spence chuckled before settling back and relaxing against my chest. I caressed his pecs, pinching his nipples as the tub filled before I turned off the water. "Did you see Senator Turner with his date?" I gently caressed Spence's chest, feeling him relax into me.

"Uh, yeah! I think everyone in that room saw him making a total fool of himself. Lucky for her, she won't have to fuck him because as drunk as he was, he'd never get it up." Spencer's deep chuckle reverberated through his body into mine.

"I hope she asked for the money up front." I gently massaged Spence's neck and shoulders. His body tensed when I joked about the money, and I knew we had to discuss my past, though I had hoped we could skip that part.

Spence seemed to be unsure of what to say, so I took the plunge. "Ask. I know what you're thinking, so just ask."

"Do you, uh, do you miss it?"

"Fucking for money? Hell no. Just to clear the air, I didn't do it very often, and I always wore a condom. I didn't let anyone fuck me. Too intimate." It was the god's honest truth, and when I felt Spencer trying to sit up, I released him and watched as he turned to study me.

Spencer rested against the other end of the huge tub, contemplating what I'd said. Finally, he reached out and touched my hand where it was resting on the side of the tub. "I don't mind bottoming..."

I squeezed his hand and slid closer to him, turning around and leaning against him. I looked over my shoulder to see the worry on his handsome face. "For you, I'll bottom all the time, Spencer. I like the idea we're both vers, and I think we're very compatible in bed. There's nothing to worry about. I've been getting tested every three months, and all my tests come back negative for STI's or HIV. I'd never put you in danger," I answered honestly.

Spencer leaned forward and kissed my lips before resting his hands on my shoulders. "Was it hard to do?"

I glanced at him for clarification. "Sleeping with people for money?"

"Yeah. I mean, we don't have to talk about this if you'd rather not."

I offered a humorless laugh. "When I was younger, I slept with people for a lot less, but at times, it wasn't easy. Like, when I was with some of the older women, they wanted to pretend it was romantic because that's what they'd missed in their lives, and I played along. I felt awful for them that they had to resort to paying for a companion, but loneliness is like poison—it'll devour you and kill you before you know what's going on. You'll take any antidote you can find to keep it at bay. I guess, I was the antidote sometimes."

Spencer nodded and kissed the back of my head, showing me love I'd craved my whole life. I'd had people who'd cared for me—my friend, Clinton Barr, came to mind.

Clint and I had become best friends because we didn't have anyone else to give a damn about us. I'd later come to learn it wasn't a weakness to want someone in my life—it was an instinct. People weren't meant to be alone.

Spencer asked a couple more questions, but when we got out of the tub, I felt he was satisfied with the answers I'd given him. We got into the large bed, and I was prepared to give myself to him, but before I could suggest it, he was asleep, wrapped around me. I must have followed him not too long later, and I slept like the dead.

We arrived at the house in Great Falls on Wednesday morning, having enjoyed a late room service breakfast and mutual blow jobs before checking out of the fancy hotel. I'd been paid cash for bartending the previous night, so I paid for our taxi against Spencer's wishes, but I was no freeloader. I always paid my own way.

Spencer let us in through the front door, immediately bellowing, "Vani!" I couldn't hold the laugh. He was a creature of habit.

"Hang on!" she called back from somewhere upstairs. Spence took my duffel and placed it at the bottom of the stairs, along with his own bag, and I followed him into the kitchen. He walked over to the one-cup coffee maker, flipping it on.

"I'm gonna have some coffee. You want a cup?" Spence went to the fridge and grabbed the creamer I loved.

"Sure. I'll make them. Why don't you go look for Vani?" I went to the sink to wash my hands. Spence kissed my lips as we passed by each other, and it made my heart skip a beat. It was like we'd been doing it for years.

It seemed so easy, being with Spencer. How had that happened to *me*?

I made myself a cup of coffee and set up the machine for Spencer's cup as I heard footsteps on the stairs outside the kitchen. "...and I'm fine in the spare room. If you and Nash aren't ready to share yet, one of you can sleep in Jay's room."

I looked up to see Vani was dressed in a woman's suit, navy with a cream-colored blouse. "I was bored, okay? I didn't want to go do anything last night, so I switched the rooms. It's no big deal, Spencer, and it motivated me to pack some of my stuff. Look, I'm going to New York for an overnight. I need to meet with my new boss, and I want to find an apartment."

I studied Spencer, quickly judging he didn't like what he was hearing. I walked to the counter and started the cup of coffee for him, staying out of it as best I could.

"I said I'd go with you!" Spencer's tone was more aggressive than I believed necessary. I could see immediately it didn't set well with Vani.

She walked to where I was pretending to ignore them, touching my shoulder. "Hi, Nash. You're rational, so I'll talk to you. I have a car coming to get me in an hour to take me to Dulles where I'll be taking a shuttle flight up to JFK, and I'll be spending the night at The Roosevelt in Midtown. I'll be back tomorrow afternoon. I've moved Spencer's things into the master, and I've unpacked your things in there as well. I've taken his old room for now, and that way, Jay can have his room when he gets home for the holiday break. If you two aren't at the place to share yet, Spence can take the pullout in the den.

"I'll leave you to explain it to the pigheaded one after I leave. Did you have... of course, you did. You look very relaxed." Vani winked before she stood on her toes and kissed my cheek.

She moved to Spencer and wrapped her arms around his neck, pulling him down to look into her eyes. "It's time, sweetheart. We both need to live our own lives, Spencer. I'll be back tomorrow evening, and we can talk then."

Vanessa faced the two of us and smiled, her eyes misting. "This is exactly what I hoped would happen. I couldn't have planned this better myself." Her phone chimed, breaking the silence.

"Ah, my driver is on the way. Spencer, start accepting this is the right step for us. Call me if you need me, boys. Love you both." She ran upstairs, returning quickly with a small suitcase in her hand and a tote bag on her shoulder.

"I could have taken you to the airport." Once the words left my mouth, I realized how ridiculous that was since I didn't have a car.

Vani stopped and snapped her fingers. She reached into her tote and grabbed something before she turned to look at Spencer with a smile. "Let Nash use my car while I'm gone and think about what we should do with it. I'm not taking it to New York." She kissed his cheek again and headed to the front door just as there was a buzzing sound by the intercom. Spencer walked over to it and looked at the small screen before pressing a button on the unit.

With a quick wave of her hand, Vani was out the front door—the human dynamo on a mission—leaving the two of us in stunned silence. I stayed where I was and watched Spencer for any reaction. When he sat down at the table, I picked up my cup and took a sip of the warm liquid as I leaned against the counter, waiting for him to react.

"I guess she's ready, then." I couldn't tell if he was saying it to me or himself. Finally, he reached for his coffee, motioning for me to sit at the table next to him. Once I sat down, he took my hand, seeming to settle into his new reality. I was still fucking stunned.

"Do, uh, do you wanna talk about it?" I wasn't sure what I would have to offer by way of comfort. I'd never been in his position, so I couldn't commiserate, but I really wanted to try.

Spencer put his cup on the table and pulled my hand to his lips, kissing my knuckles before holding it in both of his. "Not much to talk about. We always knew this day would come. I'm just glad I have you to get me through it. She knew you were perfect for me, and that pisses me off a little. She's something else."

He shook his head and laughed. I joined him, not sure why we were laughing, but it seemed to act as a pressure valve for both of us, and I was glad. Where we'd end up wasn't known, but I was damn sure we'd get there together. That was my hope.

Chapter Twenty
Spencer

"How do I look?" I asked Nash as I tightened the knot of my silver and navy tie while he sat on the side of the bed, watching me finish dressing after our shared shower.

I was more relaxed than I'd been in a long time, thanks to Nash. He was perfect at a shower blow job, and I'd admire his skills as often as he'd let me.

When I tried to return the favor, I nearly drowned myself! He laughed as I sputtered under the spray, but when we got out, I sucked him down my throat, and he wasn't laughing any longer.

I had a meeting that morning, and I'd been nervous before the shower. Sean had summoned me to meet with him at his office on the Hill to discuss his job offer. After that, I had the annual Christmas luncheon with my staffers, my last official act as a Senator in the United States Congress. I had been nervous about both functions until Nash sucked the nerves out of me.

It was ridiculous to be worried about any of it, but in his beautiful way, Nash eased my concerns so I could get my head on straight. I'd been a member of the Senate for twelve years, but I felt like Sean knew shit I didn't, and I kept waiting for the "gotcha" I was sure would come. It was pessimistic, of course, but show me an optimist in DC, and I'll show you a damn fool.

"You look like a Senator," Nash joked as he rose from the bed and walked behind me having already dressed. He tugged at the back of my suitcoat and dusted off my shoulders.

It was a move Vani had taught him when I went to buy a new suit after I ripped a pair of suit pants when I bent over to retrieve a nickel from the street while I was downtown for lunch with Mario so we could tie up loose ends. The middle-age spread had definitely caught up to me, and I was embarrassed to hell that I'd gained about ten pounds.

That night after shopping, Nash made passionate love to me, and I felt like a million bucks.

He'd offered to bottom several times, but I was coming to like being claimed by him. It helped me realize he didn't pity me for being a man looking down the barrel of fifty. He loved me, and he loved me for who I was and how I looked. It was a shot to my ego, for sure.

"What are you guys doing today?" I asked him as I turned around and kissed his lips.

"Vanessa has roped me into taking her Christmas shopping. I'll be carrying a lot of bags and nodding at her choices, I fear. Being her arm candy is tiresome." Nash laughed.

He and Vani were very close, even more so since she'd returned from her overnight trip to New York. She had found an apartment, and I'd wired her the money to put a deposit on it. I was pleased Nash and Vani got along because there was no way she wasn't going to remain one of my best friends.

It was incredible how at ease the three of us were together, and I'd even asked Vani if she was sure moving to Manhattan was the best idea for her. Of course, she'd laughed at me. I realized she was ready to move on, and I couldn't have been happier for her.

"Oh, enjoy that! Please, remind her I don't really have a job right now before she goes overboard." I grabbed my wallet and watch from the valet on top of my dresser.

Nash's things were in Vani's old dresser, and I loved to see him pulling his clothes out of the drawers. It was a reminder that we were a couple, and I relished the feeling of not being alone.

"I should be home by four. The Christmas luncheon is usually followed by drinks at O'Tooles, but I'll keep it short. I doubt many people will want to spend a lot of time with me." I knew the lay of the land. It was a tradition to take the staff out. I had no illusions that most of them would rather take a stick in the eye than attend.

"Boys, we need to go!" Vani's impatience made me smile.

"I'll be down in a minute." Nash went into the ensuite to style his hair since I'd hogged the bathroom with my primping that morning.

It was an odd setup, the three of us living together, but we were working it out as we went along. It would only be a few weeks before Vani moved, and Jay was coming home for Christmas, bringing his boyfriend before the two of them went to Cole's parents' home for New Year's. It would be our last Christmas as a nuclear family—more or less—and I wasn't sure how to feel about it. Too much change, too fast? Probably.

"Coming Mom." I rushed downstairs with Nash behind me.

Vani and Nash were dropping me off at the metro in Tyson's so I could take the silver line to the Capitol South Metro stop, which was about two blocks from the Capitol building. I was planning to take the car service home that evening for the last time, but I wanted the memory of taking the metro that morning, just as I used to do when I was a shiny new Senator on my first day that January after I'd won the November election in 2008.

Maybe I'd gotten too big for my britches when it came to my private life, thinking I was above discretion regarding who I spent time with and what we did. I'd have never done anything so stupid when I was beginning my career, so when had I let my guard down and become so damn careless as to get caught, *literally*, with my pants down?

I walked into the kitchen to see Vani with a cup of coffee in her hand. There were two cups on the island, and she had a smile on her face. "You look handsome," she offered before she handed me a cup.

I kissed her forehead and stepped back, hearing Nash on the stairs behind me. He walked into the kitchen, and Vani picked up his mug, handing it to him. He kissed her cheek and the three of us stared at each other as we sipped our coffee.

"You know, there are a lot of poly couples out there." My gaze flicked between the pair as I spoke. Vani cackled, which wasn't really a surprise. Nash looked at me with concern, so I stepped over to him, kissing his lips before we both turned to look at her.

"That sense of humor will take you far, Spencer Aaron Brady. It's a beautiful idea, but I'm not interested. I love you both, but I don't see us being a big, happy trailblazing family. I'm looking forward to a new start and knowing that I'm always welcome with the two of you makes me so happy. The three of us being together that way wouldn't ever work for me but thank you for the half-assed invitation."

Nash and I both laughed as the three of us had a group hug before Nash collected the empty mugs and put them in the dishwasher. The three of us left the house, and when they dropped me off at the metro, I could see we had a bright future as a family—just not as a poly family.

Vani was on her new path, and I would be happy for her—eventually. I was worried about losing her friendship, but I should know better. Vani would never let that happen.

I exited the metro station, pulling my topcoat closed and sliding my hands in my leather gloves. The train had been hot, so I'd unbuttoned my coat and shed my gloves, but when I arrived above ground, it was like the fucking wind could cut me in half.

As I walked toward Sean's office off Seward Square, I ran all the questions through my mind that he might ask. I couldn't officially start working for him until after the first of the year, but he wanted to meet that morning, and I wasn't one to stand up my potential boss.

I walked into the former row house on North Carolina Avenue where Sean had his offices, seeing the atmosphere was very casual. What had been the dining room was now the waiting room, so I approached the ornate desk where a handsome young man was sitting with a headset, listening intently as he made notes on a laptop. When he saw me, he hit a button on the earpiece. "Good morning, Senator. Sean will be with you in a moment. Can I get you something? Coffee or water?"

"No, I'm fine."

He rose from the desk and offered to take my coat, so I gave it to him before I went to sit down on an antique sofa that faced a gorgeous fireplace which was blazing brightly. It was a gas log set, but it looked authentic enough, and the stockings with everyone's name embroidered on the cuff were a nice touch.

I reached for the current copy of *The Hill*, the newspaper that focused on all the events that happened on Capitol Hill and scanned the cover. It was a comprehensive list of everything that would be taken up after the holiday break, and I wasn't sorry I wouldn't be returning to that bullshit in January.

Not a minute later, I heard the distinct sound of Sean's voice, the volume becoming louder as he descended the stairs. "Thank you, Megan. Have a wonderful holiday and give my best to your mother. Goodbye."

Sean ended his call and walked over to where I sat. I folded the paper and placed it on the table before rising to address the man.

"Good to see you, Senator," Sean greeted.

"Glad to be here." We shared a strong handshake.

"Let's go to my office. Byron, I'm not to be disturbed for the next hour, please. Take messages. No exceptions."

The handsome young guy nodded at Sean's barked orders before he turned toward the stairs, and I followed him to the second floor.

There were four offices from what I could see as I stepped onto the second-floor landing where there was another staircase to a third floor. Two of the offices were occupied. One was empty, and one—the biggest one—was decorated with elegant French provincial furniture, the walls a calming grey and the ceilings and trim a stark white. That was where Sean led me, closing the door when I was inside.

"Please, take a seat. Can I get you some coffee or perhaps, an espresso?" Sean offered, refilling his demitasse cup from a small French press.

"No, thank you. So, if I were to take the job with you, I wouldn't be available to officially start until the end of May. I could offer consulting assistance behind the scenes, but nothing forward facing until then. Is there anything in particular—?"

"What have you found out about your unceremonious outing?" Sean asked abruptly. I was taken aback for a moment but recovered quickly.

"Uh, accusations have been made about a member of my staff as you know, but thus far, I have nothing concrete to back them up. I've engaged someone who is trying to track the photographer."

Sean sat down in a large chair across from me, sipping his espresso for a moment before he placed the saucer and cup on the glass table next to him and sat forward. "I've always admired you, Spencer.

My boyfriend, back then, thought you were incredible, and as a small-time stringer at the *Washington Post*, he tried like hell to get time on your schedule for an interview. Oh, he was damn sure it would put him in the big time because you were a new mover and shaker in DC, and I guess he thought he could ride your coattails to fame.

"I helped set him up with powerful people to build his resume, but for some reason, I refused to set him up with you. Something told me it was a bad idea, so I kept telling him it wasn't going to happen. You were a busy man and didn't have time to sit with a reporter wannabe for an interview. That was when he started blowing me off for our dates, telling me he was busy."

That was all very interesting. However, it didn't hint at why Sean wanted to hire me. Nothing in his comment gave me any indication how he believed I could benefit his lobbying firm.

"He landed a more prestigious job, leaving me behind, but then, I was right about him, wasn't I? Next thing I know, I'm hearing through the grapevine that you're taking meetings with him and granting him access to your reelection campaign. You two met at a party, didn't you?" Sean trailed off.

My heart pounded in my chest, not sure what to say to him. I was certain he'd just set me up, and hell, maybe he was behind the whole outing thing, just to humiliate me in retaliation for some perceived transgression? *Fuck!*

"Obviously, you're talking about Blaire. I had no idea he was interested in me at the time, nor did I know he was dating you. We met at a fundraiser and started talking." I wasn't sure where the conversation was going.

"Spencer, let me be clear. I'm not out to further smear your reputation. I want to fuck Blaire over any way I can, but not at any cost to you. He was out to prove to me that he was worthy of getting the big fish, even if he had to fuck them, and it became his mission to put me in my place. Have you ever heard of Gregor Jablonowski?" Sean asked.

I'd heard that name recently. Where? "Should I?"

"Seems we were both fooled when it came to Blaire. I hope you used a condom because Blaire was fucking your comms guy—Mitchell Flora—behind both of our backs. Mitchell's former assistant, Lori Warren, married a photographer named Gregor Jablonowski. If you've found money going into Mitchell's account, you might want to look for some of it going out. I was able to get a friend from the State Department to confirm that Gregor Jablonowski's passport was used to fly to Antigua, going to the island on the same flight as Blaire, and returning on your flight back to the States after the pictures hit the papers." Sean's accusation shocked me.

Bile rose in my throat, and Sean must have seen what was happening because he rushed over to a hidden door in the room to reveal a bathroom. I barely made it to the toilet before all the coffee I'd had that morning returned.

A wet cloth was handed to me before a glass of water was presented. I quickly flushed the toilet and stood upright, sad to see my favorite tie hadn't been spared.

I wiped my mouth and accepted the water, rinsing my mouth and spitting into the sink, I moved my hand around to clean the mess before turning to Sean, who held out a hand towel.

I pulled at the tie, tightening the fucking knot to the point my shaking hands couldn't loosen it. Surprisingly, Sean slapped at my hands and quickly helped me rid myself of the offending noose before tossing it into a trash can.

"I, uh, I'm sor..."

"No, Spencer, you don't owe me an apology. I wanted to tell you what a sneaky bastard Blaire was, but I had no concrete proof of his actions. I had someone follow him and found out he was fucking Mitch Flora while he was fucking me and you, and I became suspicious. He and Flora took a lot of trips together, and Mitch only makes a shitty government salary. That's when I had someone look into Blaire's finances—not exactly legally, but I'd been stupid enough to fall in love with him.

"You see, I'd been supporting him for the three years we were together before he got the job with the NBS local affiliate. Someone helped him buy that nice house in Alexandria, but it wasn't me, and I doubt it was you either," Sean surmised.

I stepped out of the bathroom, my head swimming, and I stared at Sean, trying to see if he was fucking me over, or if he was honest. "Why did you think Mario was the leak in my office?"

"I'm not the one to tell anyone they've got a rat in their organization. I knew you and Mario were close pals, but I hoped maybe you'd start checking into your staff and find out about Mitch, his assistant—oh, she quit because she's threatening to blackmail Mitch to pay her and her husband off or they'll go to the press and implicate Mitch's unknown partner. She's a money whore, and she sang like a songbird when my guy waved five grand in front of her nose.

"You, my friend, have too much faith in the people with whom you surround yourself. Thankfully, I'm one of the good guys." Sean offered me a bottle of water from a hidden fridge that looked like a filing cabinet.

He walked to his desk and hit the buzzer on his phone. "Yes, Mr. Fitzpatrick?"

"Byron be a doll and run to Vineyard Vines and pick up a silver and navy tie for the Senator. He accidentally spilled coffee on his, and he has a meeting after we're finished. Put it on my card, please."

"Yes, sir, Mr. Fitzpatrick." Sean ended the call and returned to where the two of us had been sitting before I had to puke.

"So, uh, is this job offer just a bullshit ploy to get me to help you seek revenge?" I asked, trying to hide my humiliation, though I was sure I was failing.

Sean shook his head. "No, Senator, not at all. Your charisma and grace under pressure makes you a hot commodity in my world, and let's face it, only a few of the old pricks up the street would hold this shit against you. God knows, many a man has been taken down by a sex scandal. No, I want you to work with me because you're a good salesman, which is what all members of Congress really are.

"I just want you to see if you can get to the bottom of this mess before all the proof is erased. I've done all I can to trace it to Flora and Conner. Someone with deep pockets started this ball rolling, and you have my word, Spence, it wasn't me. Trace the money, and you'll find your enemy."

I nodded before there was a knock on the door. "In," Sean called. The handsome young Byron walked in with a maroon bag with a whale on the front of it.

"This was the only one that vaguely matched the description, Mr. Fitzpatrick." Byron opened the bag and retrieved a slender box before popping the lid to show a silver tie with navy whales on it. Sean made a motion, and Byron stepped over to me.

"Is this to your liking, sir? I can exchange it for a plain silver one if you'd prefer," the young man offered. I stood and reached for it, retrieving it from the box.

"This will do. How much..."

"It's a business expense. Byron, love, charge it against Senator Brady's expense account. Oh, get us a reservation at The W for lunch, will you?" Sean asked.

I started to protest, but I saw the look in Sean's eyes as he watched young Byron walk away, and I knew he wasn't talking about me at all. "You'll be in touch?" I asked Sean as I set about tying the silk around my neck.

"Be here on January 4 at seven to begin your first gig as a paid consultant. We'll have a breakfast meeting to get you up to speed. Your official start date will be June 2 as the Director of Political Affairs. Oh—Spencer, you didn't ask me about salary." He smirked.

I chuckled. "I'm sure it'll be fair. You know all about me, so you probably know how much I made on the Hill. Vanessa and I will be divorcing and selling the house, so my expenses will decrease. She's relocating to New York for a job in Manhattan, and it will be an amicable split, so no headlines, I hope." I owed it to Sean to be up front about the changes in my life. If he was willing to take a chance on me, then we had to develop trust.

"And, what of young Nash?" Sean asked.

In for a penny—in for a pound. "We're together, but discreetly for now. Once the divorce is final, then we'll make it public. Will our relationship prohibit him from working for your party planner?" I was unsure of Nash's plans, but I prayed they included me.

"I think we can do better than that for him. Let me make some calls, but don't say anything yet. I assume he's done with Caroline Bering-Turner, now that she's run off?" Sean asked.

I chuckled. "Yes, he told me he's done with it, and I'm more than happy. Happy holidays, Sean. I'll see you on the fourth." I shook his hand and turned to leave.

I walked out of the office and down the stairs where Byron stood at his desk with a mirror, checking his face. I stopped and smiled. "You look perfect. Have a great lunch."

I winked and grabbed my topcoat before heading out onto the street. Ah, Washington, DC would be nowhere without its scandals. Some were more shocking than others, but everyone had a secret. Some just kept them better than others.

Chapter Twenty One
Nash

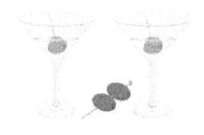

I was in the kitchen on December 22, leafing through one of many unopened recipe books I found on a shelf in the large, white oak cupboard near the table. Vani and Spence admitted they'd always catered in their Christmas dinners, but I suggested we should tackle it together. We did take the precautionary step of ordering a brown-sugar glazed ham, but the sides? I was convinced we could make them ourselves, or I thought it might be fun to try, at least.

I heard the garage door rattling, so I rushed to the laundry room to open the door. A navy pickup slowly eased into the open third parking spot instead of the sleek Mercedes Vani drove every day. The large, black SUV was still parked in the first space of the three-car garage, but when I saw the young man behind the wheel of the truck, it reminded me that Jay and his boyfriend were expected from school for the Christmas break.

I knew Vani and Spencer were meeting with their attorney that morning to draw up the paperwork for their upcoming divorce. I hadn't thought to ask Spencer what Jay knew about us, so I was momentarily paralyzed at what to say to the young man that wouldn't undermine his relationship with either of his parents.

I closed the door to give Jay and his boyfriend privacy and went back to the cookbook, continuing to peruse possible side dishes. When the two young guys walked into the kitchen, both laughing at something one of them had said, they froze when they saw me at the island. "Jay, welcome home. Cole, how are you?" *Why did I make it sound as though we knew each other?*

I saw understanding on Jay's face before he ushered Cole forward. "Nash, this is my boyfriend, Cole Glennon. Babe, this is Nash, my parents, uh..."

"I sort of run the house for the Senator and Mrs. Brady." Of late, it wasn't a lie. It was exactly what I'd been doing.

"Oh, well, it's nice to meet you, Mr. Nash." Cole extended his hand like a perfect gentleman, and I happily shook it.

"Just Nash. How's your leg?" He was in a walking cast, which was a vast improvement from just after the accident.

"I get the damn thing off after the first of the year. It itches like crazy, ya know?" Cole didn't seem at all uncomfortable with my explanation for why I was in the kitchen while Vani and Spencer weren't at home.

"I can only imagine. Jay, your bedroom is ready for you guys. Your mom's been working on redecorating it all week." I was trying to figure out what the hell else to say to the young guy.

Jay smirked, making my gut churn. "So, do you live *in*? Where do *you* sleep?"

I could tell the kid knew more than he was willing to give up, but I didn't know what, or how much. Thankfully, the garage door opened again, and I was saved. "There're your folks."

Jay started laughing and turned to Cole. "Mom and Dad had an appointment with their lawyer this morning. Nash is their third, I guess?"

"*What?* No! Oh, no! That's not it at all." The door opened and Vani came inside, squealing at seeing Jay and his boyfriend. Spence was behind her with a big grin on his face as he hugged his son after Vani.

I went to the stairwell and grabbed the boys' luggage, taking it upstairs to Jay's room, after which, I went to the master and pulled out my duffel. It was best for me to go to Tennessee to spend my Christmas with The Volunteers, so the Brady family had time to sort out everything that was happening in their lives.

I'd almost finished packing, ready to call a rental company to see if I was too late to get a car for Christmas, when there was a knock on the bedroom door. It opened without a word from me, and Spencer walked in with Jay behind him. "Where are you going?" Spence eyed my clothes in the duffel and frowned.

"I, uh, I thought it was better if I left the family to celebrate the holiday. You should get to know Cole, Senator, and it's better if there isn't a stranger here while you do it. I've been invited to Tennessee to spend the holidays with my friends, and I think that's best."

Spencer turned to Jay and tilted his head. "Jeez! I'm sorry. I was just giving you shit, Nash. Dad already told me everything about you guys, and I wanted to see what you'd say about it. You're pretty quick on your feet with that house manager bullshit."

I chuckled at seeing Spencer's eyes roll at his son's comment, but I liked the kid. "You're a shit disturber, and I respect that in a guy. I still think it's best if I go to Tennessee to see my friends, so the four of you can spend time together, what with the changes on the horizon. I'll be back the day after Christmas, and we can get to know each other then, okay?"

"Thanks, Nash. I know this is a big change for all of us, but even after Mom and Dad split, we're still gonna be a family. I look forward to getting to know you, too." Jay let himself out the door, leaving me with a very pissed off man studying my every move.

"This is news to me that you'd rather go to Tennessee than spend Christmas with us." Spencer sat on the bed and rummaged in my duffel, scanning the things I'd packed.

I went to the bathroom to gather my toiletries, taking my toothbrush from the holder where it rested next to Spencer's. I'd only planned to be gone for a few days, but if Spencer changed his mind about us after spending time with his family, I wanted to have all my shit with me. I'd learned to hedge my bets a long time ago.

"Come on! It's not like that, and you know it. Besides, you didn't tell me you'd talked to Jay about us. He seemed to think I was with *both* of you." I was trying to keep my temper in check. Nothing productive would come from a shouting match.

"He's nineteen, Nash. You don't think he's gonna fuck with you and make you uncomfortable? He told us they'd be here this afternoon, so we thought we'd have time to get home before them, but here they come rolling in at ten this morning. I'm sorry we got caught in traffic on the damn Beltway, but please, please don't leave." Spencer's voice had a pleading tone, but I didn't want that from him.

I walked over and sat down next to him on the edge of the bed. "Baby, as much as it seems like Jay's okay, this is still gonna be tough for him. The four of you need to celebrate this one together. I'll be back on the twenty-sixth, and I'll get to know Jay and Cole then. They're not going to see Cole's people until the thirtieth, right?" As much as I wanted to be with Spencer for Christmas, it felt like the right thing to do.

An hour and two blow jobs later—me to Spencer, who then returned the favor—I had the keys to Spencer's SUV, and I was on the interstate headed southwest. I'd left my sparse gifts for Spence, Vani,

Cole, and Jay to open on Christmas morning, and I sent a text to Denny.

> **I'm assuming the offer still stands for me to hang out with you bums. I'll be there about eight, if traffic isn't bad. Make sure I have a room that's clean, will ya?**

I stopped at the Supercenter to get some gag gifts for The Volunteers, along with a few cases of beer, remembering I didn't want to show up at the clubhouse empty handed.

The wrath of what The Volunteers considered practical jokes—a bag of actual shit under a bed, tires removed from a vehicle and hidden somewhere in the woods, the hot water to the adjoining bathroom turned off—were stuff of legends. They were considered harmless pranks, according to biker law. But really, those guys had been good to me when I needed a family, and I would show them all my respect.

I was standing in the beer aisle of the warehouse store, loading a cart with some of the preferred varieties of brew I could remember buying when I was with the club as a prospect. Suddenly, a distinct whistle echoed throughout the vast building, capturing the attention of those in the aisle with me.

I knew that whistle like I knew the sound of my own voice, and I chuckled when a friendly face came strolling down the aisle toward me. It was Denny—Double D, for Deadly Denny as he was known to his brothers in the club. He was wearing his leathers and a big grin, which seemed to scare off those around me.

"Little Brother! You made good time." Denny scooped me up in a bear hug, knocking the wind out of me.

"Whoa! You're gonna cripple me, man! You gotta find something else to do besides lifting heavy shit." Since I'd seen him a month earlier, he looked like he'd put on twenty pounds of muscle. The man was a mountain.

Denny laughed and whistled again, and I heard the returning whistle which meant they were headed our way. I looked up to see Hand, which was a surprise. It wasn't often the president of the club came out to see a lowly former prospect like me.

"Nash, man, it's good to see you!" Hand—Palmer Hanrahan—greeted, offering the same bone-crushing hug as Denny.

I pounded on his back in return, and when he released me, I was gratified to see the man looked happy I'd made the trip. "I was grabbing some beer to bring along. You guys need anything else?"

Hand wrapped a beefy arm around my shoulders and chuckled. "You don't gotta bring nothing. You're always welcome, and I promise, none of these bitches will fuck with your stuff. Come on! We do need beer, though." The three of us proceeded to the check out. After Denny paid, ignoring my protests, we walked outside to see Heretic, Saint, and Preacher, all surrounding the SUV.

"How'd you know that was mine?"

Denny chuckled. "It's registered to the Senator. I had Pacman run the plates for us. The Virginia tags sort of gave it away, but I wanted to double check before we went inside and gave someone else a hard time. I was gonna call you anyway. We've got some news for you."

The feeling of dread slid down my spine, but if they had any information that could help Spencer figure out who outed him and cost him the election, I wanted to know. "Is it about the money trail?"

Denny nodded, so I stood straighter and prepared myself for whatever news he had to give me. I acknowledged the fact we needed to have a conversation and hopped into the SUV, waiting for all of them to mount up and lead the way to the clubhouse.

Once we arrived at The Volunteer, the club-owned bar that was built in front of the distillery warehouse, the bikes parted, giving me a spot in front of the massive building. There were three large warehouses behind it, one for the actual distillery, one for storing supplies, and a third I'd been smart enough to never ask about.

The members of Devil's Volunteers had their fingers dipping into more pies than I wanted to know, and not many of them were legal, which was why I had to keep Spencer at arm's length from the club.

The club made its legit money from moonshine sales, now that the laws had been changed to make it legal to distill the beverage if one followed all the business regulations. Denny's grandfather, who was an old-school mountain man, taught him how to make moonshine when he was a kid. Back then the entire Wallace family lived up in the Appalachian Mountains on a family compound, making moonshine to take care of all the family's needs. They used the guise of a logging business as a front, but they burned all the wood they cut, stoking the fires under the stills that were hidden among the large trees, or so Denny told Clint and me one night.

Back then, moonshine wasn't legal, though it was still made. After the laws changed in 2009, Denny went to community college to take business classes, and later applied for and procured a distillery license. The club has had a booming craft moonshine business ever since.

There was a tasting room in the lobby of the main building, which was separate from the bar, and while the distillery could only retail its products for consumption off premises, prospective buyers could taste a little before they purchased pints, quarts, or gallons—up to a five-gallon limit.

The Volunteer also served the spirits, but that was another type of license that Hand had to obtain on his own, due to the fact he was the only senior members of the club who didn't have a prison record—aside from Denny. *Hell, live and let live!*

After I moved on from Sparta, Clint and I stayed in touch, and during one phone call in particular, he told me about the club making a lucrative off-the-books deal with several bars in the nearby counties for a bulk price on moonshine that wasn't exactly legal, since it was over the five-gallon limit. I'd determined it was probably one of the tamer ways the club made its money, so I didn't ask more questions than I wanted answered. I knew it wasn't my business to pry into the affairs of The Volunteers, but I was surprised at how many improvements had been made around the grounds.

Hand revved his Harley, and just like a dog whistle, two young guys came barreling out of the clubhouse. I saw their cuts and could see their prospect patches, which made me smile. "Pop the tailgate, Nash. Boys get the beer, the bags, and Nash's duffel. Take the beer into the family room of the clubhouse and stock the fridge. Take everything else to the blue room. Nash is here to spend Christmas with the family," Hand announced, making me feel like I was actually with family.

The two young guys nodded without question, and I chuckled. "God, I remember those days when Clint and I were your step-and-fetch boys. What are their chances of patching in?" I held out the keys to Preacher, who had always been in charge of the prospects. He was wearing a happy grin at my gesture which warmed my heart.

I knew the drill. After taking my stuff to my room, the prospects would check the Navigator over to ensure there were no tracking devices on it or hidden cameras, and then they'd park it out of sight of the local cops. Even though they trusted me, it was the way every vehicle was treated when it pulled onto club property. Moving and searching the vehicles used to be my job, and I longed for those simpler times.

Once we were inside the clubhouse, I saw a few familiar faces and a lot of new ones. I was given a warm greeting and a cold beer before Denny took my arm and led me into the chapel—the room where all senior members of the club held their meetings. I'd cleaned the room before and after the patched-in officers held church, but I'd never been inside as a guest.

Denny chuckled. "Make yourself comfortable. I need to run upstairs and grab my phone charger, but I'll be right back. The others will be in shortly. If you want another beer, just signal one of the prospects."

I slowly walked around the room, seeing the large wooden carving behind the President's chair at the table. It was what the artist perceived as hell with beings drowning in a lake of fire. There were figures standing around the devil, pushing figures into the lake, which signified The Devil's Volunteers would happily cast their enemies into the lake of fire, which reminded me of the club patch I never earned.

The founder of The Devil's Volunteers, Keith Murray—Mayhem to his brothers—had died from cancer the year before Clint and I showed up on their doorstep, and as I looked at the carving, I was reminded he'd been a carpenter. He'd been the one to buy the property in the early eighties, establishing the club and building the clubhouse by himself. The members held him in very high esteem, keeping the rules Mayhem had established in the club's charter as sacred commandments.

The punishment for breaking the rules was severe, as I'd witnessed once when a patched member was spying for a rival club. Clint and I were allowed to attend part of the ceremony—when they took the traitor's cut and destroyed his patch before we were told to leave. They also removed his club tattoo from between his shoulder blades, but thankfully, I never learned how they did it.

The door to the chapel flew open, and Hand, Saint, Preacher, Heretic, and Pacman walked into the room with Denny behind. I stood to the side as they sat around the table, Denny finally motioning for me to join them.

I took a seat next to Pacman and waited for someone to tell me what the fuck was going on. Finally, Denny pointed to the tall, slender young computer genius, who moved his laptop in my direction. "So, uh, this has been a tangled web I'm proud to say I finally unwound. This is the flow of money." The young guy showed me an elaborate flowchart highlighting how many bank accounts money flowed through until it ended up at its destination—Mitchell Flora's account, confirming he was Spencer's mole.

"Wow, that's impressive. Uh, thanks for confirming that Mitch was the Senator's mole. I'll make sure..." Pacman hit the tab and another flowchart popped up, just as elaborate as the previous diagram.

I could see all the work that had gone into the investigation, so I turned to Pacman and nodded in approval. The guy, who was probably about twenty-two and a fully patched member, rolled his eyes at me before Denny laughed. "Little Brother, look over here." He pointed to a square where there were words in red:

Ronald and Hillary Brady

I glanced at Denny for clarity. "That's the Honorable Ronald Brady and Mrs. Hillary Brady. They're the Senator's parents."

I could have been knocked over with a feather.

Chapter Twenty Two
Spencer

I was in a fucking awful mood on Christmas Eve morning. I'd spoken to Nash when he arrived in Sparta, and then the next morning, but he wasn't very talkative, and I could hear lots of noise in the background. I didn't know what he was doing or how to shake off the jealousy that he'd rather spend the holiday with his biker friends than me, but Vani told me I was acting like a two-year-old, so I tried to give him his space.

We texted a few times, and his words were upbeat. He told me he missed me and loved me, and really, what more could I want from the man? We weren't joined at the hip!

"Dad, Cole and I have some last-minute shopping to do. Do you think the roads are okay? I didn't know Mom wanted us to go see Grandma Velma on the day after Christmas, so I need to get her a gift."

We'd shoveled about an inch of snow that had fallen earlier that morning. It was still snowing, but the accumulation was supposed to be minimal, so it was more for something to do than necessity.

I pulled off my knit cap after hanging up the snow shovel. "Yeah, I think you guys will be fine. You okay to drive on it?" Jay was a good driver, but he was in a rental, since we hadn't replaced his totaled Escape, and he was driving a full-size pickup, which could be light in the back end with an empty truck bed.

"Yeah. Better here than in Blacksburg," he responded. His cast had been gone for a couple of weeks since his injury was more minor than Cole's but having had his first car accident had seemed to make him skittish.

"You guys want me to come with you?" Vani had gone to pick up the ham Nash had ordered at the store in Tyson's Corner, claiming she had a few last-minute things to pick up as well. How I ended up being the only one who was ready for the holiday was a fucking miracle.

"Not unless you need something. I was gonna take Cole to lunch after we finished shopping. We're going to the outlet mall in Leesburg, and then I thought we'd go into town and eat at Lightfoot."

Lightfoot was a great restaurant in downtown Leesburg. It inhabited an old bank building, and the wine cave was in the old vault. The ornate marble pillars and trim had been restored when the restaurant owner bought the building from a now defunct banking organization after it had been empty for about five years. Vani and I loved to go there on Saturdays when we had time for their grilled cheese special and smoked tomato soup.

"That sounds nice, Jay. You guys go and have a great day out. I think Mom wants you guys to go with her to the bell concert at Emmanuel Lutheran in Vienna at five, so text her to confirm if she still wants to go."

It was a family tradition for us, but in light of all the shit that went down, I was afraid the roof would fall in on my head if I entered the building. I'd told Vanessa to take Jay and Cole with her. I'd be fine at home.

The boys went inside to clean up, and I went to the kitchen to make myself a drink, hoping the day would go by faster if I was blurry eyed. I reached for some of the large ice cubes I preferred, pouring a healthy two fingers into my rocks glass.

I was about to head to the family room when my phone rang. It was Nash, which immediately lifted my mood. "Nash? How are you?"

"I'm fine, babe. Look, I hate to do this over the phone, but the snow is coming down too heavy for me to drive back tonight. Can you get to your computer and get on Skype?" Hell, if Skype was all I could get from him on Christmas Eve, I'd take it.

"Sure. Uh, give me about ten minutes. I've tracked snow inside, and Vani will skin me alive. I'll be there in ten minutes."

"Okay, love you," Nash offered before the line went dead.

I went to the garage and grabbed the mop to clean up the mess I'd made by not taking off my shoes when I came inside. While I was cleaning up, Vani returned home, so I helped her carry things in from the car, and then she told me we needed to talk about something, so while I helped her put away groceries, she proceeded to explain to me that she'd decided to go to the new grocery store at Reston Town Center—where she ran into Blaire and Mitch.

"And, Spence, they were wearing matching wedding rings. Do you think they got married?"

"Fuck, probably. Sean said Blaire was screwing Mitch while we were each dating him, so who knows. I mean, Blaire was clearly out for himself, and if what Sean said was true about Mitch's financial situation, then I could definitely see where Blaire would marry him for money." My mood had gone from bad to worse.

"Who did Mitch work for before he came to work for you?" Vani put some plastic containers into the fridge. Clearly, we'd abandoned any thoughts of making sides ourselves without Nash there to oversee that we didn't poison anyone.

"He worked for Representative Schneider from Ohio, but he was recommended to me by Judge Blackwell, my father's old college buddy who sits on the U.S. Court of Appeals. I ran into Blackwell at a bar association luncheon where we were both speaking, and we sat together to eat. I mentioned Tina was leaving, and he told me about Mitch."

We puttered around the kitchen for a while, me opening the mail, while Vani stacked her last-minute gifts under the tree. She came back into the kitchen with a sad smile on her face. "I wish Nash was here. It feels empty without him."

That reminded me that I was supposed to Skype with him. "Shit! He called just as you came home. I was supposed to get on Skype with him."

I glanced at the clock to see an hour had gone by. What a jackass I was to forget about him.

"He's been waiting an hour." I hurried upstairs to try to get him on Skype. I quickly logged into my account, seeing five notifications of a missed call. I tried to call back, but it went unanswered, so I reached for my cell, seeing it was dead, yet again.

I quickly went in search of a charger, finding the plug where mine usually resided was empty. "Vani!" I bellowed.

"What?" she yelled back, which made me laugh. Old habits would die hard.

I ran downstairs, nearly busting my ass on the slick hardwood in my socked feet. I found her in the laundry room folding towels. "Can you call Nash? He was waiting for me to Skype, and I missed him. My phone's dead, and my charger is missing!"

Vani sighed and went to her purse, retrieving her phone and turning it to me. "Mine's dead as well. Let me plug it in and try to call him. How could you forget?"

"You came in with groceries and... Don't start, Vanessa. Just call him, please." Vani called again, and it went to voicemail. She called a few more times, but again, all the calls went to voicemail.

"What should I do?" My heart was clenching at the fact I'd forgotten Nash needed to talk to me. Vani showed up, and I completely blew him off, which was a horrible thing to do to the man I loved.

Vani shook her head. "You're so bad at this, Spence."

"Yeah, well, you wanted to talk to me, and you're my..." My mouth snapped shut.

Vani gave me a gentle smile. "Not anymore, Spencer. You have a new priority, and he's probably wondering what happened to you." She'd plucked the thoughts from my brain.

She unplugged her phone and reached out her hand, where I placed my phone, watching her plug it in with her charger. I remembered mine was in the Navigator, which was with Nash. Damn, I had to get better at being a partner to the man, especially if I wanted him to stick around.

★★★ ★★★

I'd been calling Nash's cell phone for hours, though it seemed like days! Vani, Cole, and Jay had attended the bell concert, and after they returned home, we heated up a couple of frozen pizzas and ate together, while they told me about the concert. After, we went to the family room to relax with a Christmas movie—or so I thought. The rest of them found something else to do.

Vani pulled out the family photo albums to share photos of Christmases past with Cole. The pictures of Jay as a kid had me ready to cry as I looked at the young man that my son had grown to be. I was proud of him, and seeing how well he treated Cole, I knew he'd be a great boyfriend to the young man.

After everyone went to bed, I walked into the master and stared at the king-sized bed I'd grown accustomed to sharing with Nash. I knew his scent was on the sheets, but without him there, playing the part of my own personal bed warmer, it looked like a lonely island.

I went to the den and grabbed a book from the shelves that I hadn't read in years, and I sat down in the leather recliner, not turning on the television so as not to disturb the sleeping folks in the house.

I opened the old Zane Grey novel I'd had since high school. It had been a Christmas gift from my parents when I was fifteen and developed an affinity for the writer, mostly because I was interested in a farm boy from school who spoke the way Zane Grey's characters spoke in the books. It was a leather-bound copy of a collection of short stories that were published in the late seventies, long after the writer had passed. When I saw the handwritten message inside it from my father, my heart seized with pain.

To my son—You are my biggest accomplishment! I'm proud of you every day, and I look forward to your successes, as much as I've enjoyed my own. Love, Dad

I felt the tears fall, and of course, I blamed the liquor I'd steadily consumed all evening. No, it wouldn't make anything better, but a little self-medicating hadn't seemed like a bad idea.

I moved from the chair to the couch, my back starting to bother me from the snow shoveling I'd done with Jay earlier that day. If I wasn't so fucking lazy, I'd get up and take a hot shower.

Hell, if Nash was home, we'd take a bath, but he wasn't home, was he? He was spending the holiday with his biker friends. I didn't like it one bit. There was something about that Denny guy that rubbed me the wrong way.

I prayed that whatever he'd wanted to talk to me about earlier had nothing to do with him wanting to leave me behind for that Denny character.

I was a lot of work, but maybe if I put in more effort? Hell, I owed him everything I had inside me.

I knew he'd discussed with Vani how much damage his past could do to my reputation, but hell, I'd already annihilated it, so how much worse could it really get?

I felt a touch to my chest and opened my eyes to see Nash standing over me. He looked exhausted, but he was there. I quickly sat up, noticing there was a blanket over me. The rocks glass and bottle of Glenfiddich I'd left on the coffee table were gone, which smacked of Vani, bless her heart.

"When did you get home?" The sun was starting to turn the purple sky to baby blue.

I pulled Nash on top of me and kissed him, not minding my morning breath at all. I wrapped my arms around him and held on for dear life. I was forty-five years old, and I was in love with a wonderful young guy. I had to get better about showing him.

Our tongues swirled as my hands landed on his gorgeous ass. He wrapped his arms around my neck, holding me tight as well. Having him with me was the best cure for the Christmas blues I'd ever seen.

After frantic kisses, Nash broke the seal of our lips and pulled back, offering me a sexy smile. "It's just six thirty. Wanna go to your room?"

He was still wearing his winter coat, which made me smile. "Yeah. Let's go, and it's *our* room. Thank you for coming back." I kissed him again.

Feeling him in my arms had turned my mood from shitty to giddy. As corny as it sounded in my head, it was the truth.

Nash pulled me up from the couch, and when I stood, he hugged me tightly, which sort of surprised me. I smirked as I kissed his neck. "You missed me?"

"Yeah, I did. Come on." He dragged me down the hallway to the room we shared, closing the door and locking it after we were both inside.

I helped him out of his coat, throwing it on the chair in the corner. "How bad was the drive?" It had been steadily snowing all day and night, and the last time I'd looked at the weather report, the Weather Service was saying the roads down in southern Virginia were barely passable, which had me feeling guilty again for missing Nash's Skype call.

"I'm so sorry I missed your Skype calls. Vani came home from the store, and I helped her carry in groceries. She saw Blaire and Mitch at the store as well." It was a feeble excuse at best. I owed him more than that, but he didn't seem interested in conversation.

"Don't worry about it. Let's go to bed. I want you to fuck me, Spencer." Nash's voice was demanding, which was unlike his usual easy-going demeanor. I stared at him and saw he was serious.

"Okay, but is something wrong?" His request to speak earlier in the day, and now his determination to have me fuck him had me more than a little worried. We were equal-opportunity lovers, but why it was suddenly important for me to top Nash had me worried. Was it the last bow before he left me behind?

We undressed each other quickly, my heart beating out of my chest with worry. It was on the tip of my tongue to ask him what was going on, but I wasn't about to be the one to ruin our time together.

Nash dropped onto the bed and pulled me with him, settling under me, which was a thrill. It would be the first time I'd topped him, and I prayed it wasn't the last. "How would you like me?" Nash whispered as he studied my face.

I rested on my elbows, looking into his beautiful hazel eyes. "I wanna feast on that gorgeous ass, and then I wanna look into your beautiful eyes when I stake my claim."

Nash chuckled. "Let's take this to the shower first, Senator. Your plan sounds like there's no need for debate."

That comment made me laugh. I pulled him up with me, and we went into the master bathroom. I turned on the shower while Nash retrieved towels from the linen closet. Once the water was at the right temperature, I walked into the shower and motioned for him to join me. The little blush on his cheeks revved my engine perfectly.

I turned Nash toward the spray and stood behind him, whispering, "Why didn't you wait to come home until tomorrow?"

"I was stupid to leave you guys in the first place. Jay's gonna think whatever he wants about us, but I need you, Spence." I hit the button on the dispenser for body wash.

Oh, I wasn't about to deny him anything. I washed his back as he ducked his head under the spray. I slid my soapy fingers down his crack before I reached under and washed his balls and taint, feeling him relax a bit more.

I used the conditioner in the dispenser next to the body wash to loosen him a bit and turned him to rinse his ass. "Nash, love, is something wrong?"

He rinsed the shampoo from his hair. "No, Spence. I just... I want you to make me yours. I liked seeing my friends, but I belong here with you. I love you, and I want to feel you inside me." His words were all I needed to hear.

We quickly finished our shower and dried off. I brushed my teeth, noticing Nash's toothbrush was missing. I rinsed mine quickly and handed it to him, receiving a grin in return. I hung the towels over the rack and walked out of the bathroom to turn down the covers on the bed.

I turned off the ceiling light and turned on one of the bedside lamps so I could see his gorgeous naked body. Watching myself slide into him would be a dream come true.

Nash came out of the bathroom in all his naked glory, falling onto the bed with me. "I love you, Spencer, but if it's too much for you to give up Vani and Jay, then tell me, and I'm gone."

I'd started working my way between his legs, but I stopped. Clearly, we needed to have a discussion before we went any further.

"What the hell happened? Did those bikers do something to you? Are you okay?" I couldn't imagine why he would want to leave me when I'd just found him.

"It's nothing that can't wait until later. Please, make love to me." How could I deny him?

I reached into the nightstand and found the lube and a condom, hating the idea we needed to have anything between us. Nash was insistent because of his previous profession, but I was determined they'd be gone after the first of the year.

I placed my hands under Nash's muscular ass and lifted it to my mouth, diving in for my first taste, hoping and praying it wouldn't be my last.

He was beautiful, and the next time we were together in such a fashion, the coconut conditioner wouldn't be what I smelled as I feasted on him. I wanted his natural scent, and I'd damn well get it next time.

I swirled my tongue over his hole before I attempted to push inside. Nash moaned, and his noises had me doubling down on him. I opened the lube and slicked my fingers before I began working my index finger inside him as I sucked on his balls and ran my tongue over his taint. I nipped it before I pushed further inside him, up to the second knuckle.

"Please, Spence." Nash pressed against my finger. I put him through the paces, fucking him with my tongue and my fingers before he begged me to stop.

"Baby, I'm about to blow. Please, suit up." Oh, I was happy to oblige.

I pushed the head of my cock against his entrance, resting his legs on my thighs. "I'll go slow."

I gently pushed in to test the waters. Nash, however, wasn't in the mood to go slow. He angled his ass just right, pressing back on my cock, which slid in without hesitation.

"Ahh! Yeah, Spence. Fuck me." His gasp fed my ego.

From my side, I was ready to come, so I stilled him. "Baby, give me a fighting chance! It's been a while for me." I took deep breaths to back off the fucking edge.

Nash's ass was made for me, and I needed to claim it properly. I wasn't a thirty-second man, but the luxurious feel of him wrapped around me had me nearly ready to blow.

Nash chuckled. "Okay, Senator. I'll give you some time." He wrapped his hand around his gorgeous prick and began pumping.

"Fuck no. You're not going without me." I rested on my elbows that were next to his ears to gain control.

I nipped at his soft lips, so grateful to have him as mine. I finally slid my tongue into his mouth, tasting my toothpaste and closing my eyes to concentrate solely on Nash and everything about him.

THE SENATOR

His taste... His sounds... The feel of his hands on my shoulders... Wrapping around my neck and pulling me closer to him. It was a heady feeling to have the gorgeous young man want me. If I was a betting man, I'd have never put a dime on it.

Unfortunately, the longer we kissed, the more my urge to fill him grew, and suddenly, I could stop myself. "Fuck, I can't..." I groaned as I pounded into him.

Nash wasn't shy, pushing back in perfect rhythm. I felt as if I'd died and gone to heaven, as I wrapped my fist around his hard cock to take him with me.

"Oh, fuck!" His loud moan let me know I'd hit that spot inside him, just as he hit inside me every fucking time we made love.

"Let's go." I pounded him and jacked his hard rod in time. When Nash shot off, the white stream covered his chest and ran down my hand like lava. I thrust into him three more times before I couldn't stop myself, filling the fucking condom.

I couldn't form sentences, so I leaned forward and gently kissed his soft lips. "I love you."

"I love you too." That was exactly what I needed to hear. As long as I had Nash Lincoln, I could weather any storm.

Chapter Twenty Three
Nash

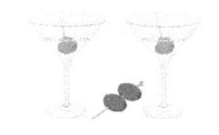

Feeling Spencer fill me that first time—even with the condom—had turned me into an addict, but after what I had to tell him, I wasn't sure how he'd feel about anything, much less me. The whole fucking thing had gone off the rails, and learning his mother and father were behind him being outed and losing the election? I had no idea how he'd take the news.

The drive from Sparta took hours. When I couldn't get Spence on Skype, I left The Volunteers, much against the advice of the club, but what I'd learned couldn't wait. Spencer deserved to know the truth about who had instigated and funded his downfall.

When I finally arrived at the house in Great Falls, I let myself into the gate and drove to the house, opening the garage door and driving inside. I hoped to hell I didn't wake Vani, Jay, or Cole, but I damn well planned to wake Spencer.

I went upstairs, following the light to the den where I found Spencer sleeping on the couch with a throw over him. He had a peaceful look on his handsome face, so I watched him for a few moments, hoping what I had to tell him wouldn't break his heart.

He'd mentioned a few times he didn't have a relationship with his parents, but I wondered how much it weighed on him. I didn't have parents, but he'd had his for years, and it would hurt him to learn his parents had instigated his political demise. I hated the idea I'd have to be the one to deliver the shitty news.

After Spence and I made love, we settled into the big bed. I figured the day after Christmas was soon enough to tell him how fucked up his parents were, so I made myself at home in his arms, playing the little spoon and praying my revelation didn't wreck us.

I knew Spencer would never reclaim his reputation as long as I was in his life, so I was going to leave him once he was on secure footing. Spence had a family to worry about, and I was just a diversion. I got it, and I wouldn't raise a stink about it.

"So, what were you so frantically trying to tell me earlier today? I'm sorry for fucking up the Skype thing. Tell me now." Spencer's hot breath on my ear brought a shiver down my spine as his cock nestled into my crack.

I faked a yawn, having drank five energy drinks as I made my way through a blizzard to get to Spence after Pacman, Hand, and Denny explained how the Judge and Mrs. Brady had set up Spencer's downfall. They'd offered to drive with me to explain that shit to Spence, but I knew keeping the club away from Spencer was for the best.

Denny made me promise I'd call him if I needed anything, and one of the prospects followed me until I reached the highway. It was slow going, but I made it, thankful to be in the Senator's arms again—before it came crashing down.

"We can talk tomorrow, Spence. Get some sleep." I evened my breaths so he thought I was asleep. My mind wouldn't stop spinning, because I had no idea how to begin to break the news to him.

I'd considered seeking Vani out, but it occurred to me that I couldn't continue to count on her as a crutch. She was Spencer's wife, yes, and it was completely fucked up that I'd ask her for advice. I needed to learn to talk to him on my own, without her intervening on my behalf.

"I really missed you, Nash." Spencer's breathing became even, comforting me as I listened to the sound in the quiet room. He pulled me closer, and I did my best to relax, but the idea that I had to be the one to tell him his parents had been behind the scheme to fuck him over? Not the best spot to be in, ever.

After Spencer fell into a deep sleep, he turned onto his back and loosened his arms around me, so I gently extricated myself, pulling on my jeans before I went downstairs, determined to get my duffel out of the SUV so I didn't have to keep using Spence's toothbrush.

I walked into the garage and grabbed my bag from the back seat, trying to be quiet when I walked back into the house. I was surprised to see Jay standing at the refrigerator, scratching his ass as he leaned over the door. He was shirtless and wearing a pair of grey sweats, and I could see I'd startled him when I came into the kitchen.

"Sorry." I placed my bag on the island so he could see I wasn't doing anything shady.

Jay chuckled. "It's okay. You want something to drink?" He pulled out a Gatorade and held it out to share from the bottle, which surprised me.

"I, uh, I'm okay. Everything okay with you?"

"Well, I'm a little dehydrated, and I thought you might be as well." Jay gave me a sarcastic smirk.

"Ah. Too loud. I hoped we weren't." My cheeks heated with embarrassment.

"Don't worry about it. Cole's usually loud, but he was asleep. When did you get back?" Jay took another gulp from the energy drink.

"Uh, about an hour ago. Can I ask you something?"

Jay shrugged, so I stepped out on that limb. "Are you close with your grandparents? I mean, uh, Judge Brady and Hillary?"

"Fuck no. They were against my parents adopting me. They thought Mom and Dad should have a bio kid, and they never accepted what happened to Mom." Jay's scowl supported his comment.

"I, uh, I know some stuff, but what do you mean?" I tried to determine how much the young man knew about his parents getting together.

"Do you and Dad do *anything* other than fuck?" Jay chuckled. "Mom wasn't able to have a kid, so they decided to adopt me. Judge and Hillary never accepted it, though based on recent revelations, they probably wouldn't have one anyway since Dad's gay." He did have a point.

"So, they won't drop by with presents?"

Jay chuckled. "Hell no. They're both assholes, and we never see them. I remember once when they came here to give Dad shit about the way he voted on a bill, and they got into a shouting match. Ron said Dad was too liberal, and Dad told him to fuck himself. I'm sure the neighbors enjoyed the show. Ron and Hillary left, and I don't remember seeing them after that."

I nodded. "Merry Christmas."

"Look, Nash, I wasn't sure how you played into this situation. I remembered seeing you at the hospital after the accident, but nobody explained it to me until Dad finally told me the score.

"Mom also talked to me about their divorce, which wasn't so much of a surprise as everybody seemed to think it would be. Hell, I don't ever remember them sharing a room, and the excuse that Dad snored was bullshit. I know he doesn't, but you know, as a kid, there's shit you don't wanna think about your parents—you know, like my dad plowing you like farmland." Jay's joke made me laugh.

I heard moving around upstairs, and glanced down to see I wasn't wearing a shirt. "I'm gonna go get decent. Are you people early morning gift exchangers?" I walked to the coffee maker to set it up, knowing it wouldn't be long until everyone was awake.

"Hey, I'm going back to bed, but if you can keep Mom and Dad down here for a while, maybe I can get my Christmas present before breakfast." Jay waggled his eyebrows before he ran back upstairs.

I heard the snick of a bedroom door, so I left the light on over the sink and grabbed my duffel, heading upstairs to change into something nicer than a pair of ratty old jeans. When I opened the door of the bedroom, I saw Spencer was leaning against the headboard, his shirtless chest enticing me to climb back in with him. Maybe I could get another Christmas present myself?

"Where'd you go?" He stifled a yawn.

"To get my bag out of the Navigator. I started the coffee." I opened my bag with the intention of unpacking, but then, I remembered what I needed to tell him, and I decided to forego it. I reached inside and grabbed a clean Henley, tossing it on the chair where Spence had put my coat.

Spence pulled back the covers to reveal his naked hip, and he smirked at me. "Come back to bed."

I laughed. "I think Vani's up. Seems bad form for us to be fucking like rabbits in here while she's downstairs making breakfast."

I did, however, drop my jeans and step out of them before climbing into the bed with him and straddling his groin. He was rock hard, just the way I liked him. My cock was growing at a quick pace with his short public hair rubbing against my balls. Spence had sparse tufts of hair on his chest and a nice happy trail that was sprinkled with sexy grey strands. He didn't have washboard abs, but there was muscle there, and it turned me on like a switch.

I captured his mouth with mine, feeling his whiskers scrape against my short stubble. I pulled away, looking at his handsome face. "You planning to let this grow?"

Spence's cheeks turned a little pink. "I saw your biker friend had a goatee, and I thought maybe you liked that sort of thing."

Okay, Denny didn't just have a goatee, he had a bushy half-ass goatee that was in desperate need of beard oil, but Spencer was such a good-looking guy, and the goatee only made him hotter.

"It could be quite sexy, but I don't want you worrying about Denny, Spencer. He was in love with my best friend who died in an accident. Denny's still trying to get over Clint, and I worry he might never.

"When they came to Blacksburg after Jay and Cole had that accident, Denny agreed to do a favor for me if I'd sit up with him all night and tell him stories about Clint growing up, and that was all we did. He misses my friend like he's missing part of his heart. He makes moonshine—well, legal moonshine. He's an interesting man, but I want you to be as far away from him as possible. Not everything The Volunteers do is exactly on the up-and-up, so I never want you two associated."

He squeezed my ass cheeks. "Look at you, watching out for my reputation that's been completely obliterated."

I chuckled. "Hell, you probably shouldn't be associated with a whore either. You've got a long enough fight ahead of you to get back your reputation. You don't need me bringing you down." I stared into his beautiful brown eyes.

I teared up at the thought of leaving him, but he came first. What was best for him came first.

Spencer reached for the nightstand where the lube was sitting since we'd made love earlier. "I've got a job lined up, Nash, and fuck my reputation. I'm not worried about it. DC has a short memory."

He whispered those words against my skin before he kissed my neck.

All talking ceased, and riding the high of feeling his hands on me took away any thoughts of what I needed to tell him. It was Christmas, after all. Bad news could wait.

Chapter Twenty Four
Spencer

With Nash's return, the plans for cooking were back on, and even though Vani had bought some premade sides, Nash made a few dishes to add to the feast. Cole even helped him, which was great.

Vani and I sat at the table watching the two of them cook while Jay cleaned up after them. It was amazing that we all seemed to hit it off easily as we did, and I looked forward to more festive times with my family, which now included Nash and possibly

Cole, if he and Jay lasted. They seemed to love each other, but they were young. It remained to be seen.

Vani turned to me and smiled, "This is nice, huh?"

I placed my hand over hers, squeezing for a moment. "It is. You'll come back to see us, right? When do I need to be out? Are you listing it, or do you want someone else to do it?" I was referring to the house.

We'd been moving in that direction, and in the divorce papers, we agreed to sell it and split the profit. She had contractors scheduled to begin painting and doing minor repairs after the first of the year, but I wasn't sure of the timeline.

Vani giggled softly. "I'd say you should buy me out, but this house has a lot of memories, so maybe it's for the best that we do sell it? Any idea where you want to live? I can get you some listings. The contractor doesn't start until the tenth of January, so you could find a place and get out before construction starts."

Jay turned from his place by the sink. "Who's taking my stuff?"

"Well, let's discuss it. I know this might not be the best timing, but I plan to get a place with a few bedrooms, so I can take your furniture until you have a place of your own."

Vani moved her hand and walked over to Jay. "My place in the Upper East Side has two bedrooms, and I'll buy furniture. You'll have a place to sleep when you come see me." She hugged around his middle as he held a skillet in his hands in the dishwater.

Jay dropped the pan and reached for the towel over his shoulder. "Mom, just get a pullout couch, okay? Make the room into a den, and I can sleep there when I visit. It's gonna be alright. We're still a family, you know." Jay's reminder was a relief.

Nash stood at the stove, a worried look on his handsome face. "Okay, no talk of moving and shit. We need to open gifts, and are you people ever going to get some food on the table?" I tried to lighten the mood before we all ended up in tears.

Nash laughed, which made my heart sing. "Alright, cranky. I think it's ready. We just need some serving dishes." He looked at me, so I got up and started opening cabinets to find whatever was handy to put the food in so we could eat.

"Spencer, go to the butler's pantry— *Ugh!* Come with me." I followed Vani into that strange room between the kitchen and the dining room where I never went.

I watched her open cabinets and drawers, handing me various dishes, cloth napkins, and placemats. She turned to me with a smile. "Should we eat in the kitchen? I don't want to be formal, do you?"

I stared at her, certain there was a look of disbelief on my face. "I think the time for formal has flown right out the window." I laughed hard at my joke and pointed to all the stuff in the cabinet. "You're taking all of this, right?"

"I'm not talking about that today." Vani loaded another platter onto the stack of shit I was already carrying.

I followed her to the kitchen where we placed everything on the island like an assembly line, or a buffet, as Vanessa schooled us. Nash and Cole placed the food in the serving dishes, Vani set the table, and Jay took the pots and pans to the sink to soak. Like always, I watched.

Once the food was set up, we all filled our plates. The variety of dishes was surprising, but I figured I could work off the food since I didn't start consulting until the first week of January. I was planning to eat everything in sight and as much as I wanted.

Once we were all seated at the table, I looked around to see the faces of people I loved, or in Cole's case, cared about. Most Christmases it was Vani, Jay, and me sitting at the dining room table with a catered meal served by people we didn't know. The relief of having something normal was overwhelming.

Nash filled our wine glasses and took a seat next to me, and I felt the need to say something. I started to tap my knife against the water glass to get everyone's attention, but there were only five of us. "If you'll give me a minute, I want to make a quick speech. I guess not getting to stand at the podium in the chamber has spoiled me, but I won't pontificate for long.

"I'd like to make a toast to Vani and Jay. We've had a hell of a year, and here we are, still standing. To Cole, we are so happy to have you join us. I'll feel better when you get that cast off, but I'm glad you're here with Jay to celebrate with us.

"Last, but certainly not least, to Nash. You fit into our family like a hand in a glove, and I'm grateful to have you. I love you all, and I wish us the happiest of New Year's! Here's to us." We all touched glasses, wishing each other a Merry Christmas.

We laughed, we ate, we bonded, all of us. It was exactly what I wanted the holiday to be—time spent with those people who meant the most to me.

THE SENATOR

Leaning against the headboard of the bed, I admired the new health and fitness tracker Jay and Vani had given me for Christmas. I pushed the buttons on the side to see what they did as I glanced through the small brochure that accompanied it. It was a thoughtful gift.

Nash bought me winter running gear—a base layer, ear warming headband, insulated gloves, and a thermal beanie. I smelled a theme among my family, but it was given with love, I was sure.

"What's taking so long?"

Nash was in the bathroom, but I wasn't sure what he was doing. I'd given him a watch and smartphone on my account, and I was going to talk to him about our housing needs. As far as I was concerned, we'd already crossed the hurdle of us living together. All we needed to do was find a place that was convenient to both our jobs, though I was hoping Sean would come through with a job for my guy.

Nash stepped out of the bathroom wearing a pair of flannel lounge pants from my drawer. I loved seeing him in my clothes. "You okay?" The expression on his face had me worried.

Nash sat on the edge of the bed and faced me. "I have something to tell you, and it's bad, Spence. I love you, and I'd rather cut off an arm than hurt you. I've been trying to figure out the best time to tell you what The Volunteers found about you being outed."

I held out my hand for him to come closer, but he didn't move. "There's nothing you can tell me that will come between us, Nash, I promise."

The expression I saw was skeptical, so I crawled to the end of the bed and took his hand. "Tell me. I can't fix anything if I don't know what's broken."

Nash scooted closer. "Babe, it's not something you can fix. It's done. I hate that I'm the one who has to tell you this."

After a deep breath, I took his hand and kissed it. "Just tell me, Nash."

"I had Pacman—a guy from the club—continue tracking the money from Mitch Flora's account. It went through him to an offshore account and led to the people behind the pictures. The source of the money was from someone you know, Spencer."

I knew a lot of people, so I wasn't surprised. "Tell me it's not Mario."

Nash gave me a sad smile. "No. It's not Mario. Blaire was involved, but it wasn't him either. The money started with... It was your parents."

For a moment, I couldn't breathe. *My parents? My fucking parents?*

I swallowed. "Are you saying that Ron and Hillary had me followed, photographed, and leaked those pictures to the press? My own parents did this to me?"

Nash unlocked his old phone and handed it to me. The screen was small, but the information was huge. I scrolled through the various charts he pointed out, and when I got to the head of the snake, my parents' names were there... not surprisingly... in red.

"Motherfucking son of a— Why am I surprised?" I sat there, paralyzed, as my mind tried to process the information.

Nash took his phone and tossed it on the bed. "I'm sorry, Spencer. I hoped it would be someone else. Maybe Pacman got it wrong?"

I glanced at Nash... the beautiful man who held my heart. "I doubt it. This is exactly something my parents would do. Are you okay being connected to me when we start going out in public together?"

Nash stood and paced. "Spencer, I should leave. I can find work somewhere else. I can't take you down, babe."

"You can't... What the hell do you mean, Nash?"

"I mean, I'm going to leave town. I want you to have a great life, Spence. I can't be the reason you're not respected after the way your parents had you outed. I won't contribute to you not getting your life back."

Was he serious? "Where are you going? You can't leave, Nash. I need you."

"You need *me*? No, Spence. You *need* Vani and your family. I wish I could be a part of it, but I'm nothing but trouble for you. As you said, the city has a short memory. Me with my history? You don't need a revolving scandal when your enemies find out I slept with some of them, and they need ammunition against you for one reason or another. If I leave before anyone finds out we're together, then I take that stigma with me."

"Stigma? The stigma of finding a handsome man and falling in love? There's no stigma to that. Goddammit, Nash. I need *you*. I'll accept all your secrets and mistakes and successes, and I want you to do the same for me. I was a US Senator. Do you think I don't have skeletons in my closet? Please don't walk away from me." Now I was begging, but what the hell else could I do?

I'd crawl across broken glass to keep Nash Lincoln. He was the key to my future, and I was sure of it.

Chapter Twenty Five
Nash

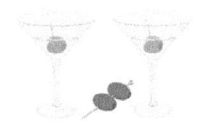

As much as I believed it was best if I walked away from Spencer Brady, I was struggling not to cave when he begged me not to leave. "I don't want to be a problem for you, Spencer. It's not like I'm not known around town. I can't get a fucking job because I have no skills. I'm a whore, and that's all I'll ever be."

Spencer got up from the bed and stepped in front of me to stop my pacing. He took my face in his hands. "No. No you're not, Nash. You're a beautiful person who was trying to get by the best way he could. Sex work is nothing to be ashamed of. You had a good that was highly marketable, and you sold it. Hell, I was no different in my job as a senator. Your business with Caroline Bering-Turner was the same shit I was dealing with on Capitol Hill when it came to her husband. I had a vote that he wanted desperately, and I used it to get what I wanted from him. Please don't walk away from me because of what I did." My chest pounded at his heartfelt plea.

"You have a chance at a new life, Spence. You have a family who loves you, and a real opportunity to make something great working for Sean Fitzpatrick."

"None of that matters if you leave me. *I* love *you*." He was so fucking sincere I wanted to drop to my knees in front of him because I worshiped the ground where he stood. I'd never loved another person the way I loved Spencer Brady.

There was a knock on the door, which brought our conversation to a halt. "Jay heard us having sex this morning. I hope he's not hearing this conversation."

Spence opened the door to reveal Vanessa standing there in her robe. She came inside and closed the door.

"I'm here on behalf of Jay and Cole. Can you two keep it down? What's going on? You're obviously not in the throes of passion." She had a smirk on her face.

I ran my hands through my hair because it was too damn surreal. Why the fuck couldn't I find a regular guy to fall in love with?

"I wish to hell that's what's going on. Now, I'm begging Nash not to leave me. Ron and Hillary are the ones who had me outed. They funded the whole thing. Nash, show her what you showed me."

I pulled up the documents Pacman had sent me and handed the phone to Vani. She flipped through the charts and when she landed on the most telling, I thought she was going to throw the phone. Considering I was giving Spencer back the Christmas gifts he'd given me—except the nice robe because that would always remind me of him—I had to snatch the phone away from Vani.

"That's fucking twisted, Spencer. I knew they were bottom-feeders, but this is low, even for them." She pulled him to sit on the side of the bed with her.

I went into the closet and grabbed the first shirt I found, which happened to be his, and I left the room. It was yet another example of me not fitting into their close-knit lives. They would never be able to let each other go. I could see it clearly, even if they couldn't.

"Hey, sorry for ratting you guys out last night. Did she put you in a time out?" I opened my eyes to see Jay standing by the couch in the den where I'd fallen asleep. My neck was killing me because of the odd angle.

I sat up, placing my feet on the floor, and gently rolled my head until I heard the expected pop. "It wasn't what you think it was. You'll need to talk to your folks about it."

Before I'd dozed off, I'd made up my mind to call Caroline Bering-Turner to see if I could get a referral from her to another escort business. I'd decided maybe Atlanta was a good place to start over, and considering Caroline had contacts everywhere, I hoped she'd help me out.

"Jay, Dad wants to talk to you. Where's Cole?" Vani stepped into the room, her eyes red and swollen.

Jay turned to her. "Damn, Mom. You look like hell."

The lifted eyebrow she gave him made me grin. "Where's Cole?" She meant business, that was for sure.

"He's in the shower. What's going on?" He glanced in my direction, but I wasn't saying anything. It wasn't my news to share.

"Your grandparents were behind my public outing. They gave money to Blaire and Mitch Flora to get evidence that I was gay, and then they leaked it to the press." I glanced toward the door to see Spencer had walked into the room.

He sat down next to me on the couch. "Why didn't you come back to our room? This affects you too."

"I'm going to Atlanta. You deserve a fresh start, and you can't have it with me as a millstone around your neck." I stood and left the room without waiting for comments.

I went to the bedroom and placed the Christmas gifts Spence and the family had given me on the dresser. I emptied the dresser of my clothes and shoved everything into my duffel. I dressed and went to the ensuite to get my toiletries.

Once I had everything, I grabbed my coat. I'd given no thought to where I would go, but there was an all-night diner two miles away. It would be a cold walk, but it was best for everyone involved.

I opened the bedroom door and listened, hearing Jay, Vani, and Spencer down the hall having a heated discussion, so I put on my coat and grabbed my bag and shoes. I quietly walked down the stairs and stopped at the door to slip on my boots.

"Where are you sneaking off to?" Spencer's voice didn't sound happy.

"I'm not sneaking. I didn't want to track dirt through the house. I'm going to the diner on Georgetown Pike to get a cup of coffee and figure things out. I'm sorry if I ruined your Christmas."

Spencer went to the closet by the front door and slid on a pair of boots, tucking his pajama pants inside before he pulled on a sweatshirt and a thick coat. "Let's go. I want pumpkin pie."

So much for my quiet getaway.

★★★ ★★★

The Friday after Christmas, Spencer had a breakfast meeting with Sean Fitzpatrick at the same Georgetown hotel where Sean held his birthday party last fall. "Sean wants to talk to you, too, so come with me. He was going to call you later, but we can handle everything with one breakfast."

I was busy folding towels. Jay and Cole had gone to meet Cole's family to spend New Year's with them on a ski trip to the Pocono Mountains, and Vanessa was busy packing things she wanted to take with her to New York. Spence had ordered boxes to pack up the rest of it, and we were supposed to go apartment hunting over the weekend.

My idea of going to Atlanta had flown the coop when Spencer sat down at the diner and ordered a whole pumpkin pie for us to split. We ate it out of the pie tin and laughed like loons.

"Why would Sean want to talk to me? I know nothing about the lobbying business." Man, that was no joke. I'd overheard Spence on a phone call with him the day after Christmas, and they were talking about some press conference Sean was planning to hold on January third. I wasn't sure what it would be about, but I wondered if Spence did.

"I'm not sure, sweetheart. I told him when he called that I could bring you along with me, and he agreed. He mentioned something about a business proposition he had for you."

Spence was wearing jeans and a sweater, so I went upstairs and showered. I pulled on black jeans, a tan sweater that had been a Christmas gift from Denver, and my black boots. I dried my hair and put finishing spray on it, and I walked down the hall to find Vanessa in the den looking through the bookshelves.

"Do I look okay? I'm going with Spencer to meet Sean Fitzpatrick for breakfast."

Vanessa turned to me and smiled widely. "You look handsome. I think that sweater is perfect. So did Spence say why Sean wants to see you?"

"A business proposition, but that's all. I'm nervous. I'm not sure what skills I have that—" I froze. There was no way Spencer would be okay if Sean was planning to pimp me out, was there?

"No, no. Don't even think about it." Vanessa touched my shoulder. "If you're thinking what I think you're thinking, I can tell you Spencer won't go along with it for any amount of money. He'll lose his mind if Sean even hints at asking you to do anything of the sort."

I took a deep breath, hoping she was right. "I hope so. Anyway, you'll be here when we get back, right?"

Vani giggled. "Yes, I will. The truck isn't coming until the thirtieth, so calm down. You're as bad as Spencer."

I hugged her and left the den, heading to the kitchen where Spencer was rinsing our mugs to put in the dishwasher. "I'm ready."

When Spencer turned around, his eyes scanned my body, making me self-conscious. He walked closer and put his forearms on my shoulders. "You, my love, look fantastic."

He leaned closer and kissed my lips. I wrapped my arms around his waist, feeling his strong body next to mine. How could I ever think of leaving him? I must have been out of my head.

Before the kiss could turn into something I didn't have the power to stop, Spence ended it with a soft nip of his teeth on my bottom lip. "Come on. I'm anxious to find out what Sean was so excited about."

Yeah, I was anxious about that myself, though I doubted it was the same thing Spencer was thinking. My stomach tied itself in knots at warp speed.

***

We headed into DC, Spencer holding my hand as he drove. The radio played a smooth jazz station that filled the silence as my mind raced. After we crossed the Key Bridge into Georgetown, we hit a red light, so Spencer stopped.

"I have a question. What if Sean wants to pimp me out? Use me to get dirt on some of your former colleagues or people in the elite Washington set?" The words came out fast, and Spence did a double take.

When the light turned green, he turned right onto M Street and pulled into the curb lane, turning on the emergency flashers. There were angry horns and a few middle fingers, but Spencer didn't see them because he was staring at me.

"What are you talking about? Sean pimp—there's no fucking way I'd let him even hint at something of the sort."

Spencer turned in his seat to face me. "I love you. We're going to make a life together, and I would never stand for Sean to ask something like that from you. If I catch a whiff that he's thinking along those lines in any way, we'll leave. We'll figure out our next steps, but we're doing it together. You feel the same, right?"

I swallowed the lump in my throat. "I still think—"

Spencer put his finger over my lips. "It's a yes or no question, Nash. You feel the same way, right?"

I kissed his finger before pushing it away from my lips. "Yes, Spence, I feel the same way. I love you and want to make a life with you, but I think you'd still be better without me."

He chuckled. "I can assure you, I wouldn't."

Spencer checked the rearview mirror and the side mirror before pulling into traffic, seemingly satisfied that we'd put the argument to rest.

I was sure something would happen that would prove to him I was right.

Chapter Twenty Six
Spencer

I valeted my SUV at the Four Seasons Hotel in Georgetown, and I took Nash's hand and led him inside. We made our way through the lobby to the Seasons Restaurant. We stopped at the host stand. "Spencer Brady to meet Sean Fitzpatrick."

The host scanned the reservation list and nodded. "Follow me, please."

We were led to a square table next to windows that faced the outside terrace, which was closed for the winter. Sean was sitting with his back to the windows, facing the room. I expected no less. Someone like Sean didn't like surprises, much like me.

Sean stood as the host led us to the table. "Senator. Nash. Good you could both make it." He extended his hand to each of us, and we shook before we sat down. Menus were left for us, and the host returned to the entrance.

Sean lifted his hand, and a server stepped over. "Coffee, gentlemen?"

"Uh, I'll have coffee, please." I turned my cup over for the server and glanced at Nash. He appeared to be nervous, so I reached under the table and squeezed his thigh. Nash waved her off, gulping down his water.

"Thank you for coming. Senator, you mentioned in our brief call that you knew who was responsible for your outing."

"Call me Spencer, please. If we're going to be working together, can we be less formal?"

Sean stared at me for a moment before he grinned. "Good point. So, about your unceremonious outing?"

I sighed. "Seems my parents happily started the ball rolling by contacting Mitch Flora, my former head of communications. He confirmed that Blaire would be accompanying me to Antigua, according to the digging a friend did. Mitch's former assistant had a brother who is a photographer, so Mitch hired the man to follow me to Antigua after Blaire told him where we were staying. There are transfers of nice sums of money through the accounts. My friend created a meticulous record of the transactions.

"Oh, by the way—I believe Mitch and Blaire are married. Vanessa saw them in DC, wearing matching gold bands. Seems we were both duped, Sean."

"And what do you want to do about this, Spencer? Are you going to keep it under wraps, or are you willing to publicly identify them?" That was a very good question.

Part of me wanted to let the whole thing die down and let the public forget, but the part of me that was pissed at all the people involved in my outing wanted me to...

"I'm considering a press conference on the steps of the Capitol and naming all the individuals involved. If there are any other members of Congress who aren't out, they should see that we must be strong and support each other. And those who would contemplate doing anything like what was done to me should see that there are consequences."

"A press conference?" Sean's expression of surprise had me second-guessing myself.

"A *press conference?*" I turned to see Nash was even more surprised.

"Yes." No way was I backing down now.

"Spencer, I think it's a gutsy move. If you're interested in doing it, I've already got airtime scheduled for the second. We can flip the content and go with your story. When do you want to do it?" Sean's head was pivoting between Nash and me.

Nash reached out and touched my arm. "Think about this. You'll torch any relationship you ever had with your parents. Hell, not just you but Jay, too. You'll be putting him right back in the spotlight the way he was in November when you lost the election. I'm all for going to see your parents to confront them in person for outing you to the entire country. Doing it publicly, though? You better really think through the ramifications."

I smirked. I *definitely* had a type. Nash was the kind of guy who would keep me from making horrible mistakes. He had a strong moral compass, and as much outrage as he knew I had for my parents and what they did, he didn't want me to implode my life, yet again. He was much like Vanessa, though not at all in one very *important* way.

"And that's why I love you. You're right. I can't put my family through anymore than I already have." I picked up Nash's hand from where it rested on the crook in my left arm and kissed his knuckles.

Sean chuckled. "It's good to have a conscience—even if it's external. Anyway, I have a roundabout way of still making it happen without it reflecting on your family... well, I hope not. You can discuss it with your ex-wife and your son, but this is my need for revenge."

"Oh, yeah? What's your plan?" I took a sip of my coffee as Sean reached into his messenger bag hanging on the back of his chair and pulled out a folder, sliding it over the table to me.

I flipped open the cover to see the title at the top of the paper.

Interview with Caroline Bering-Turner

"No."

"What, *no*?" Sean was smirking at me.

"You're not going to throw Nash under the bus, Sean."

Nash took the paper out of my hand. He seemed to be reading the entire paper, whereas I hadn't gotten beyond the title.

"Hear me out." Sean held up his hand.

"Oh, shit! Are you kidding about this? Her husband, Senator Turner, knew about her business the whole time and used her services quite often free of charge. And Blaire Conner was one of her boys back in the day? How do you know that?" Nash was completely stunned, as was I, at the news.

"Will Nash's name come up in the interview? Who's doing it?" It was kind of vengeful of me to encourage Sean to do the interview, but only if Nash wasn't mentioned. Man, I'd pay money to see that shit on purpose.

"No. Here's how this came about. I was at Penn Quarter having a steak sandwich one night when Caroline came in and sat at the bar next to me. She got two glasses of Chardonnay and shotgunned them one after the other before she turned and smiled at me."

I only knew Caroline Turner from functions we'd attended while I was in the Senate. I didn't have long conversations with her, just a friendly hello and an air-kiss on each cheek. Vanessa didn't like her at all.

I nodded and Sean continued. "I asked how her day was, and she told me her husband was a lying cheater. She showed me pictures of him with a woman a quarter of his age, the two of them in a small apartment Turner was keeping for her on the Hill. She explained her suspicions to me, and then she explained her business to me, which everyone knows in town, and she said she wanted to burn him. When she mentioned Blaire Conner was a good friend and he would back up her accusations because they were besties and told each other everything, I went into publicist mode."

I chuckled. "Obviously, they didn't tell each other everything if she didn't know you and Blaire were an item."

Sean gave a humorless chuckle. "True. So, she agreed to sit down with a journalist friend of mine and answer questions I had prepared. I want it done before you officially start working for me, so there's no tie to you, Spencer, and I won't allow her to use Nash's name in the interview." That was a relief.

Nash released a heavy sigh, squeezing my arm again. "Thank you, Sean. I appreciate you keeping me out of it because I don't want my past to come back on Spencer." His sincerity made my heart clench.

Sean chuckled. "Just my luck. It shoulda been me instead of Spencer. Give me a second." Sean stood and walked out of the restaurant.

My attention turned to Nash. "My love, I'm grateful you talked me down. I know you may not find this complimentary, but you're like Vani in the way you remind me that I have people I want to protect in life. You are the *man* I've craved my whole life.

Please, please, don't try to leave me again." My eyes teared without my consent.

Nash took his napkin and pressed it against my eyes with a sweet smile. "I won't bring it up again. I love you."

"I know, and I love you too."

I noticed Sean coming through the restaurant with a very attractive woman following behind in precariously tall heels. She appeared to be quite sophisticated and looked familiar, though I couldn't place her.

"Gentlemen—"

"Naomi!" Nash stood and walked over to the woman, who hugged him in return.

The two spoke quietly until Nash led her to the table with a big grin. "Senator Spencer Brady, this is Naomi Chu. She's the Event Coordinator for the Four Seasons Hotel. I've worked with her several times for parties Sean has hosted, among others. Naomi, this is my friend, Senator Brady."

I stood and extended my hand to the young woman, finally placing her. She'd consulted with Vani for an anniversary party for her old real estate firm. "It's a pleasure to see you again, Ms. Chu."

The woman smiled and shook my hand. "It's nice to see you again, Senator. How is Mrs. Brady?"

I glanced at Nash, who chuckled. "Vani's incredible. She's getting ready to move to New York in pursuit of new opportunities. Sit, please." Nash should have been a politician. He handled that question like a pro.

Ms. Chu joined us, and the server brought her a glass of ice water and poured her a coffee. Sean took his seat and grinned. "Naomi, do you have something you wanted to discuss with Nash?"

Ms. Chu turned to Nash and smiled. "I've worked with you more than once for events here at the Four Seasons. We have an opening for a junior event coordinator that I'd like to offer to you. You've already proven yourself valuable to me the times we've worked together. I have no doubt your work is exemplary.

"Here's the package Four Seasons is prepared to offer you, Nash. I'd love to have you on my staff. Think about it and call me after the first of the year." Ms. Chu handed over a folder and stood. We all shook hands before she left us.

Sean motioned for the server. "Shall we order, gentlemen? I'm starving."

We ordered breakfast, and when we left Sean that morning, I had a better feeling about my future than I'd had before the election. I accepted that my time in the Senate was over, and I was fine with it.

My future was wide open, and I couldn't wait to see what was next.

Chapter Twenty Seven
Nash

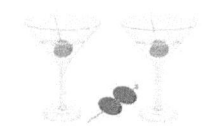

Spencer and I shared breakfast with Sean, who talked about pending anti-LGBTQIA+ legislation that I wasn't familiar with; their conversation easy. Spence wasn't intimidated by anyone, and I admired the hell out of him for it.

I leafed through the folder Naomi had given me. The offer she'd made was generous. The salary mentioned had my eyes nearly bugging out of my head.

When we left, I shook Sean's hand. "Thank you, Sean." I followed Spencer out and stood behind him under the heat lamp while the valet went to get the SUV.

"Are you going to accept the job?" Spence nuzzled up behind me, kissing my neck as he slid his hands into the pockets of my coat. I rested against him, relishing in feeling his affection right out in the open.

"Not sure."

"You okay?" Spence removed his hands from my pockets and turned me to face him, a worried grin on his handsome face.

"I'm a little overwhelmed by the offer from Naomi." Overwhelmed was far away in my rearview mirror.

The SUV was brought around by the valet, and Spencer opened the door for me. I climbed in and he went around to slide into the driver's seat. Spence turned to stare at me with a big smile.

"What do you think about me working there?"

Spence grinned. "Sweetheart, you should do what you feel is right. If the offer interests you but you need more, you can negotiate with her to get what you want. Clearly, they want you, Nash."

I had to wonder if that was true, but the bigger question was would I be able to work for Naomi and not have people staring at me. "Do you think they'll see me as a whore?"

Spencer drove us out of the entrance of the hotel and made the left onto M Street to take us back to Great Falls. He said nothing, which made my stomach roll.

When he pulled into a public parking garage in Arlington, I glanced his way. "Where are we going?"

"We're going for cheesecake. This place has the best peppermint cheesecake. Come on."

Clearly, the man's brain was ruled by his stomach, so I followed him into a popular restaurant. We went to the bakery case, and we each chose a favorite slice of cheesecake, and Spence ordered an extra slice of chocolate cheesecake. Once we had the bag, we left, returning to the SUV.

"So, you're not going to give me your opinion?"

"Oh, I have a lot of opinions, but let's get home, okay?" Spence kissed my lips as he opened the door for me. I took the bag of cheesecake and slid into the seat.

When we arrived at the house in Great Falls, Spence drove into the garage, and we both hopped out and went inside. The house felt empty to me, but I said nothing.

Spence, however, did what he always did. "Vani!"

I saw the envelope on the counter as he stomped up the stairs. "Nash and Spence." I picked it up and flipped the unsealed flap, pulling out the note inside.

> *My darlings –*
>
> *I am so happy you found each other. I know you'll be fine. Please give me a little time to get settled, and then come see me.*
>
> *I'll be staying at Warwick on 54th in Midtown. My apartment won't be ready for a couple of weeks, but I'm starting my job after New Year's, so I'll be calling a four-star hotel home. I'll be in touch about the movers' schedule on the tenth. Of course, I still have my cell, but Spence, look for things before you call me. Nash—I wish you the best of luck with that one!*
>
> *I couldn't leave with you here because I can't imagine waking in the morning and not having coffee with you, so I'm taking the coward's path and leaving while you're gone. Remember, I love you both.*
>
> *Love each other. We all deserve the next steps in our lives. Make them count.*
>
> *Xoxo,*
> *Vani*

I held my breath for a moment, but I knew she was doing what Spencer couldn't do. She was taking control of her life and striking out on her own. I admired her for it.

"Nash!" I was guessing that would be his go-to phrase now that she'd left. I understood her logic in waiting until Spencer was on solid ground with his upcoming job. I'd probably take off when he was gone, too. I would still miss her.

I climbed the steps and found Spencer sitting on her bed. The sheets were folded and laying on the end, as was the comforter. Her pillow was gone, but I understood that. Nothing like your own pillow.

Vanessa's closet was empty, but there were six boxes stacked in the corner. They were taped shut with notes on the front listing their contents.

Spence whispered; his voice filled with pain. "She's gone." I sat down next to him and wrapped an arm around his shoulders as he broke down.

"She left a note." I handed it to him, but I was sure he couldn't focus on the letters because of the tears. That was fine. He would grieve her leaving for a while because they had been best friends since they were kids.

That was okay. I'd be there waiting for him, and eventually, he'd realize she was just a phone call away.

I kissed the top of Spencer's head as I held him and gently rocked us both. The house was so quiet that it was creepy, like the house knew Vani was gone and was mourning like Spencer.

We sat in her room in silence for a while before Spencer stood and wiped his eyes with the heels of his hands. He stepped into her bathroom and returned with a length of toilet paper, chuckling before he blew his nose. "She took the tissues."

I didn't add, "And both of our hearts." We both knew it. No use in stating the obvious.

New Year's Eve was quiet. We dressed up and went to a French restaurant in Potomac, Maryland, for a cozy dinner, just the two of us. A couple of people stopped by the table and spoke to Spence, just staring at me. He didn't introduce them, and I only gave polite head nods as they left.

Later, when we returned home, we changed into sweats and went to the den to watch the celebrations in New York and Los Angeles. "You think Vani ventured out into the crowd?" Spence poured each of us a few fingers of bourbon and sat on the couch, pulling me around and sliding in between my legs, his back resting on my chest.

"Cheers." I touched my glass to his before taking a sip. "I don't see that as her kind of fun, but maybe I'm wrong. I wouldn't do it."

Spencer chuckled. "You and me both. We took Jay one year when he was in middle school. You couldn't have a backpack or a purse, so you can imagine Vanessa without her purse. We didn't make it to midnight."

"I guess that's stuff real families do. My fosters never wanted to take us anywhere."

Spence sat up and turned to face me, pulling my left leg over his lap. "You don't talk about growing up in foster care. How bad was it?"

That wasn't anything I talked about... ever... but if we were becoming each other's family, then I supposed I needed to give him some idea of my life before I met him.

"I hated it, but mostly because I didn't belong anywhere. I wasn't accepted into the families where I was placed, and I acted up because of the rejection. Once I accepted that the families only saw me as a paycheck, I decided it was easiest to just do the time without causing trouble. I met Clint at the last placement. He phased out a year before me, but he came back to get me the day I turned eighteen, and he took me to Sparta where he'd met Denver and the Devil's Volunteers. They became as much family as I'd really ever had."

"Were they hard on you? Abusive?" His expression showed he was interested, so I girded my loins and took a trip down memory lane.

"Some were. One couple rented us out as a cleaning crew. There were six of us, and we were told if we said anything to the social worker, they'd make us sleep in the barn which didn't have heat or air conditioning. I was twelve at the time, and after I got beat because I broke a vase at a home where we cleaned, I called the cops and turned the couple in. We were out of there by that night, and they lost their side hustle, the rat bastards."

For the next thirty minutes, I gave Spencer snippets into my shitty childhood. At five minutes before midnight, his phone rang. He glanced at the screen and grinned before putting it on speaker. "Hello, son!"

"Hey, Dad. Hey, Nash."

"Hi, Jay. Happy New Year. How's the skiing?"

We chatted with Jay and Cole for a few minutes before hanging up at thirty seconds to midnight. Spence turned to me. "I should have bought champagne. I love you and I'm grateful you came into my life. Happy New Year, my love. I have a good feeling about it."

As the grandfather clock in the hallway struck midnight, we put our glasses on the coffee table and kissed as if the world was ending. A minute later, Spencer surprised me with a condom and a bottle of lube as he was taking off his sweats.

"My boy scout." I quickly undressed and grabbed a throw from the back of a leather recliner where Vani used to read, and I spread it on the couch before I took a seat.

Spencer prepped himself as I slid the condom over my throbbing cock. I took Spencer's hand and helped him onto my lap. He held my cock steady and slowly slid down my shaft. "God, that feels good." We both sighed when his ass was resting on my thighs.

He slowly began to roll his hips, sliding up and down in the most erotic way. "I love you Nash. We're gonna fuck all over this house before we move out."

I chuckled, putting my hands on his hips to guide him on my dick so it hit his prostate with every drop of his ass.

I reached for the lube on the couch and squeezed a few drops into my palm. I wrapped my hand around his dick, sliding my fist in time with his movements. "Fuck! I'm not going to last." My eyes were fixed on the leaking purple head in my hand. The slick fluid lubed my hand, and I sped my pumps to get him to the edge with me.

Finally, he shot all over my chest, and moaned my name. His ass spasmed around my cock, and I followed him into the bliss of a fantastic orgasm.

What a way to ring in the new year!

Chapter Twenty Eight
Spencer

Nash and I had picked an apartment in downtown DC on Mount Vernon Street. It was a new building, which was great for us—no previous residents and a fresh place for us to begin our life together. We'd signed the lease on December 30 with a move-in date of January 3, the day after the interview with Caroline Bering-Turner aired.

On advice from Sean, I hadn't been there when his friend, Ingrid Mohr, sat down with Caroline, but he sent me the unedited cut, and Nash and I watched it together. The woman didn't hold back anything.

At the end of the interview, I felt wonderfully vindicated and couldn't wait for Senator Turner to see it. I knew the networks would be clambering for his response after the piece aired on NBS's Sunday morning show, and the old goat wouldn't know what the fuck hit him. I wished him the best of luck.

"How much longer? I could use a bottle of water." Nash had been reading through the contract he was going to sign with Naomi Chu, and I'd been daydreaming.

It was New Year's Day, and we were driving down to Portsmouth, Virginia. I'd vowed to myself that I would rid myself of the burden of being angry with my parents over what they did to me, years ago and now. I was going to confront them about outing me and tell them goodbye forever.

I took the exit ramp that led to the gated community where my parents' large home was located. I was dreading the quarrel, but it was something I should have done a long time ago. I'd let them bully me my whole life, and it was time I stood up for myself.

There was a convenience store on the right side of the street, so I pulled into the parking lot. Nash unbuckled his seat belt and turned to me. "You want anything?"

I smirked. "For this to be over and for you to give me road head."

"I see a future where both things can happen." He laughed as he went into the store. My dick and I contemplated the idea of road head, and we were both on board.

Slowing the SUV, I flipped the blinker on to make the left into my parents' circle drive. The house was ostentatious by anyone's tastes, looking far too much like a plantation than a home.

When I stopped near the wraparound front porch, I shut off the motor and turned to Nash. "Don't be offended by anything you hear them say. They are bigoted people whose minds are stuck in the 1950s, and remember I love you. You don't have to come inside."

We'd argued about it for most of the drive, the prudence of Nash coming inside with me to witness the showdown. "As I've said for the last three-and-a-half hours, I want to be there to support you. If you believe they'll say something you'd rather I not hear, then I won't go in, but I'm worried about you going in there alone, Spencer." His love for me solidified my resolve.

"Okay. Let's go in." We both hopped out and met in front of the SUV.

I took Nash in my arms. "Thank you. You're my new hero." I gently kissed his lips and took his hand, leading him to the large brick home with the stone front porch. I rang the bell and took one more deep breath.

When the door opened, I was surprised to see my mother standing in front of me instead of the housekeeper, Matilda. Her bright smile quickly shifted to the frown I was more used to seeing. "What do you want Spencer?"

Nash's hand slowly tried to slip from mine, but I grasped it tighter. "I wanted to update you on what's going on in my life. Is Dad home?" No use telling it twice or leaving things to Hillary Brady's interpretation.

"Your father is on a conference call, and we're expecting guests for lunch. What do you want, Spencer."

Much to my surprise, Nash reached up and pressed the doorbell a dozen times in rapid-fire succession. Matilda came running into the hallway, and my father stomped in right behind her.

I turned to Nash. "Thank you, my love." He winked.

Now that the gang was all there, I stared at my mother. "Aren't you going to let me in? Or do you want the neighbors to hear your dirty laundry?"

"For god's sake, Hillary, move." Dad stared at me. "You've got five minutes."

"I've worked with less time before." Nash and I stepped inside, and I closed the door. They hadn't invited us to sit down, but I wasn't surprised.

"Okay, first things first. Vanessa and I are getting divorced. She's already moved to New York, and we're moving to DC in a few days. We're selling the house in Great Falls. Neither of us need all that space." Their faces showed no response, leading me to believe they already knew. I'd have been a fool if I didn't think my father had spies all over the metro area.

"I thought we made it clear to you that we didn't care what happened to you after the election." My dad was a son of a bitch.

"Yes, you did, but you didn't tell me it was because you conspired with someone on my own staff to out me and leak the story to the press before the election." *There's the surprise I wanted to see!*

"Wha— Wha— How dare you accuse us of something of the sort. No one was more shocked to see those pictures than we were," my father blustered indignantly. Mom said nothing, and Matilda reached behind her and untied her apron.

"I bet. For what you paid Gregor Jablonowski, he should have taken better shots. You almost couldn't tell it was Blaire Conner I was fucking at the time." Mom's gasp at my use of the f-word was comical. Nash chuckled quietly next to me.

Matilda turned to my mother, her eyes narrowed in anger. "What did you do to your only child?"

"This is none of your business." The haughty nod of my mother's head almost had me laughing.

Matilda had worked for our family for so many years I couldn't remember a time when she wasn't there. She tolerated my parents, but she had always cared for me. It was when I got elected to the Senate that we grew apart. It was my fault.

I stepped over and gave Matilda a hug. "I'm sorry I haven't called for a while. I'll rectify that, I promise. Matilda, this is my partner, Nash Lincoln. Sweetheart, this is the woman who raised me, Matilda Jones."

Another scoff from my mother, but I didn't pay attention. Matilda hugged Nash. "It's a pleasure to meet you. You take care of this man. He's like another of my children." Then she turned to me. "I understand that a senator has a lot on his plate, but now you've got time to give me a call when you can."

She patted my cheek before she took off the cap Mom made her wear when they were having people over. I'd always made fun of it, and I knew Matilda hated it.

She plopped it on top of my mother's shampoo-and-set hair, and she draped the apron over Dad's shoulder. "I quit."

With that, she stomped into the kitchen and came back a moment later with her coat, scarf, and gloves. She stopped in front of me and smiled. "Don't be a stranger. I'm thinking of moving to Alexandria where my daughter lives."

Nash smirked. "We'll have you over once we get settled in our apartment. I'd love to hear stories about Spence as a little boy." He walked over to the front door and opened it, closing it once Matilda was outside. That was an unexpected pleasure!

I turned back to my parents, who were now furious, my mother glaring at me. "Look what you've done."

Nash stepped in front of me, which was a surprise. "No, Spencer had nothing to do with that poor woman leaving this circle of hell. You obliterated Spencer's life when you betrayed him. Jay, Vanessa, and I will help him put it back together.

THE SENATOR

We're his family, and you are only an embarrassment to a man with integrity."

I wanted to say to him that maybe integrity was the wrong word, but I was so touched by his defense of me that I put my arm around his neck and pulled him close enough to kiss his temple.

"So, yes, I know what you did and how much you spent to do it. I'd say I'm surprised, but I'm not. There's another scandal brewing in DC, and mine will be long forgotten, but I'll never forget what you did to me. I hope you have someone you trust when it's time to pick your nursing home. You won't like where I put you."

I turned to Nash. "Ready to go? I'm hungry, and I know a great place on the way out of town to eat." We clasped hands, and we were out the door before anything more could be said.

"Spence! Come here quick!" I was hanging our clothes in the wardrobe boxes that had been delivered to Great Falls. Nash and I were finally moving into our new place in DC. We'd taken a few days to disappear to Key West to celebrate the new year and my new freedom.

Nash had signed his contract with Four Seasons, and was set to begin his training on January 20, so we had some time to just be, which was something I hadn't done in a long time. I don't think Nash had either. We had a damn blast, and nobody gave a tinker's damn who we were.

I ran down the hall to the den where Nash was busy boxing up my books and he had the television on. "What?" I stepped over to where he stood, eyes glued to the screen.

There on the screen was Blaire Conner being hounded by Ingrid Mohr. "Is it true you used to work for the DC madame, Caroline Bering-Turner? Did you sleep with Senator Turner? Is it true, your husband participated in the conspiracy to out Senator Spencer Brady last year which caused him to lose the election?"

"Shit!" Nash grabbed his phone from the bookshelf and immediately hit a contact, putting it on speaker.

"Hey, Nash. How you doing kid?" It was Denver Wallace.

"Denver, you guys didn't leak the source of Spencer's outing, did you?" Nash's face was flush with anger, but I had the feeling his friends had kept their word.

"What's with these accusations? Of course we didn't. We don't turn on our own, and you know this, Nashville. I'll accept your apology in chocolate chip cookies from Trina's Treats." The line went dead.

I took his phone and smirked. "It didn't cross my mind that they'd have even considered going to the press. And I don't think Sean had anything to do with this either."

My phone rang at the same time the front door opened. I answered as I headed downstairs to find Vani. It was the first we'd seen of her since she'd moved right after Christmas.

I held up my finger to her. "Hello?" I hadn't even looked at the number on the screen of my phone.

"Mom there?" It was our son.

"Yeah, as a matter of fact, she just walked in. You okay?" I put the phone on speaker as Nash came downstairs.

"Mom, glad you made it. Did they see it? It's the lead story on all the news channels here in Blacksburg."

"Yeah, I got a call for comment from Ingrid. I said that my family deserved privacy and any illegal activities related to your dad's outing were the product of collusion between The Honorable Ronald Brady and his wife, Hillary Brady."

Vani stared into my eyes as she said it, and I felt the tears. "Why would you do that?" I couldn't believe her kindness to me in the face of the embarrassing mess I'd made.

"I also told Ingrid that our marriage was nobody's business, I was aware you were gay from the beginning, and we're still friends."

Nash went over to the large television in the living room and flipped it on, turning to NBS's cable channel.

"In a statement given by Senator Brady's former wife, Mrs. Brady implicated the Senator's parents in the conspiracy to discredit the Senator before the 2022 election and confirmed that she'd known the Senator was gay for many years. She refused to comment further, saying it was nobody's business and that the two remain close friends."

Nash looked at us, before walking over to put his arm around the two of us. "It's not a lie." He kissed my cheek and then Vani's as I let it all soak in.

He was right. It wasn't a lie. We were still close friends, and I loved them both with all my heart. Last August, my life was a dumpster fire after being outed. All the events following could have made me jump into the Potomac—which was disgusting—and I wasn't sure if Vanessa could have kept me from doing it.

Then, on a cold night early in the fall, an angel walked into my life and those bad times are distant memories. Who knew a beautiful young bartender could save The Senator.

Epilogue
Nash

Thanksgiving, one year later...

"Remember, our flight leaves at six from Reagan, so don't cut it close like last time."

"I promise, my love. I packed this morning, so I'll swing by the house and pick up our bags and meet you at the airport like we agreed."

Spencer had a morning meeting on Capitol Hill before we went to New York for Thanksgiving with the family. Jay was adamant that we not miss the flight as we'd done for Memorial Day weekend earlier in the year. Spence was starting his job on Tuesday and had a bunch of reading to do. Vani called him and ripped him a new asshole—after I got done ripping him one myself. This time, I'd asked Spence to take the day off so we wouldn't cut it close. Meetings on the Hill always seemed to run long.

"Okay, but you'll face the wrath of Vani and Jay if we miss the flight. Love you."

"Love you, too, and I swear I'll be there. I love you too. Have a great day."

We hung up and I went back to the inventory sheets that had been dropped off after the Langers Holiday party so I could submit the orders for the Christmas season.

My job at Four Seasons was everything I never imagined I could do. I made a great salary—enough that I could pay half of our living expenses and save money to put down on the new house we were planning to buy in the spring. Spence had the money from the sale of the Great Falls house, but I wanted to contribute too.

Spencer's job was going great guns. He was the rising star of the Washington lobbying world, just behind Sean Fitzpatrick, and I was proud of him for turning around the shitstorm he'd suffered when he was in the Senate. The assholes who demonized him were now lining up to kiss his ass, and we laughed about it all the time.

"Mr. Lincoln, there's a man here to see you. He's in the lobby." I glanced up to see one of the desk clerks who was new to the hotel, though I couldn't remember her name.

"Thank you, uh..."

"Gretchen. My name's Gretchen, but don't worry about it. You were in a meeting when I was introduced to the rest of the staff."

I stood and walked over to her. "Gretchen, please call me Nash." We shook hands and I followed her out to the lobby.

After glancing around and seeing no one I recognized, I turned to Gretchen who pointed to the guy in the leather jacket by the windows. I recognized those broad shoulders in an instant.

I hurried to where he was standing and tapped him on the back. "How may I help you, sir?"

Denver turned around with a huge smile on his face. "Kid! I wouldn't have recognized you in a suit."

We hugged, and I led him over to a seating area, pushing him into a chair. "How've you been? I'm sorry I didn't make it to the club's anniversary party in October. We've both been crazy busy. How've you been? How's the club?"

"The club is fine, but I've got some news. The, uh, the club changed its bylaws and we're becoming

LGBTQIA+ inclusive. Turns out I wasn't the only queer in the—"

"Damn, Denny, you should see the bathroom. It's fancy as shi— Oh, hey, Nash."

I studied Pacman for a minute before I glanced at Denver to see his cheeks were red, but he was gazing at Pacman as if he hung the moon. "Pacman, it's good to see you. How've you been?"

We hugged quickly, and I eyeballed Denver. "Something you wanna tell me?" If he was finally in a place where he could love someone, I would be more than happy for him. Getting over Clint had been nearly impossible. It had taken so long I thought it was a lost cause.

"Yeah, uh, Henry and I have been seeing each other for a couple of years. We've decided to get married, and I wanted to see if you'd be my best man." I hugged them both. I was thrilled for them.

"When?" We sat down, Pacman and Denver on the couch and me in the chair.

"I'm going to be a June bride." Pacman batted his eyelashes at me and rested his head on Denver's shoulder. I laughed at the two of them. They were so cute.

Denver put his arm around Pacman's shoulders and smiled at him. "Baby boy, will you go get me a coffee?" Denver gave me an imploring look.

"Oh, uh, yeah. The café is down the hallway near the concierge desk. Tell Tony to put it on my tab." I pointed the direction and after Pacman left, I turned to Denver.

"I'm sorry to spring this on you. I wanted to tell you, but I wasn't sure if you'd understand. I loved Clinton more than I ever imagined loving anyone. When he died, I wanted to die with him. Thought about it a couple of times, but then Henry came along, and he annoyed and needled and taunted and got under my skin so deep that next thing I know, we're dating and I'm falling in love with him.

"You know I'd never betray Clint. I still love him, and I'm convinced I always will, but hanging around Henry reminded me that I only get one life. I want to live it with him, and I want you to be okay with that."

I stood from the chair and sat next to Denver on the couch. I took one of his hands and held it between both of mine. "I'm very happy for you, Denver. I know for a fact how much you love Clint. I know he wouldn't want you to be alone for the rest of your life. He was a happy guy, and he'd want you to be happy too. I'd be honored to be your best man."

Denver kissed my cheek just as Henry returned with three drinks. "Everything okay, guys? Nash, I hope—"

I stood and took the paper tray from him, handing it to Denver. "I'm so happy for you guys." I hugged Pacman again. "Where's the wedding going to be?"

They both laughed. "The club won't let us have it anywhere other than Sparta. Think your man will come down to the country to see how an MC celebrates?"

I shook my head. "I'll do my best to prepare him beforehand."

Spencer

Nash and I arrived at JFK on time, and when we came out of the security area, we were surprised to see a man in a suit holding an iPad with *Brady Party* on the screen in Helvetica Bold.

"Did you arrange a car service?" Nash held my hand and pulled his suitcase while I carried my messenger bag with a lot of work inside I hoped to get done sometime over the long weekend and dragged our shared garment bag on the other side.

"I didn't think about it. I'm not that familiar with New York, sweetheart. I just assumed it would be easy to get a cab."

"Okay, then, let's go ask the man. Maybe there's another Brady family."

We approached the man. "Hi, uh, I'm Spencer Brady. Are you waiting for another Brady?"

"Do you know Jay Brady?"

I chuckled. "Yes. He's my—"

"He's here." We both turned to see Jay and Cole wheeling luggage behind them.

"Wait, I thought you guys were already here. What's going on?" I looked at them, and they appeared to have tans? That made no sense.

"Where are you coming back from?" We all exchanged hugs. The driver took the garment bag from me and the suitcase from Nash, and we all headed to the parking garage.

The lights flashed on a black Suburban sitting close to the parking garage. "So, what's your name?" Seemed rude not to know the name of the man making the airport run.

"I'm Josh, Senator." Okay, Josh was a man of few words.

He opened the back and put the third-row seat down to fit our bags inside. I sat in the front seat with Josh while Cole, Jay, and Nash sat in the middle row. The three of them chatted about college.

"Do you like being a driver? I bet you get a lot of crazies, huh?" What did one talk to a driver about? I was such a dick. When I used the service at the Capitol, I was usually on the phone or reading work stuff, so I didn't worry about talking. Now, I felt like an asshole.

"I'm not actually a driver. I'm a contractor. I've worked with Vanessa on some renovations for some of her clients, and she asked me to do her a favor." All talking in the back seat stopped.

"Ah. Well, that's... you're a good friend. The airport pickup is a hell of an ask. Thank you for agreeing."

Josh was about five-ten. He had a full beard and bright blue eyes. His hair was short, and he had full sleeves on both arms. I could see the dark ink under the white-dress shirt he was wearing, and the sleeves were rolled up, which gave him a cool vibe that was beyond me.

"This yours? It's a beast. I have a Tahoe, but it's not this big."

"Yeah. I have a son who plays hockey and I end up driving his team around, so I needed the space." Josh merged into the lane leading to Midtown.

"Your family live in Manhattan?" I noticed the guys in the back seat were oddly quiet.

"My, uh, my ex-husband lives in Williamsburg, Brooklyn. My son lives with him, and I live in a guest house in the backyard. Since Felix started playing hockey, I've been helping out as much as I can because Grant travels for his job. He's a pilot for Delta. When he's working, I stay in the main house or Felix stays in the little house with me. It's a work in progress."

"Oh, I see. I truly understand a work in progress. Vanessa and I had to work through a lot of things too. It takes a while to find your groove. How long have you been—no, I'm sorry. I'm nosy. What position does your son play?"

You're an idiot, Spencer!

"No, it's okay. Grant's very much a part of my life, but he has hard feelings for how things shook out. Anyway, we've been divorced for seven years. He's dating a really nice girl, but I think he's gun-shy. I mean, I understand it, but you can only beat a dead horse for so long."

I was really confused, but we turned into an alley, and Josh reached up to the sun visor and pressed a button, opening the garage door of Vani's apartment building.

It took a minute, but then something occurred to me. "You, uh, you're gay?"

Dear god, did my best friend not learn her lesson about being tied to a gay man? Jesus H. She'd already wasted twenty years of her life on me. I hoped she'd know better than to repeat herself.

"Uh, Dad. Why don't you wait until we get to Mom's. Josh, how'd Felix do in his game Sunday?" I did a double take as Josh slid into a spot near the elevator that had Vani's apartment number on a post.

We all got out of the SUV, and Jay came around the front to where I was standing. "Look. Keep an open mind. He's a great guy."

"He seems like a nice guy, Jay, but he's gay. Did you hear him say ex-husband?"

I stared at my son for a moment before he glanced away. I knew that look. "What do you know that I don't?"

Nash grabbed my arm and led me to the elevator. "Come on, babe. Let's go see Vani." I grabbed my briefcase and the garment bag. With that, we took the elevator to the twenty-third floor.

Nash and I had been to Vani's place a couple of times, and she'd been to our apartment a few times, so I knew which apartment was hers. It seemed Josh did too.

Josh rang the bell, and Vani immediately opened the door with a huge smile. "My guys!" She hugged Jay and Cole first and then she hugged Nash, giving him a kiss on the cheek. I was next with a kiss and a tight hug.

I pulled back. "Vani, you look fantastic. How have you been, love?"

"Come in. Come in." I stepped inside and pushed my suitcase into Jay's room. Nash and I were staying at the Marriott across the street, but we could check in later. I wanted to know what the hell was going on with that Josh guy.

"Mom, what are you cooking?" Jay sounded nervous, and I could see he was stalling.

"It's not me. Josh made lasagna this afternoon while I was finishing up a closing. Tell me how Bermuda was, boys." Vani was staring at Jay, and that answered my question about where they'd been.

"You guys went to Bermuda?" I sat at the dining room table Vani had in her small dining room.

"Seriously, Jay, you haven't kept your father informed?" There was that mother bear I was used to seeing.

"They were busy with new jobs, and I thought it would be better to talk to them in person. How about you, *Mom*?"

Vanessa's eyes moved to Josh, who came over and stood next to her. He wrapped his arm around her and stared at me. His face showed he was ready for battle, but I wasn't trying to fight with him. I was protective when it came to Vani, sure. I loved her as I always would.

Vani stared at me. "You know I love you. You're my best friend, but I had to take some time to figure out things for myself." She stepped closer to me and touched my face. "You and me? We will always be family, and you know that."

She stepped back, and Josh wrapped his arm around her with her coaxing. "Josh and I started working together on my first project. He's an amazing contractor, and we hit it off immediately."

I nodded and stared at them. Nash moved closer and touched my shoulder. "Spence, honey, I think Vani's trying to tell you that she and Josh are in a relationship."

My eyes moved from Jay to Cole to Nash. "Did you all know this? Why wasn't I let in on the secret?"

Josh chuckled. "They're all dancing around the truth, Senator. I'm a trans man. I met Vanessa at a house she was trying to sell. Her boss has worked with me before, and when Vanessa told him there was a problem with the kitchen, he contacted me. I've been a contractor for years, and I'm good at my job, but I'm not going to try to win you over. Vanessa and I are seeing each other, and she thought it was time we met."

I was shocked. "You and Vani? You're in a relationship?"

Josh chuckled. "Well, I'm trying, but I'm having a hard time getting around you."

"Spence, let me talk to you in private." Vanessa stepped closer and took my hand.

I followed her to her bedroom and stared at her as she closed the door, waiting for an explanation.

Vani paced. "You know I've had a difficult life. I love you Spencer, but we're best friends. You're gay, honey, and we both know it. We made a life together, but it wasn't the life either of us wanted, was it?"

I didn't exactly agree with her, but I understood what she meant. "I didn't think you hated our life, Vani." I sounded hurt, and maybe I was a little.

She smiled. "Spencer, you and I have had an interesting relationship, haven't we? I've always known you were gay, and you've always known I was ace. I appreciate the fact you and I found a way to make a family, but we were always meant for something else, don't you think?

"You met Nash, who is perfect for you. I met Josh, who I'm so happy I've gotten to know. He's incredible to me, Spence. You've got to understand that I'm trying to make my own life, right?"

It smacked me in the face. The truth was right there, and it made me grin.

Vanessa and I had found our own paths, and it seemed she'd found the perfect person for her. I couldn't say I didn't like Josh. I didn't know him, but if he was the man who made Vanessa's heart soar, then I wouldn't stand in the way. I wasn't that much of a selfish ass.

I chuckled as I pulled her into my arms. "I'll be happy for you after I get over being jealous. Our life hasn't been easy, has it? I will always love you, and we'll always be a family. If this guy is who you want, I'll get to know him, and I'll be supportive. Just don't keep me out of the loop, please?"

Vanessa hugged me and stared into my eyes. "When are you going to marry that man?"

I laughed. "Gimme a break. I just got out of a marriage."

Vanessa laughed. "Yeah, I get it. But look how great both of our lives have turned out. You've found the love of your life, and I believe I've found mine."

Seeing the smile on her face was all I needed. I had one question. "Does Velma like him?"

Vani giggled. "Not at all." I knew in that instant that Josh and I would get along spectacularly.

I had finally found my road to happiness. Years ago, it had seemed endless, but I'd finally arrived at the destination meant for me. How fucking great could life be going forward? I couldn't wait to find out.

♥♥♥

About Sam E. Kraemer

ABOUT SAM E. KRAEMER

I grew up in the rural Midwest before moving to the East Coast with a dashing young man who swept me off my feet. We've now settled in the desert Southwest where I write M/M contemporary romance. I also write paranormal M/M romance under "Sam E. Kraemer writing as L.A. Kaye." I'm a firm believer that love is love, regardless of how it presents itself, and I'm proud to be a staunch ally of the LGBTQIA+ community. I have a loving, supportive family, and I feel blessed by the universe and thankful every day for all I have been given. In my heart and soul, I believe I hit the cosmic jackpot.

Cheers!

Other Books by Sam E. Kraemer/L.A. Kaye

Books by Sam E. Kramer

The Lonely Heroes Complete Series
RangerHank
GuardianGabe
CowboyShep

HackerLawry
Positive Raleigh
Salesman Mateo
Bachelor Hero
OrphanDuke
NobleBruno
Avenging Kelly
ChefRafe

On The Rocks Complete Series
Whiskey Dreams
Ima-GIN-ation
Absinthe Minded

Weighting... Complete Series
Weightingfor Love
Weightingfor Laughter
Weightingfor a Lifetime

May/December Hearts Collection
A Wise Heart
Heart of Stone
Whatthe H(e)art Wants

A Flaws & All Love Story
Sinners' Redemption
Forgiveness is a Virtue

SwimCoach

Men of Memphis Blues
Kim& Skip
Cash& Cary
Dori& Sonny

Perfect Novellas
Perfect
2Perfect

Power Players
TheSenator

Holiday Books
MyJingle Bell Heart
Georgie'sEggcellent Adventure
The Holiday Gamble
Mabry's Minor Mistake

Other Titles
WhenSparks Fly
UnbreakHim
TheSecrets We Whisper To The Bees
ShearBliss
Kiss Me Stupid
Smolder

ADaddy for Christmas 2: Hermie

BOOKS by L.A. Kaye

Dearly and The Departed
Dearly & Deviant Daniel
Dearly & Vain Valentino
Dearly & Notorious Nancy
Dearly & Homeless Horace
Dearly & Threatening Thane
Dearly & Lovesick Lorraine

Dearly and The Departed Spinoffs
The Harbinger's Ball
The Harbinger's Allure
Scotty & Jay's First HellishAdventure
Scotty & Jay's Second HellishAdventure

Other Titles
Halston's Family Gothic - The Prologue
The Mysteries of Marblehead Manor
Mutual Obsessions

Milton Keynes UK
Ingram Content Group UK Ltd.
UKHW040817141124
451205UK00001B/15